A Silent Child

A Silent Child

Claire Sheldon

Book 2 – Lisa Carter Files

Stories that inspire emotions!
www.rubyfiction.com

Copyright © 2022 Claire Sheldon

Published 2022 by Ruby Fiction
Penrose House, Crawley Drive, Camberley, Surrey GU15 2AB, UK
www.rubyfiction.com

A CIP catalogue record for this book is available from the British Library

ISBN: 978-1-91255-067-8

Printed .A.

For Andrew, Alex and Melanie.

Acknowledgements

Book two. Who would have thought it? And there are no doubt so many more people I need to thank:

To those authors who are pretty much killing it and still have the time to support and cheer me on: J M Hewitt, Louise Jensen, C L Taylor, Roz Watkin, Lucy Mitchell, Rebecca Bradley, Rachel Burton and Angela Clarke.

Holly Lord, for her knowledge of social working and Kevin Tedds, for his knowledge of the fire service. Any mistakes are purely my own.

Richard Parkin, for sharing his diagnosis story with me.

Professor Nikos Evangelou, for taking the time to answer my drugs and neurology questions.

The Bond Girls and colleagues of Insolvency Risk Services. What a year we've had! I'm looking forward to celebrating and thanking you all in person soon (hopefully).

Team Cliki forever!

To the early reviewers who took *Perfect Lie* into their hearts: Lucy Mitchell, Lesley Budge, Cathryn Northfield and Angela Watt, and not forgetting the Tasting Panel readers who said 'yes' to *A Silent Child* and made publication possible: Dimitra Evangelou, Steph Price, Mel Appleyard, Sally Pardey, Bee Master, Barbara Wickham, Jenny Mitchell, Jo Osborne, Lorna Baker, Jenny Kinsman and Carol Botting.

My editor, who is never short of fairy dust to
sprinkle to make sure my stories work.

My Choc Lit and Ruby Fiction family, who
continue to support this novice author from
Nottingham, who is pretty much still winging it.

Jimmy Eat World, who continue to
see me through any edits.

To those that I call family; how did I end up
with such a great bunch of supporters?

Alex Sheldon, who continues to compare me
to his teachers with some amazing authors
I can only ever hope to emulate.

Melanie Sheldon for her continued excitement and, of
course, Andrew Sheldon who is the only person I know
who is still willing to love, support AND put up with me!

Prologue

Dana

I never thought it would end this way ... I'd been drug running for several years before it happened. I had been promised a safe place to rest my head away from my war-torn home, and I jumped at the offer. I didn't realise what I'd have to do to stay in the United Kingdom. I was always treated well, and I had enough money for the things I liked. Mr Crawford was so nice to me – he even managed to get me a forged UK passport. When that happened, I couldn't thank him enough. Finally I would have the freedom to travel the world, and I had identification to open a bank account and get a mobile phone. He said I was his favourite, and he would take me out to parties and on holidays ... it was just a shame that I had to swallow condoms full of drugs every time I came back to the UK. He used to tell me it was my way of paying him back, travelling alone with a belly full of drugs. But the more I did it, the bigger the buzz I got when I made it through customs without a hitch.

When I first started, we were trained and had it drilled into our heads what we had to do if we were pulled over. I used to see them looking at me as I walked through customs. I'd have my head held high, clicking along in my three-inch heels. If we looked happy and confident, they told us that nobody would suspect, but the first time I got pulled over for a baggage check I was so scared I thought I was going to be sick. I'm surprised the security officer couldn't hear my heart racing as he searched my bags, asking me why I'd come to America. I knew the lines and what I needed to say by heart, but all I wanted to do was

1

run. I knew someone was waiting for me just behind the two-way screens, and if I screwed this up the punishment wasn't even worth thinking about. Somehow, I managed to get through and was met by one of George's men, who questioned me about why it had taken me so long to arrive. They told me I must have done something to make the security guard pull me aside, that they didn't just do random searches. No matter what I said I wasn't believed and, as I expected, the punishment came ...

Chapter One

DI Chris Jackson and DS Julie Ryan pulled up beside the football club. There had been calls earlier that morning about something suspicious floating in the River Trent, and some officers had been sent to investigate – but when Chris got a call from the city's top pathologist asking him to attend the scene, he knew straight away that something more serious was going on.

'Any clue as to why we're here, boss?' Julie asked as she got out of the car into the full force of the hot sun that was beating down from above. 'We don't usually get a call out for somebody's old sofa floating in the Trent.'

'None at all.' Chris followed her with his insulated coffee mug in one hand and several headache pills in the other, and they began to make their way over to where everyone seemed to be congregated. 'Any idea why we've been called?' Chris asked as they approached one of the officers.

Chris and his small team worked as part of the Special Ops department, which was responsible for all major crimes that happened in the East Midlands area. He and his colleagues worked out of the Nottingham city centre police station and had their fair share of violent crime to deal with.

'DI Jackson, we've been waiting for you,' a familiar voice shouted from inside the tent that had been erected around the scene. He downed the pills and took a swig of coffee as he entered.

'Amanda.'

'Sorry for calling you both out so early.' Dr Walsh greeted them both.

'Not a problem. What you got for us?' Julie asked.

'I think you might find this one interesting,' Amanda said as she lowered the sheet that was covering a swollen female body. 'My team have just pulled this poor lady out of the Trent.'

'So, this is our suspicious item?' Julie muttered grimly.

'We get our fair share of suicide attempts here, but this one seems different.'

'She looks like she's been in there for a while,' Julie commented.

'Exactly. I would say she's been under there for about a week, and she's only resurfaced due to decomp.'

'So how does it differ from any other suicide?' Chris asked as he moved closer to the body.

'Usually people surface a lot quicker in the Trent, or they're reported missing so there's already a search under way for them,' Amanda explained.

'So, we could be looking at murder?'

'Possibly, though I'll leave that one for you to figure out,' Amanda answered, giving Chris her knowing smile.

'Do you know when you'll be able to perform the autopsy?'

'Once we recover her back to Derby Royal, I'll be able to give you a more exact time frame.'

'Thank you.' Chris moved away from the body and let the team continue to make the recovery.

'Do we know who found her?' Julie asked one of the officers who was positioned outside the tent.

'The groundsman, ma'am.'

'Do you know where he is now?'

'He was taken into the stadium by one of his colleagues. PC Wilks is with them. I'll radio ahead and let him know you're on your way.'

Chris looked up at the stadium that towered above them.

'You a fan?' Julie asked as they approached it.

'Oh no. That would be treason, seeing as I live in spitting distance of Derby County's stadium.'

'I can't say I miss working match days when Nottingham Forest and Derby were playing,' Julie commented.

'It sometimes felt like we were going into war.' Chris laughed.

'Football fans, alcohol and rival teams – a dangerous mix!'

Chris and Julie walked around to the main entrance and, as they passed through the stadium car park, Chris admired all the expensive looking cars.

'Players must be here.'

'I wish I was on the same salary as one of these footballers,' Chris muttered as he peered through the car windows.

'I'll let *you* bring that one up.' Julie laughed as she held open the door and followed Chris into a brightly lit reception area.

'Sir, ma'am.' A young PC approached them both. 'William Drake, the groundsman, is in his office with one of his colleagues.'

'Thank you ... Officer?'

'Wilks, ma'am.'

'Have you managed to get much out of him yet?' Julie asked.

'He was in a state of shock when we arrived, so we decided just to get him inside, give him a drink and take the statement when he was ready.'

'Do you mind showing us to his office?' Chris asked.

'Of course. It's a bit of a walk – right on the other side of the ground, I'm afraid.'

'Not to worry, it'll give DS Ryan a chance to see if she can spot any footballers hanging around.' Chris smirked at his partner as they began to follow the PC.

'Do we know the location of the players?' Julie asked as they skirted the pitch.

'They're currently in a meeting with their manager. Do you think you'll need to speak to them?'

'I doubt it. Unless any of them saw anything suspicious?'

'Not that I know of ... but I can go and check,' PC Wilks offered.

'No, it's fine, Officer. I think DS Ryan will be more than happy to take on that job.' Chris continued to look around the grounds as they passed through. He noticed the large screens at either end of the pitch playing cartoons to an empty stadium and wondered vaguely why they were still on – the amount of electricity those things must waste being on all the time! It was hard to imagine how, on most weekends, the stadium would be filled to capacity, when right now all he could hear was the passing of traffic outside.

PC Wilks led them back inside and towards a set of offices, all with brass name plates on the doors.

'Sorry, I did say it was a bit of a walk,' he commented, turning to them as he knocked on one of the doors before entering. 'Detectives, this is William Drake. He's the groundsman here.'

Chris introduced himself and Julie and then held his hand out towards the man who seemed to have shrunk into himself.

William's office was filled with football memorabilia; maps of the football pitch were attached to the walls, as well as a calendar listing all the year's fixtures and other events taking place in the stadium.

'Can I get you a drink or anything?' William asked as he stood up and moved over towards the kettle, hidden away in one of the corners.

'I'm good, thank you.' Chris took a seat while Julie walked over towards the small window.

'Sorry, Detectives,' William said, letting out a long sigh before continuing. 'I just can't get the image out of my mind.'

'Why don't you take a seat?' Julie suggested, reaching into her pocket and pulling out her notebook. 'Are you comfortable talking us through what you found?' she asked as Chris got up and put his hand on William's shoulder, guiding him gently back towards his desk.

'Every morning before I start, I always take a tour of the outside of the stadium. I pick up the odd bit of litter and just do a general inspection. It's something I've done since I started as a groundsman, thirty years ago.' William stopped and reached over towards the drink that was already sat on his desk. He took a sip and looked thoughtful for a moment, before taking a breath and continuing. 'As I was doing my usual tour earlier, I noticed something in the river and went over to take a closer look. I thought it might be, you know, some rubbish that somebody had dumped ...' William's voice broke, almost like he was about to burst into tears.

'Mr Drake, we can continue this later if it's easier,' Julie offered kindly.

'No, no ... I went to the edge and looked closer and saw the body. I immediately pulled my phone out and rang you guys. Do you know ... how long she's been in there?'

'We're not sure at this point, Mr Drake.'

A silence fell across the room, and William shifted uncomfortably in his chair, clearly unsure what to say next.

'Mr Drake, I'm afraid we know very little about the victim at this stage, but please take comfort in the fact that you did the right thing in phoning us,' Julie reassured him.

'I just have so many questions. We see our fair share of suicide attempts here next to the Trent ... it's just sad that no one saw her go in, or could have at least tried to talk to her before she jumped.'

'I don't want to put any more added pressure on you, so we'll leave it there for now. Would you be okay to come down to the station later today so we can take a full statement?'

William looked around and shakily opened his diary. 'Yes, yes ... of course.' He snapped the diary closed quickly and started to rise again. 'I'm not sure what time it'll be. I'll finish up here and pop down.' Something in the way William moved made Chris stand up again – he was worried the man was about to fall over or pass out.

'PC Wilks will take some contact details from you and we'll arrange for someone to escort you to the station when you're ready.' Julie smiled encouragingly at the man.

'Thank you, officers. Would you be able to keep me in the loop, once you know what happened to her?'

'I'm sure we can arrange something,' Julie replied, 'Here, take my card. If you have any further questions, you can contact me on that number.'

William glanced at the card. 'Let me see you back to reception.'

'I'm sure we'll find our way, Mr Drake. You stay here and I'll get PC Wilks to join you shortly.' Julie put her hand reassuringly on the man's shoulder.

William sat back down heavily, rubbing his hands over his face.

'Are you okay finishing up here?' Chris asked PC Wilks, who had been hovering outside the office.

'Of course. Do you want me to stick around so I can escort him to the station later?'

'That might be a good idea. Give him your contact

number so you're not smothering him whilst he's trying to work.'

'Okay, boss. I'll re-join the others once I've finished up here.'

Chris and Julie began walking back towards the entrance, trying to retrace their footsteps.

'What do you think?' Chris asked, once they were a safe distance from the office.

'I think our victim is going to haunt Mr Drake for a very long time,' Julie responded grimly.

Finally making their way out of the stadium, they noticed a flurry of forensic officers combing the area, while the underwater team were already checking nothing had been missed. Whether this was a crime scene or not, it was important to make sure they collected everything that might help identify their victim and figure out how she'd come to be floating in the Trent.

Chris sat back in his office chair. His headache was ever-present as he counted the hours until he could take something else. Trying to distract himself, he thought about the full-on weekend he had just had. He still wasn't used to getting home from work and finding a naked undercover detective in his bed, but that was how things worked with him and Hannah. He would go for weeks without hearing from her, but then, one day, he'd come home and she'd be there. They both worked for the service one way or another; it was just her career choice was more chaotic and intense, which left Chris never knowing when she was going to appear. He kind of liked it that way: no commitment, just a nice surprise to see her at the end of a shift. He would take her out, wine and dine her and then she'd disappear the following Monday.

'Chris, I've just heard from Amanda. She doesn't

think she's going to get time to do the autopsy today but promises to be on the case first thing,' Julie said as she stood in the doorway of his office.

'Thanks for letting me know. Have you said anything to the team?'

'Not as yet. They know we were called out this morning. Do you need me to round them up?'

'There isn't much to tell at the moment, so let's leave it till tomorrow. All being well, we'll have a better picture then.'

'Well, if you need me I'm with the rest of the team catching up with paperwork,' Julie said as she turned and headed back to the main office.

No one should feel that their only option was to jump into a fast-flowing river, but the fact that nobody had been recently reported missing in the local area concerned Chris. In a way, he hoped it was nothing more serious; that this woman was just another victim of the dark side of depression. His attention returned back to his computer as the weekly review email from the head of Special Ops dropped into his inbox. This gave him a chance to see what everyone else was up to in the area and any operations that required assistance. There was also information regarding the next quarter meeting, which all detective inspectors were duty-bound to attend. Chris added it to his Outlook calendar and hoped it would sync with his phone at least.

The rest of the day would be spent filing paperwork and tidying the chaos of his desk. A new case would no doubt mean more paperwork, and Chris was running out of space.

Chapter Two

Jen Garner

Jennifer Garner looked up at the clear blue sky, her head rested on James' chest as it rose and fell with his breathing. As the summer sun shone, she lay perfectly still, enjoying the calm before the storm.

Jen had decided that this weekend her family wouldn't be staying at home and using electronic devices. Instead, they'd go to the local park and enjoy the sunshine. The kids were running in and out the water fountains, coming back occasionally to check they were both still there or to dry themselves off, only to go back in again five seconds later. Things between her and James were getting better; finding out your wife was a former undercover detective was hard enough, but the fact that she had disappeared for almost a week without a word to her husband had been proving a bit more difficult for them to overcome as a couple.

They'd tried couples' therapy – although that hadn't been easy, given Jen's past. James' parents regularly took the kids away to give them space and Rita, James' mum, had told Jen that she was there if she needed to talk. She felt bad talking to Rita about her marriage issues, no matter how impartial she said she'd be. James wasn't the problem in the marriage – she was, along with her lies and the disappearing act that had almost torn her family apart.

Jen had promised James she would tell him everything and answer any questions he had, and she had. One good thing that had come out of last year was she had seen more of her former boss, Max, who the children adored.

Max had begun to wind down from his role at the Met and the search for his replacement was galloping on. She'd also heard from Hannah, who she had worked closely with the previous year. It seemed she was now in a relationship with the local DI who had been involved in the case, and she often sent Jen messages with tales of domestic bliss.

Jen felt content as the warm sun kissed her skin and she listened to the distant excitable screams coming from the fountains. But then the peace was shattered.

'Jen, what happened to your parents?' She turned her head and looked at James, trying to process the question. Though she had pretty much told him everything else, every time her parents had been brought up, she'd sort of glossed over it. It was easier just to say they were dead, and James had always accepted it – up until now.

'What do you mean?'

'You've never talked about them. You told me they're dead, but that's all you ever say.'

'To be honest, I don't know where they are … if they're still even alive,' Jen replied, sitting up and looking at James through her large sunglasses.

'You can tell me the truth, Jen. You've told me so much about your past life in the service … but you've never really talked about the other stuff.'

Just then she felt something heavy and soggy hanging around her neck.

'Mum, can we have an ice cream?' Alex asked.

'I tell you what, you and your sister go and play for a bit longer, then we'll get you both dry and grab an ice cream to eat on the way home, okay?'

Clearly not wanting to waste a moment of his last remaining play time, Alex ran off to report back to his sister, who more than likely had sent him to ask in the first place. By now, James was sat up and had reached over to pull Jen towards him. She knew she couldn't avoid the conversation much longer, and he already knew everything else. It was only right to give up her last secret.

'Let's just say I didn't have a great childhood. It was made clear to me at a very young age that I was an accident, and they'd never wanted me. I put a damper on them partying with their friends, so they used to send me to bed and have them over instead.' Jen looked up at James but was unable to meet his eyes as he took hold of her hand. 'Then, once I hit puberty, I started to become interested in boys and drinking in the park with my friends. I used to steal alcohol from my parents for the sessions. I guess I rebelled a bit ... like every teenager.'

As she took a breath, she searched James' face for some sort of emotion, but there was nothing other than his piercing blue eyes. He reached over and removed one of the hairs that was dangling in front of her sunglasses, pushing it back behind her ear and lifting her face to his.

'So, I was lucky. I sailed through school and then went on to college and pretty much sailed through that, but as I got older, I partied more and started to experiment with drugs.'

'What about your parents? Didn't they even try to stop you?'

'They didn't care, James. I was out from under their feet, so they could go back to their own partying lifestyles.'

James shook his head in disbelief as she continued.

'I would go from one drug and alcohol fuelled party to another, until one day I woke up and I was surrounded by people who had crashed out on the same floor I had. As the hangover and the comedown began, I looked around and thought to myself, "there must be more to life than this".' Jen could feel the tears forming at the corners of her eyes, but she wasn't going to cry – she was stronger than that. James hadn't interrupted her story or asked questions – he was getting good at just listening and not judging her for the mistakes she had made. She felt the reassuring squeeze of his hand, so she continued.

'So, I packed up everything I owned into a rucksack and left. I had enough money to keep myself afloat for a while, but I knew I needed to get a proper job as soon as I could.'

'Did your parents never even try to look for you?' James asked, breaking into Jen's thoughts.

'I don't think so. They were probably just glad to see the back of me. Not their problem any more.'

'Where did you go?'

'Manchester.' Jen took another deep breath before continuing. 'So, to cut a long story short, I was applying for jobs and came across an advert for the police force. I applied for a laugh, to be honest.'

'I guess you got the job.'

'Yeah, it was the turning point in my life. After graduating from Hendon and being headhunted by Max, he became the father figure I never had. I had purpose.'

Jen looked over at James, waiting for some form of response, but she knew from the look on his face that he was mulling it over. It gave her a chance to breathe before the onslaught of questions that usually followed. Looking around the park, she noticed the kids still playing happily ... having the childhood she never had.

'So, what changed?'

'What do you mean?'

'You just said that the Met gave you a purpose. Why did you decide to leave that whole life behind?'

'I fell in love, James.'

'Who was the unlucky guy?' James joked as Jen

continued to hide behind her sunglasses – at least he couldn't see her trying to fight back the tears.

'You remember when we first met, in that nightclub?'

'Like it was just yesterday.'

'You were out on one of your mate's stag dos, and I was in the club with Chloe, letting our hair down.'

'And I came along and swept you off your feet?'

'Kinda. You were the first guy I'd gone home with after a night out who seemed to care about me. You didn't treat me like some sort of conquest – yes, we slept together, but there was more to you. I left the next day wanting to see you again. So, I gave you my real number and didn't give you false promises about meeting up again.'

'And we lived happily ever after?' James laughed softly.

'We did, James. Everything was perfect ... before I screwed it all up.'

An awkward silence fell between them. James couldn't argue and tell Jen she hadn't, because wasn't that the elephant in the room? Jen began to tidy everything around them away, ready to call the kids over for ice cream and the walk home. Why was James suddenly so interested in her past? Why hadn't he just believed the story that her parents were dead?

'So ... who are you really?

The question startled her. 'I don't understand what you mean. I'm Jennifer Garner – your wife.'

'But you can't be.'

'What do you mean?'

'Well, Max sometimes calls you Lisa. I've only ever known you as Jen ...'

'Does it matter? Max was so used to calling me Lisa that it's just become a slip of the tongue. If it concerns you so much, I was born Marie Stephens. When I joined the service, I became Lisa Carter. But they don't matter any more.'

'Why the name changes? Why just not stay as Marie Stephens?'

'When I left my parents, I wanted a new life. People knew Marie Stephens as a party girl who'd do anything for a good time. So, when I joined the force, I became Lisa. When I met you, I was Jen, and you knew no different.'

'There seems to be so much more about you that I don't know,' James said as he rubbed his face.

'You see, when Chloe and I used to go out we'd change our names, so I couldn't exactly turn round to you and go, "oh by the way, my name's Lisa, not Jen". It would have led to too much explaining.'

James continued to study her face. Perhaps he was wondering whether he should have brought this up at all.

'I've put Marie in a box … she's in the past. The same way I did with Lisa when I left the service to move to Nottingham with you.'

Why was he questioning who she really was? Wasn't being Jen enough? Did he doubt their whole relationship? What did she need to do for him to completely forgive her?

'James?' Jen questioned as he stood up and began to fold the blanket they'd been sat on. He was brooding – maybe it was best to just leave him, but she couldn't cope with the silence and awkward atmosphere. It just made her feel more guilty and more dirty for the past lives she'd lived.

Chapter Three

DI Chris Jackson

'Thanks so much for seeing us first thing, Amanda.' Chris greeted her in the reception of the Pathology department.

'Not a problem. We've got ourselves an interesting one here.'

'Oh?'

'I'm afraid this one isn't looking like our regular suicide.'

'And there was me hoping for an open and shut case.' Chris sighed as he held open the door for Julie and Amanda.

'I decided it was best if we talked in one of the meeting rooms, as the autopsy was pretty straightforward. There are no obvious signs of anything criminal,' Amanda explained as they walked down the corridors of the Royal Derby Pathology Unit; the neutral-coloured walls and scent of flowery air freshener – to disguise the smell of disinfectant and chlorine – were now so familiar to Chris.

'Take a seat,' Amanda said, inviting them into one of the meeting rooms. 'I asked one of the team to provide us with some coffee, so help yourselves.' Amanda sat at the table and started to arrange her notes.

Chris offered around the coffee as he took control of the decanter before finding a seat alongside Amanda and waiting for her to begin.

'I think you're going to thank me for making sure the scene was as preserved as possible,' she started as she glanced towards them. 'Right, so, starting at the beginning. Our victim, as you will both be aware, is a female. I would put her approximately around the age of forty, but I can't be totally sure as her teeth show a lot of damage, but this could be due to poor diet or dental care. She is of Asian, possibly Middle Eastern, descent, around fifty-five kilograms and five-foot-seven.'

Julie scribbled away on her notepad.

'Cause of death is drowning as suspected. I have sent samples to the lab of the water in her lungs and a sample from the Trent, but I'm not expecting any big surprises,' Amanda continued as she referred back to her notes. 'I got Riley to run her DNA, and this is where it gets interesting. We got a match to one Dana Antwar. She is a known sex worker and, from investigation of her cervix, it looks like she has given birth in the past.'

Chris readjusted his position in the chair as he felt panic in the pit of his stomach. 'Can you tell how long ago?'

'I'm afraid not. Due to the shape and there being no visible damage, I would say it wasn't a recent birth – so, not in the past year – but you'll have to contact social services on that one.'

'Do you have any ideas on time of death?'

'I would take an educated guess that she would have been down there for about a week due to decomp.'

'Were there any signs of trauma suffered prior to her death?' Julie asked.

'I found some bones that hadn't healed properly, but there were no signs of recent sexual intercourse, whether consensual or not.'

'So, we've got a dead sex worker who's given birth at some point in her life?' Chris sighed.

'Yes, if you want to break it down like that.'

'Thank you, Amanda.' Julie jumped in

'Not a problem. We've sent her blood samples off and if anything pings, I'll let you know.'

Chris stood up and downed his lukewarm coffee.

'Thanks again,' he said, offering his hand .

'You okay?' Julie asked as they began their journey back to the car park through the hospital building.

'Yeah, I've just got this killer headache. I just can't shift it, no matter how much pain relief I take.'

'What have you been taking for it?'

'Oh, the normal over-the-counter stuff.'

'Is it even worth asking if you've seen a doctor about it? It could be something serious.'

'When I saw him last year, after the Garner case, he suggested that it was probably all down to stress. He said I should take some time off and maybe get my eyes checked out, just in case I needed glasses or something.'

'And did you?'

'Yup, perfect vision. Nothing to worry about.'

Last year, what had started with a dead woman found in a ditch in the small town of Long Eaton had led to a large-scale, multi-agency investigation and the seizing of millions of pounds worth of newly branded drugs. Though Chris and his team couldn't take credit for the whole of the investigation, he knew they'd been a big part of it and their achievements had made him proud. However, there was no doubt in Chris's mind that the case had taken its toll on his health.

'Well, maybe you should go back again Chris – before you get swept away with the next big case that lands on our doorstep.'

It was like Julie had read his mind. 'I'm probably just tired after a busy weekend with Hannah,' Chris lied, knowing full well the headache had been present long before the weekend. He was just getting far too good at ignoring it.

As they broke free of the hospital's stagnant air and found their car, Julie checked in with the team. They'd gone through some changes in the past couple of months with DC Sally Croft moving across to work with DI Manson on the drugs task force. This left the team with only four members, with promises of more officers if needed.

'Chris, I have the guys on conference call,' Julie said as they got into the pool car to head back to the station.

'Great. Put them on the hands free.' Chris jumped into the passenger seat as Julie transferred the call.

'We're all here.'

'Sorry for having to do this over the phone, but I want to hit the ground running with this one.' Chris could hear mutterings in the background. 'Okay, once this call is finished, I'll email you over a photo of our victim, Dana Antwar. She was pulled out of the Trent yesterday afternoon. Julie and I have just been with Amanda for the results of her autopsy.' There was no response over the phone, so Chris continued. 'Julie can fill you in on the details of Amanda's findings once we're back. Trudie, Dana was a known sex worker. Could you look her up on the system, please, regarding her criminal record?'

'Do you have anything further I can use, Chris, other than her name?' Trudie asked.

'I'm afraid not. We know very little about her at the moment, but Amanda said that her DNA pinged because of her career choice, so you shouldn't have too much of a problem. All being well, Amanda will have updated the system with Dana's vital statistics.'

'Okay, thanks.' Trudie still didn't sound completely convinced.

'Greg, Amanda tells me Dana has given birth in the

past. Can you work with Trudie and see if anything on Dana's records mentions the birth of a child and where he or she is now?'

'Not a problem.'

'Colin, would you check through all the recent reports of suicide attempts in the area surrounding the football grounds in the past couple of months? I'm wondering if Dana tried to jump before, but maybe someone had been around to stop her.'

'Will do.'

'Julie and I are on our way back, so if you could all make a start, then I'll check in with you in about an hour or so.'

'Sir,' they all echoed as Chris ended the call, before looking out of the window for inspiration.

'What do you really think?' he asked, turning towards Julie.

'I think we might be in for a bit of a challenge, in all honesty.'

'I don't like briefing the team over the phone. I have images of them all sitting there nodding but playing on Candy Crush, or putting us on mute so we can't really hear what they're saying.'

'While the boss is away,' Julie joked as they continued on their way back to Nottingham.

'Right, what have you got for me, team?' Chris asked as he entered the incident room.

Greg was sat at his desk and immediately started giving Chris a run-down. 'Okay, so Dana gave birth to a son called Mikel approximately six years ago. She appeared out of the blue at Nottingham's Queen's Medical Centre maternity unit in the late stages of labour.'

'Was she not registered under any midwife care?'

'Nope, this was the first they knew about her apparently. She hadn't attended any prenatal scans or appointments.'

'I'm guessing that means she wasn't registered with any doctor then?'

'Correct. She was completely off the radar of the midwifery team and the local GP.' Greg read from his notes 'She gave birth to a healthy baby boy weighing seven pounds and five ounces on the 19th June, six years ago.'

'Where does this fit in with her criminal record, Trudie?'

'Looking at the computer, she was caught up in a police raid of a brothel in April of that same year,' Trudie shouted from the back of the room.

'So, by my calculation, nine months prior to June is …' Chris looked at the ceiling while he did the maths.

'September, Chris,' Trudie called.

'September. Do we know if she was still a sex worker at that point?'

'I can't see anything after the April raid, but we have no way of knowing.'

'A pregnant sex worker wouldn't be good for business?' Chris mused.

'I'm not sure. People are into all sorts these days.'

Chris grimaced. 'So, what happened to them after the birth?'

'According to the notes, they kept her in till they were sure there was a safe place for her and the baby to go to.'

'Anything on why she hadn't sought medical advice before the birth of the baby?'

'She claimed to have not been aware of her pregnancy, but the team who were first responsible for her noted that there was no way she wouldn't have been aware.'

'Okay, so what happened next?'

'Dana and her baby left the hospital and returned to

where she was apparently living: a small flat at Regatta House near the Castle Marina retail park. She was passed on to the local midwife team who were happy with her and the baby's progress, and she was then fed through to the health visitor team.'

'All good then?'

'It looks that way, sir.'

'So where is this baby now? He must be six.'

'This is where it gets interesting. Dana confided in her health visitor that she was an illegal immigrant and that she was on the run from her pimp. The red flags went up, and she was then referred back to social services.'

'Do we have a contact?'

'Yep, somebody called Holly Lord. I'm just trying to get through to her now,' Colin shouted over with the phone glued to his ear.

'Her records state that Dana and the baby seemed settled and were doing everything right. The baby received his injections and, by all accounts, was a healthy and happy little boy,' Greg continued.

'Okay, so what went wrong?'

'Well this is it ... just after her son's third birthday, Dana and the child vanished.'

'Vanished?'

'She had missed a couple of appointments and meetings with the social worker who was helping her find a job and gain residency in England. So, she went over to the flat and she was gone – all personal effects had been completely cleared out.'

'So, where did she go?'

'This is where the trail goes cold. Nobody knows, sir.'

'Missing person's report logged?'

'Yes, her social worker logged her disappearance. But it looks like she just got lost in the system.'

'Great, so now we have a missing child.' Chris sighed as he rocked back on his chair, feeling his headache starting to re-emerge.

'According to the records, she wasn't considered a risk to herself or the child so ...' Greg trailed off.

'Do we have a timeline for Dana? From her first appearance in Nottingham?'

'Working on it now,' Julie said as she started to add the information to the incident board.

'The period between the child's third birthday and when we found Dana – we definitely have no information?'

'It's looking that way.'

'Do we know if she was soliciting during the period of those three years?'

'According to the social worker's report, she had turned her life around.'

'I think we need to speak to Ms Lord and find this child.' Chris studied the timeline.

'I've just arranged for you to meet Ms Lord in the next hour, boss. If that's okay?' Colin announced as he put the phone down.

'Thanks, Colin. I know you were also looking into whether Dana had tried to take her life prior to this. Did you have any luck?'

'I contacted the mental health teams at both hospitals and they have no records of anyone that matched Dana's description, but they are also *really* understaffed at the moment, so the lady I spoke to promised she would enquire amongst her colleagues just in case something had yet to be filed.'

'Thank you, Colin. Hopefully Ms Lord will be able to shine some light on the whereabouts of Dana's son.' Chris surveyed the room, wondering how best to direct his team next. 'Trudie, will you take Greg and go and visit Regatta

House to see if you can find any information on Dana's tenancy? How she was paying, that sort of thing.'

'Okay, boss. We'll take my car.' Greg turned to Trudie. 'Unless you fancy a walk?'

Chris carried on. 'Colin, I'm wondering why Dana ran. Greg said that she confided in her health visitor about her immigration status. Can you contact immigration and see what you can find out about her application?'

'Will do.'

'Julie and I are going to meet up with Dana's social worker and see what she can tell us about Dana's wellbeing ... and hopefully the location of her child.'

Holly's office was situated in the shadows of the city centre. Knowing they would struggle to find parking, Chris and Julie had taken the short walk from their office to meet her.

'Ms Lord,' Chris said, holding out his hand as she greeted them both in the main reception area.

'Officers, please call me Holly.' She spoke to them in a sing-song voice that Chris wondered if she always used.

'Thank you for seeing us at such short notice,' Julie said, taking Holly's hand and introducing herself.

'I wasn't sure where the best place for us to meet was, seeing as my office tends to be very busy. But I have managed to book one of our family rooms, if that's okay?'

'Not a problem,' Chris said as he and Julie followed Holly along a series of corridors and up a flight of stairs into a large room which was furnished with green sofas, a large coffee table, a television, which was securely fixed to the wall, and, weirdly, waist-high plug sockets.

'We have to keep certain things out of reach of little hands.' Holly had obviously noticed Chris's confused expression. They took a seat on opposite sofas as Holly laid out a series of folders and logged into her tablet. 'I've asked for some drinks to be brought over shortly, so they should be with us soon,' Holly said as she pushed her shoulder-length hair behind one of her ears and opened her notebook. 'How can I help you? The person I spoke to on the phone mentioned a body ...'

'We pulled what we thought was a suicide victim out of the Trent yesterday, and we have identified her as Dana Antwar.' Holly nodded as Chris spoke. 'We learned from her post-mortem that she had given birth in the past, and my team's investigation led us to you.'

'Yes, I remember Dana well,' Holly began as she looked through her paper files and started typing onto her tablet. 'Dana and her son, Mikel, were fed through to us via the health visiting team in Nottingham city. Dana had disclosed to them that she was an illegal immigrant, and she had some concerns about her former pimp.'

'Did you have any concerns for Dana and her son's safety?' Julie asked.

'As Dana was a known sex worker and due to what she'd disclosed, she was subject to weekly visits and meetings so we could keep a close eye on the care Mikel was receiving.'

'Did she know who the baby's father was?'

'I'm afraid that wasn't disclosed. She was uncomfortable talking about anything to do with her pregnancy and how she found herself in that situation. I did my best to be there for her and provide any support that I could.'

'Can you tell us what happened from there?' Chris pushed.

'I continued to work with Dana and Mikel for the next year until she was signed off as not a risk to the child. Our meetings then went to monthly – I wanted to help the two of them build a better life.'

Just then the drinks arrived and gave them the welcome interlude they all needed to sort through their notes.

'Are you able to tell me anything about her asylum request? How long had she been in the country illegally?' Chris asked, once the drinks had been served round.

'I can only disclose what was on her application. Anything else, I'm afraid you'll need a warrant for.'

'Anything you can tell us would be great.'

'At the time of her son's birth and the date of the application, she'd been here illegally for five years.'

Julie and Chris exchanged glances with each other as Holly continued.

'Her application stated that she had been brought over from Iraq and promised a better life which, as I'm sure you can imagine, didn't materialise.'

'So, what happened next?'

'She was called for an interview.'

'Did you attend the interview with Dana?' Julie asked.

'I wasn't allowed to as it was between Dana and her case worker. But I met her afterwards, and she seemed pretty positive about the experience.'

'So, where does this all fit in with her disappearance?' Chris asked.

'Dana made her asylum application prior to her son's first birthday, and I reported her missing, if I remember rightly, a week after what would have been his third birthday.'

'Would her claim not have been finalised at this point?'

'Yes, her claim would have been finalised for a while.'

Chris knew that Holly would be tied by client confidentiality and Colin would be able to fill them in on their return to the office anyway, so he decided to change tack. 'What can you tell us about her disappearance?' he continued.

'She had missed a couple of appointments and, because of the type of person Dana was, I took it upon myself to go over to her flat to see if she was okay.'

'I'm guessing this is when you discovered she was gone?'

'Yes, the flat was completely cleared out. It was like she had vanished into thin air.'

'Is there a standard procedure you follow in these circumstances?'

'I reported it to my manager and also to the police. I was concerned for her.'

'Okay, so what happened next? It seems Dana was never found.'

'You need to understand, Detective, that Dana's case was special, and I had personally gone out of my way to keep her on the books longer than the standard period. She was free to come and go as she pleased. There was no legal reasoning to keep me informed as to her plans and whereabouts.'

'So, there wasn't much you or your team could do?'

'I'm afraid not. It was logged, and I personally made sure she was reported as missing but, other than that, there wasn't a huge amount I could do.'

'So, I'm guessing you have no idea what happened to either her or her son?'

'In the beginning I checked once a month or so to see if there had been any news, but after a while …' Holly tailed off. 'I'm sorry I can't be any further help, Detectives. There will be meeting notes and further details on her case for asylum but, like I said, you would need a warrant.'

'Understood. We'll go back to the station and get someone onto the magistrates for that.'

'I'll get the files ready for you. It's the least I can do.'

'If you wouldn't mind, we'd really appreciate it,' Julie said as she began to gather her things.

'One more question. We recovered Dana's body yesterday but, as for her son, I don't suppose you're aware of any lost six-year-olds?' Chris asked, keen to continue the line of questioning and hoping for that bit of extra information.

'Nothing has been reported, but I'll get in touch with you if I hear anything.'

'Okay. Thanks, Holly,' Chris said, rising to his feet and passing over one of his business cards. 'If you think of anything else, my contact details are on the card.'

'I'll be sure to get in touch.' Holly led the officers from the building and into blinding sunlight as the midday sun hit from behind the arena.

'What do you think?' Chris turned to Julie, who was struggling to shield her eyes from the sun rays as they left.

'If things were going so great for Dana, why did she up and disappear?'

'I think that's what we need to find out. I'll ask somebody at the office to get a warrant application processed so we can get hold of Holly's files as soon as we can.'

'I'm wondering if she was denied asylum and thought her only option was to run?'

'Possibly,' Chris agreed as he began to search his pockets for some pain meds. He must have gone long enough now to be allowed to take some more.

'You okay?' Julie enquired as she watched him search his pockets

'Just struggling with the change of light. My vision blurred for a second.'

'You still got that headache?'

Chris nodded his response. He knew already what Julie would say.

Chapter Four

Chris was relieved as he headed into his air-conditioned office. *Summer was definitely here.* His phone rang as soon as he sat down, and he answered.

'Inspector, it's Holly Lord phoning from social services.'

'Ah, Holly. Did we leave something behind?'

'No, no. I was sorting my files ready for you to pick up and I got talking to my colleague. Apparently, there was a young boy found walking around Nottingham last week, asking people if they knew where his mum was.'

'Do you think it's connected to our case?'

'Quite possibly. From what my colleague has said, she thinks he's around the six-year-old mark.'

'How do we go about seeing and speaking to the child?'

'My colleague is just looking up the information now. I'll give you a call back as soon as I've got something.'

Chris hung up his phone and ran his hands over his face. *Time to see what the team have unearthed,* he thought as he heaved himself up from his desk and headed to the incident room.

'What you got for me?' he asked as he walked in.

'Trudie and I went to Regatta House and spoke to the letting agent.' Greg kicked things off.

Chris moved to pick up a pen to start writing on the incident board.

'According to the letting agent, the flat was paid for a year at a time in advance.'

'Okay, so did the money just stop coming in?' Chris asked in amazement. *How would somebody like Dana have been able to pay that much in advance?*

'This is it, it didn't. The letting agent thinks she left mid tenancy.'

'So how did they discover she'd gone?'

'It wasn't until Ms Lord went looking for her that they discovered the flat was empty.'

'So, you're telling me they have no idea when she left, but they definitely weren't chasing her for money?' Chris started to scribble on the board, hoping his handwriting would be readable. Moments later, he felt someone come up beside him and gently take the pen away from him.

'I'm afraid it is looking that way. The flat was rented, part furnished – and those items still remained – but Dana and the child were gone,' Greg explained.

'So, we have no time frame of when she might have run then?' Chris sighed, re-taking his seat at the front of the room.

'Holly should be able to help us with that. She'll have kept better records,' Julie reminded the team as she continued to write notes on the board.

'Did you manage to speak to any of her neighbours?' Chris asked, hoping that someone might have seen Dana leave.

'Sadly they rent mostly to students who don't stick around too long.'

'Does the landlord keep a list of the tenancy?'

'Yes, and he's also tracing where the payments for Dana's rent were coming from.'

'If I'm honest with you, boss, it all sounds a bit suss to me,' Trudie offered as she picked up her mug of coffee. 'Who can afford to pay a year in advance these days?'

'I was thinking the same thing,' Chris said as he stretched out and crossed his ankles. 'Do you have any better news, Colin?'

'I'm afraid not. I spoke to our contacts at the immigration service and Dana was refused asylum.'

'How come?'

'Dana was very open about her past on her application, and it was decided that it was no longer unsafe for her to return to her home country. It was felt that if she was granted asylum, there was nothing stopping her from going back on the streets.'

'So, where does that fit in with our timeline?' Chris pressed as he stood up again.

'Well, Dana then made an appeal that she subsequently lost. She was due to be deported back to Iraq with her son.'

'Did her application mention anything about the child's father?' Chris asked, hoping that a name might have been given that he could go on to trace.

'Afraid not. But she did divulge it was somebody from the UK, so it's possible her son had a right to be here at least.'

'It's a shame they didn't think the same about her.' Chris sighed again. 'Okay, team. We have a six-year timeline here from when her son, Mikel, was born to the date Dana was found in the Trent. Julie, have you been able to find when Dana was reported missing?'

'Just adding it now.'

Chris turned and looked at the board, trying to find some logic in the mess. 'Colin, did you get anywhere with a warrant for Holly's case files on Dana?'

'I'm due in court in the next hour.'

'Great. I'm waiting on a call back from Holly regarding a child who was found walking the streets of Nottingham and asking for his mum about a week ago.'

'Does she think that it's Mikel?' Greg asked.

'She isn't sure, but it does seem like a coincidence.'

'It would fit with the fact Amanda thinks Dana had jumped approximately a week ago,' Julie chipped in.

'What I'm struggling to understand is if Dana was instructed to leave the country, why did it then take three years for her to appear in the Trent? As harsh as it sounds, she must have been doing something in that timeframe. But what? And why wasn't she picked up?'

It just didn't make sense to Chris, and he knew then that this was another case that was going to be keeping him up at night for a long time to come.

Chapter Five

Dana

I knew a girl once who I would only see at parties, and one night she just dropped dead on the dance floor next to me. I was in a state of shock as Mr Crawford's men ushered me away and into a cab back to the house. I used to ask him what had happened to her, but he wouldn't tell me and would get angry. I overheard him on the phone not long after the incident. He was saying something about a burst package and the loss of thousands of pounds worth of drugs. He was so furious that day that I stayed away from him; he scared me when he got like that. After that, I knew in my heart what had happened to the girl that night, but each time I swallowed the packages I told myself I wouldn't make the same mistakes as she did.

I had just flown back into the UK after one of our trips abroad. I had that buzz because I had, once again, made it through customs without an issue. I met my driver, and we headed back towards Kent from Gatwick and to the house where I knew Mr Crawford would be waiting for me. He always sent the same driver and, as we pulled off the M25, I asked if I could walk for a while and get some fresh air. To my surprise, he agreed and let me out up the road from the place I now called home. I walked along, enjoying the view, and as I turned the corner towards where we lived, I noticed that the place was swarming with police officers in bright yellow jackets. My road was blocked off by police cars and officers with guns strapped to them. I thought I recognised one of the officers who seemed to be calling the shots; she looked like one of the girls who was always around George – but there was no way it could have been her. I casually turned around and walked back up the road the way I'd come, hoping to see my driver ... but he'd vanished. He'd obviously also seen what was going on and turned around and driven off instead of returning me to the house. With a stomach full of heroin and cocaine, I turned and ran. My survival instincts kicked in, and I knew I had to get away from the area and find somewhere to hide and plan my next move.

Chapter Six

DI Chris Jackson

'Morning, boss,' Trudie shouted as she approached Chris' office door, unaware he already had visitors.

'Morning Trudie. Good night?'

'Yeah, nothing much happened really. Watched a bit of telly, read for a bit, you know …' She trailed off as she noticed the other people in the room.

'This is Holly Lord, Dana's social worker, and her colleague, Jill Stokes.' Chris introduced the two women who were sitting in his office.

'Can I get anyone a drink?' Trudie asked, once the introductions were over.

'Mine's a coffee, please. Holly, Jill?' Chris said, glad of the excuse for more caffeine.

'Water, please. Unless you have decaf.' Holly and Jill spoke almost in unison.

'I'll see what I can rustle up.'

Trudie left, closing the door behind her, and Chris flipped over to a fresh sheet in his notebook. 'Thank you for coming here to meet me.'

'Not a problem. Like I said last time you visited, there isn't really anywhere in the office to hold meetings. It made sense to come here,' Holly responded as she turned on her tablet. 'Jill is responsible for all of the children who are either found on their own, or where something has happened to their parents and there is no one left to look after them. This is why I wasn't aware of the situation when you first came to my office.'

Chris turned his attention towards Jill. 'I was wondering if you'd be able to tell me the circumstances in which this young boy was found?'

Jill readjusted herself in her seat as Trudie came back with the drinks and handed them round. 'Thank you,' Jill said, taking the glass from Trudie. 'Holly filled me in with the case on the way over. The police became aware of a child wandering the streets of Nottingham about a week ago. Our CCTV team first picked him up talking to random passers-by. As you can imagine, they were rather concerned to see a six-year-old on the streets of Nottingham alone, so an officer was dispatched to his location to check the situation.' Jill took a sip from the water. 'When the officer approached the boy, he appeared to be well looked after. He said that he wasn't lost but that he was looking for someone, and he wouldn't give the officers his name.'

'Have you managed to trace his mother at all?' Chris asked.

'When asked about his mother, the boy got very animated and insisted he couldn't go anywhere until he had found somebody called Lisa Carter.'

'Sorry, can you repeat that again for me?'

'The child was walking around Nottingham, asking people if they knew where Lisa Carter was.'

'Is the name familiar to you Chris?' Holly asked, clearly noticing the change in Chris' body language.

'Quite possibly. I'm guessing the fact that the child is still in your care means you haven't found this Lisa Carter, or his mother for that matter?' Chris needed to know if the Lisa he was thinking about was the same one Jill was looking for.

'No, no luck yet. He won't communicate with anyone. He just sits in his room asking for Lisa Carter.'

'Do you think Lisa is his mother?'

'I don't know, but I'm hoping, whoever she is, she might be able to provide us with some answers as to why he was left wandering the streets.'

Chris turned and looked over to Holly. 'Does the boy resemble Dana's son Mikel?' he asked, doing his best to change the subject. Chris thought he knew very well who Lisa was but, as yet, hadn't worked out what he was going to do about it.

'Quite possibly, which was another reason why I knew we needed to speak to you as soon as we could.'

'Jill, would we be able to get a saliva sample from the boy? I can get it compared with the DNA we have on the system for Dana. We might even come across the father while we're at it.'

'I don't see why not. I'm not sure about how legal it is to use it to search for the father, but I'll leave that up to you.' Jill gave Chris a knowing smile.

'What I don't understand is this Lisa Carter angle, though,' Holly continued.

'He won't tell anyone anything. His emergency foster mum has tried all sorts of things to get more information from the boy, but he's just completely fixated on Lisa Carter,' Jill said with a sigh.

'Chris, can't you check your missing persons' database and see if she pings from your end?' Holly asked.

'Shouldn't be too much of an issue. I'll get one of the team on to it straight away.' Chris shifted in his seat uncomfortably.

'Do you think he could have been brainwashed?' Holly asked suddenly.

'What do you mean?' Chris was slightly taken aback.

'I'm not an expert in that sort of thing, but maybe this Lisa isn't the be all and end all?'

The three of them sat in silence for a moment as they all sipped their drinks at the same time, processing the new idea.

'So, you think Dana and the boy are connected, Holly?' Chris asked, breaking the silence.

'I think it's a strong possibility.'

Jill nodded her head in agreement.

'What can my team best do to support you, Jill – and of course the child?' Chris asked, clicking his pen, ready to make notes.

'The boy is as fine as he can be. He's with one of my best emergency shelter families and, other than this Lisa Carter business, he's safe and well.'

'If I arrange for one of my officers to accompany you to meet the boy, we'll get the ball rolling on the DNA comparison.'

'I think it would also be an idea to try and locate Lisa as well,' Jill reminded Chris.

'Like I said, I'll get someone to see if we can trace her on our systems. Holly, did your office get the warrant for your files?' Chris asked, quickly changing the subject once again.

'I have them in the boot of my car, if I can borrow someone to help me bring them in?'

'Of course.' Chris suddenly had another thought. 'Has a child psychiatrist had a chance to access the boy?'

'We are in the process of getting one organised, but there is a slight delay given the budget constraints.'

Chris stood up. 'If there's anything else we can help with, you know where I am.' He handed Jill one of his cards.

'Nice to meet you, Detective. I suspect we might be seeing more of each other as this case carries on, but I think we made some progress today.'

'I'm just grateful to Holly for linking the two cases initially,' Chris responded. 'I'll find someone to help you with those files, Holly, and get someone to follow you back with a DNA kit.'

*

Chris returned to his office, having seen Jill and Holly out of the station, and turned his PC on. This case was about to get very complicated – all because of Lisa Carter, a former undercover detective and missing person. He wasn't sure where to turn for advice. He had no way of contacting Hannah and, other than turning up on Lisa Carter's doorstep, he was at a loss. The last time he was on that very doorstep, he'd had a warrant in hand and was leading her kids away from the ensuing chaos.

'You okay, boss?' Julie asked as she stood in the doorway to his office.

'Yeah, sorry, just lost in thought, trying to decide what to do next,' Chris responded, looking up from his notebook.

'Do you want me to rally the team?'

'Yeah. It'd be good to see where everyone is at,' Chris said, getting up from his chair. 'And I can feed back from the meeting with Holly and Jill.'

'I'll get everyone into the incident room. I think Colin's finished bringing the boxes up from Holly's car.'

'I'll grab another coffee, then I'll be with you.' Chris followed Julie out of his office and towards the incident room and the strategically placed kitchen. Once he'd made his coffee, he headed in to meet the team, only to be greeted with multiple boxes stacked on the table and Colin looking rather out of breath.

'Thanks for that, Colin.' He smiled at him.

'I didn't realise when you asked for help it would involve carrying so many heavy boxes. I might think twice about volunteering next time.' Colin plonked himself on one of the spare chairs.

'I didn't expect there to be this many, to be fair.' Chris looked uncertainly at the five boxes he had been presented with.

'Three years' worth of meeting notes, though,' Julie reminded him as she overheard their discussion.

'True. Right, everyone here?' Chris asked, surveying the room, just as Trudie and Greg walked in and took their places. 'Who wants to start us off, then?' Chris perched on the end of one of the tables. 'Any luck with the tenancy payments, Greg?'

'I'm planning to chase them up as soon as we're finished.'

'Colin, anything more on her asylum case?'

'Yes and no. As mentioned previously, her application had been refused, but she claimed that Mikel was born in the UK to a British father, so she needed to stay here to look after him as there was no way of tracing him.'

'Okay, so what happened from there?'

'Nothing really ... because she vanished.'

'And ended up in the Trent three years later,' Chris muttered. 'Can you keep on at them and see if you can find out how she managed to stay in the country and not get deported back?'

'I'll try my best.'

'Okay, so that just leaves me ...' Chris wasn't sure how much he was going to reveal about his meeting but, as he had promised himself from the very beginning, he would always be honest with his team. 'So, I had a meeting with Holly and Jill from social services about Dana's child. As I'm sure you've all heard by now, a child of around six years old was found wandering the streets of Nottingham last week.' Chris looked around the room at the others for their reactions. 'He's currently in an emergency foster home till they find his mother but – and this is where it gets really interesting – he was walking around Nottingham asking for somebody called Lisa Carter.'

'Has he not said anything else?' Greg asked.

'According to Jill, he just sits there asking for Lisa Carter. He won't say anything about where he came from, or how he got into Nottingham. Just that he needs to find Lisa Carter.'

'Is this the same Lisa Carter you were trying to locate last year, boss?'

'It's beginning to look that way,' Chris acknowledged.

'Doesn't your lady friend know where she is?' Greg asked with a smirk.

When Chris had returned to the office last year, all he'd told them was that both Lisa Carter and Jennifer Garner had been located and that it was a closed case. He'd managed to field the questions that followed, but mostly the team were happy to know that Jen had been returned to her family safely. 'Hannah? I can ask her, but all this Lisa Carter stuff was before her time.'

'What are social services doing?' Trudie asked.

'Holly thinks that the child is possibly Mikel, but I've sent an officer back with Jill to get a DNA sample to see if he's related to Dana.'

'And if he is?'

'I guess we begin the search for his family.'

'Easier said than done.'

'As you've no doubt all seen, in front of us are the notes Holly kept regarding her meetings with Dana. We might not find anything we don't already know in there but, until we get a confirmation on the DNA either way, I suggest that this is where we start.'

'But what are we looking for?' Julie asked.

Chris realised he didn't really have an answer. 'Go through the boxes and learn about Dana and her plight. We still have unanswered questions regarding her tenancy and where she and Mikel were the three intervening years before we found her body.' Chris stood up from his seat and felt himself wobble slightly as his vision blurred.

'You okay, boss?' Trudie seemed to notice the wobble and looked concerned.

'Yeah, think I just stood up too quickly.' Chris had to admit, he felt strange. But he didn't have time to worry about his health right now – he had a case to solve. 'I just need to pop back to the office for something. I'll let you all take your pick and I'll do whatever's left.' The whole team laughed at Chris' obvious attempt to get out of document checking.

Chris tried to laugh along, but he didn't feel too good. The sudden loss of balance and blurry vision had scared him slightly. When he got back to his office, he quickly picked up the sandwich he had on his desk and took a bite. Maybe he was just hungry? He didn't really *feel* that hungry, though. Having battled with a headache the day before, he hoped and prayed that this was just a side effect of the pain medication he was taking.

Chapter Seven

Jen Garner

James hadn't said much since their conversation in the park the day before. Jen knew to give him the space to work things through, but at the same time she was scared that her lies were becoming too much for him to handle. Was this the beginning of the end of their marriage?

She had just returned home from her daily run. James seemed to understand the reason she ran every day now; keeping her fitness up was what she had been trained to do for most of her life. He just let her go and endured the sweaty kisses and hugs on her return. As she let the water run over her, she heard the doorbell ring and, moments later, voices from below followed by her name being shouted repeatedly.

'I'm coming. Who is it?' she shouted back at them.

'It's the DI from Nottingham. You know, the one who arrested me and searched the house while you were gone?' Jen wished she could see James' face as he shouted up to her. When he came out with things like that, she had no idea whether he was joking or seriously pissed. She wrapped her hair in a towel, rushed to put on a clean set of clothes and headed downstairs. As she reached the bottom, James met her.

'Try not to get me arrested this time,' he said, kissing her forehead. James' arrest the previous year was still a sticking point between them. Jen supposed that it was understandable that he still struggled to come to terms with the fact that he had been arrested whilst she had been safe and well in London.

Jen opened the living room door and greeted the

inspector. 'Detective.' She held out her hand and he shook it with a firm grip. Though she had meet him once before at the poorly lit Silverdale Gateway on the night it all kicked off, she didn't know much about him – other than the graphic details Hannah shared with her about their sex life, of course. Jen sat down opposite him and studied his appearance. He seemed a lot younger than she'd remembered, but he was definitely fit – and she most certainly understood why Hannah was attracted to him.

'So, you're the man who tried to track me down then?' she said wryly.

'Afraid so. Am I okay addressing you as Lisa? Or Jen? Or something else?'

'Jen is fine. I left Lisa back in London.'

'Jen it is. Can we talk? I wasn't sure what the situation would be between you and your husband.'

'It sort of depends what you want to talk about. Do I need a lawyer present or something?'

'Oh no.' The detective appeared slightly taken aback. 'Maybe you've seen the news recently? The body of an unidentified female was pulled out of the Trent a couple of days ago.'

'I think I saw something on the local news.'

'Well, to cut a long story short – she had a son, who we think is currently living in emergency sheltered accommodation.'

'Right … and what does that have to do with me?'

'Well, the thing is, before the police found him, he had been walking around Nottingham city centre, um … asking for you.'

'Excuse me?'

'Well, not you – Lisa Carter.'

Jen looked at Chris in disbelief. 'I don't understand. No

one here knows me as Lisa. Are you sure you have the right person?'

'Well, you're the only Lisa Carter *I* know and, given your history ...' Chris trailed off.

Jen was still in shock, trying to figure out what was going on.

Chris continued speaking. 'The body we pulled out belonged to Dana Antwar, originally from Iraq and here as an illegal immigrant. Her past is a bit sketchy, but she has a six-year-old son who, if we're correct about his identity, won't speak to anyone ... unless they're Lisa Carter.'

'Have you spoken to anyone else about me?' Jen asked quickly.

'No, most certainly not. When your name was mentioned by social services, I didn't feel comfortable revealing your identity until I'd spoken to you.'

'So, you think the body in the Trent and this boy have something to do with me and my past?'

'Right now, Jen, you're the only lead I have.'

'Sounds like you know more about me than I know myself ...' she said vaguely, just as James walked into the room.

'So, you off leaving your family again?' he asked, looking over at Jen. Once again, she couldn't tell if he was joking.

'What? No, of course not.'

'But you've heard what the detective said as clear as I did. Someone is looking for you, Jen, or Lisa ... or whoever the hell you are.' Now she knew he wasn't joking.

'James!' Jen couldn't believe his tone.

'Whatever. Can you at least let me know where you're going this time, so I don't waste any more police time looking for you?'

Jen looked over towards Chris, who was beginning to stand up. 'I'm sorry. I shouldn't have come. I can see myself out.' At that point, James laughed and muttered some comment as Jen left the room, following Chris to the door

'Detective, I'm sorry about James. Things are ... well, you know.'

Chris nodded his response, clearly not wanting to comment on what was going on in front of him.

'I'll contact Max and get him to look into it. I'm sorry I can't be any more help but ...' Jen stood for a moment as she watched Chris leave, get into his car and reverse off the drive. Then she stormed back into the house and into the kitchen. 'What the fuck was that all about, James?'

'Mum?' Melanie looked up from where she was doing her homework at the kitchen table.

'Come on, James. Spit it out! I'm waiting.'

'Dad?' Melanie was looking worriedly between her parents.

'Pull the other one, Jen. You were lapping it up. The world needs saving – quick, let's call our local undercover detective!'

'It's not like that, and you know it.'

'What's going on?' Melanie was getting more and more upset.

'You've changed, Jen. Ever since you walked out on us last year, you're not the woman I married.'

'I'm the exact same woman you married!'

'Come off it. We were just some mission to you.'

Jen raised her hand and slapped James round the face as Melanie stood on a chair with tears in her eyes and shouted at them both to stop. James lifted his hand to his face, and the room fell silent for a moment before Melanie's sobs became louder, and the realisation of what

47

had just happened hit them both. Jen moved towards Melanie and tried to pull her across for a hug, but her daughter pushed her away, got down from the chair and ran towards her room, slamming the door.

Jen looked at her husband. *What had gone wrong between them? Where had the trust gone? Where was the "for better and for worse" of their marriage vows?*

'James?' He didn't answer as he, too, left the kitchen and headed out towards his car. The next thing Jen heard was the squeal from his tyres, and suddenly the house was silent again. She questioned again where it had all gone so wrong. She thought things had been sorted between her and her husband, but that was obviously not the case. It seemed it really was too much to expect him to accept her past. Had she been wrong to return and assume things would go back to normal? Was she doomed to be alone for the rest of her life? Because if her own husband couldn't deal with her past, who could? Should she accept that all she could hope for was a relationship like Hannah had with the detective, seemingly just based on sex? Maybe she should be the one packing a case and leaving ...

She sank down onto a chair and put her head in her hands. This was a mess, and there was no one she could talk to who would know a way out. She took her phone from her pocket and tried phoning James; as she expected, it went through to voicemail. Instead, she scrolled to Max's number, and her finger hovered over the green dialling symbol. She couldn't give up that easily, could she? Just then, Jen heard a crashing coming from upstairs and remembered she had a daughter who had just watched her mum and dad tear strips off each other. She put her phone back into her pocket and quickly returned to mother mode as she went to check on the heartbroken Melanie.

James had driven around aimlessly for hours. He had initially decided to visit his parents in Wetton, only to make it to the top of their drive and change his mind. After that, he'd returned to Nottingham and gone to where Harry, his best friend, used to live and watched a loved-up couple – he assumed the new owners – enter Harry's old house. He and Jen had been like that once, hadn't they? He'd thought everything was perfect between them, but maybe it had all been too perfect to be true? As he sat outside his best friend's old house, he tried to figure out why he'd become so angry. He knew Jen's history; he just hadn't expected, after last year's events, to be still be facing hurdles six months on. She had told him about her parents and her partying, she had answered every question he'd asked. He had met Max and Hannah and heard stories about Chloe. But the threat that she may up and leave again at a moment's notice broke him.

It was late when he pulled back onto the drive. Though the house was dark, Jen had left the porch light on. He crept silently into the house to be greeted by a lone figure sat on the stairs, holding his teddy.

'Daddy.'

'What's up, mate? Shouldn't you be asleep?'

'I've been waiting for you to come back. Melanie is really upset and wouldn't stop crying and shouting. I knew that you'd be able to make it better, so I've been waiting for you to come home, so I could tell you and you could make everything all right.'

James' heart broke. 'I'm here now. You go and get into bed, and I'll go and see if Melanie is okay.'

'Mummy is in there with her, Daddy. She's been quiet for a while, but Mummy hasn't come out of her room.'

'Not to worry. You need me to come and tuck you in?'

'No, Daddy. Melanie and Mummy are more important.' Though he'd been dismissed, James still followed Alex into his room and tucked him and teddy into bed.

'Thank you, for waiting for me. You did a good thing for your sister tonight. You'll be the man of the house in no time.' James kissed his son's forehead and crept out of his room.

He went to his daughter's room and stood in the doorway. Jen was balanced on the end of the single bed, cuddling Melanie. They were both sound asleep, and he worried that if he tried to go in, he would only end up falling over something and waking them both. So, he just stood there and watched. Finally, he decided that maybe it was time for him to find his bed too. Hopefully tomorrow would be a better day, and he and Jen would be able to start again.

He woke to the sound of his alarm and noticed that Jen had returned to bed at some point in the night. He sat on the edge of the bed and wondered if he should say something to her, or just get up and go to work and leave an air of unsaid words. He tried to creep out of the room when Jen began to stir.

'What time is it?' Jen muttered in a sleep-drenched voice.

'Six-thirty. I'm just going to start getting ready. Do you want me to wake the kids and tell them to get ready too?'

'Yeah ... it's not like they'll get up.'

James bent over the bed and kissed her on the forehead. 'I love you.' His words were met with silence as he left the room and headed in to wake the kids, or at least give them their first "wake-up warning".

Jen had been awake when James had kissed her. In truth, she had been lying awake since she'd moved out of bed with Melanie. She felt like she needed to run for miles before she could even begin to clear her head. Things really were a mess. She started going over it all in her mind, trying to make sense of the chaos.

When she and Hannah had caught up with Jessica at the Silverdale Gateway and the links between George Crawford, Jess and herself had become clear, it soon became obvious that neither of them knew that Jen and Lisa Carter were the same person. Jessica and George hadn't spoken to each other since Jessica was a child, so they hadn't shared their combined knowledge. Jessica had never known Jen as Lisa Carter and never would, and George was none the wiser about Lisa's change of identity and wouldn't be getting out of prison any time soon anyway. So, to find DI Jackson at her door telling her a child had been asking around Nottingham for Lisa felt like a kick in the teeth, and James' reaction had just made her feel more guilty. But if this really was another life she'd affected, then she needed to put things right again …

Chapter Eight

Dana

I realised I didn't even know Kent that well as I hopped on one train and then another. I found a cash machine and emptied it of what little money I had. I knew it wasn't safe to use the card Mr Crawford had given me, so I found a cheap, grotty hotel, booked myself a room and hid. I never opened the curtains, scared that I would be seen. I would spend days with my back up against the door, listening for people coming up the stairs to my room, but no one ever came. I remember squatting in the bath one night as I passed the packages that had been hidden away safely inside me. As each one emerged, I sobbed. I was alone and scared and, as the stomach cramps kicked in, I curled into a tiny ball and stayed there till I was sure I was still alive.

Once I felt safe and convinced myself no one was coming, I retrieved the packages from the bath, cleaned them and laid them out on the desk. I had seen Mr Crawford's men do this a thousand times over, and somewhere in my brain I had an idea. Scraping together my remaining money, I left the hotel for the first time in over a week and went in search of some food and some small packets. I was living in what I was stood up in; I decided I needed some new clothes to look like I meant business. I was scared as I walked around the town centre, checking in every doorway and waiting for someone to jump out on me, but it never happened and my confidence grew.

I sat at the desk of my hotel room, and I cut the drugs like I had watched so many times before. I turned on the television and began to watch Mr Crawford's trial play out in front of millions. This had been the country's biggest drug haul, and it spread like an epidemic across the country. But here I was, sat in this grotty hotel room with a plan. When I'd walked the streets, people looked down on me, but suddenly I saw a way I could command respect. It was like I'd been reborn, and this time I wouldn't make the same mistakes.

Using some of Mr Crawford's old drug networks, I managed to shift all the drugs in my possession. I started looking to move on somewhere new, where a girl like me would be welcome, and that's when I saw a programme on the telly about Leeds. I somehow knew that that was where my future was, and it would no longer be about drug smuggling. I could be anyone I wanted to be ... and I was.

Though I didn't need the money, I found a cash-in-hand job in a small café, so once the money from the drugs I'd sold on had run out, I'd at least know I was going to be able to support myself. For a while, everything was just how I imagined it would be when I first came to the United Kingdom.

Chapter Nine

DI Chris Jackson

Chris was back at his desk with one hell of a hangover, despite the fact he hadn't had that much to drink the night before. His cat, Fluff, had woken him up early with yowls and licks, and he'd moved her aside just as his alarm had sounded.

The overwhelming feeling of a hangover certainly didn't help his already troubled mind. He was completely torn about what to do after the meeting with Jen. There were clearly some issues between her and her husband, although, if he was honest with himself, he wasn't sure how he'd behave if he was in James' shoes. Should he disclose to social services that he knew who Lisa Carter was and where she was, or was it his duty to protect Jen and her past?

'Excuse me, boss.' It was one of the PCs, Nikki Haywood, knocking on his open office door.

'Come in, Nikki. What can I do for you?'

Nikki walked in and stood uncomfortably in front of his desk. 'I'm sorry to disturb you, but this really weird thing has just happened,' she began as Chris signalled over to her to take a seat. 'I was working on the front desk when this lady came in. She was dressed like she'd just been to the gym. But, anyway, I looked up at her to see if I could be of any help, and I could've sworn blind that it was the missing woman we spent last autumn trying to track down stood right in front of me.'

'Okay.'

'Well anyway, she asked for you by name. When I asked her what hers was, she kind of looked at me blankly, like

I was supposed to know who she was.' Nikki fidgeted in the seat. 'So, I asked her to wait while I came to get you. Are you free to speak to her?'

'So, you think Jennifer Garner is in reception wanting to speak to me?'

'Quite possibly, yes. Are you expecting her?'

'I went to see her last night and gave her my card.' Chris stood up from his desk, his thoughts going a hundred miles an hour. If this was Jen, did it mean she knew more than she had said the night before?

Following Nikki down to the front desk, he was greeted by the sight of Jen as she sat surrounded by others in her running gear. A sense of despair radiated off her.

'Jen, good to see you.' Chris held out his hand. 'Is everything okay?'

'I'm sorry about last night and James,' she said, taking his hand.

'I hope I haven't caused any further issues between you two.'

'Can we talk somewhere else?' Jen asked, looking around uncomfortably.

'Of course. Will my office be okay?'

'Yeah.'

Chris nodded over towards Nikki, skipped the formalities of getting Jen to sign in and led her up the stairs to his office. He wondered if the word would spread about Jen's arrival and his office would become a fish bowl, as everyone congregated to check out the former missing person.

'Can I get you a drink?' he asked as he ushered Jen into the office.

'Some water would be good, thanks.'

'I'll be back shortly,' Chris said as he went in search of refreshment.

Jen didn't know what on earth she was doing at the police station, let alone sat in DI Chris Jackson's office. She surveyed the room, which was rather bland and standard office-like. Other than the stacked-up paperwork, which she assumed were case files, the space gave nothing away about the DI himself.

'Sorry about that, someone hadn't refilled the kettle,' Chris said as he came back into the room. He handed over a glass of water while cradling his coffee. 'No biscuits, I'm afraid.' He settled back down behind his desk.

'I usually run to clear my mind,' Jen took a sip from the glass, 'but the more I thought about this poor boy losing his mother and asking for—' she hesitated, '—Lisa Carter, the more I realised that I had to come in and see you.' She paused again. 'But away from the house and all the complications with James.'

'I'm not really sure what more I can tell you at this point. As I said yesterday, we pulled Dana out of the Trent a couple of days ago. During her autopsy, we learned she was a known sex worker.'

Jen knew there was no point trying to hide anything as she felt her face giving away her emotions.

'When we started looking into the case, we then discovered this little boy had been found around the same time we believe Dana went into the Trent.

'And he was asking for me?' She could sense that he was holding something back, but what?

'Yes, well … Lisa. He won't speak to anyone. Social services have tried all sorts of things to get him to talk, but he won't.'

'Okay. I just don't understand … no one in Nottingham should know me as Lisa Carter. Well, except you and maybe some of the officers you work with.'

'I can assure you, Jen, I'm the only one who knows about your second identity in this office.'

'So, what do you want from me?'

'I'm not even sure myself. I was just following up leads.'

She sat there for a moment, trying to work out what she could do and where Lisa Carter fitted into all of this, when her phone beeped. Knowing exactly who it would be, she ignored it for a while until it beeped again.

'Sorry, I need to look at this,' she said, taking her phone from the case she used when running, which was attached to her arm.

Meet me at 1p.m. I'll be in the Holiday Inn. Room number 504.

As she read the message, her mind went into overdrive.

'I'm sorry, Chris. Everything is such a mess at the moment, with my home life and now this.'

'I'm sorry for dragging you into it all.'

'Look, I need to go.' She stood up from the chair and looked towards the office door.

'Thank you for coming in to see me, Jen,' Chris said as he also stood up. 'I can show you out the back entrance if that's easier?' he offered as he led her out through the station.

'Thank you.' She turned and looked at Chris. 'Sorry again.' And with that, she began to run.

Jogging away from the station, she knew exactly what those messages from James meant. But hadn't the days of random sex in hotel rooms on his lunch break become a thing of the past? She didn't bother texting him back, knowing that she had to just go and face him. The two of them needed to talk. She'd gone out on her run and, just by following where the paths led her, had ended up at the Nottingham police station. She hadn't planned the visit, but the thought of a little boy out there alone, never mind the fact he was asking after her, almost guided her way there. So much for running to clear her mind; it seemed to have made thing ten times worse.

She arrived at the hotel just after 1 p.m. and, as instructed by the text, she made her way up to the room. She hadn't dressed for the occasion – if anything, sex was the last thing on her mind, and she knew what would be waiting for her behind the door of room 504. Bracing herself for another possible argument, she knocked on the door and awaited her fate.

Chapter Ten

James Garner

James had known that this was a long shot when he'd booked the hotel room. The chances of Jen even turning up were slim, never mind being interested in having sex with him. He had to try to make things work, and if going back to the start was the answer then so be it. So, once his office clock had slowly made its way to 1p.m., he headed over the road and checked in to the hotel – under a fake name like they used to. He ordered room service and then sat on the edge of the bed and waited. The excitement wasn't there any more like it used to be. The thought of making love to his wife, the excitement of which outfit she would turn up in this time didn't thrill him and make him crave her touch. The magic had well and truly gone. What was he even doing sat in this hotel room, anticipating the knock on the door? Maybe he was wrong, maybe Jen still felt the excitement and she would present herself in some newly acquired outfit? There was only one way to find out, and the answer would lie behind the knock on the door.

'Hey.' James greeted her with a kiss.

'Hey.'

There was silence and an awkwardness between them that neither of them had ever felt. James moved out of the way and let her into the room. She wasn't hiding anything under her coat as she took it off and laid it on the bed.

'Sorry to disappoint,' Jen said as she noticed him looking at her.

'I'm sorry about last night,' he began, but his words were met by an icy silence. He watched Jen as she moved around the room. Then she stood opposite him, looking directly at him as she started taking her clothes off.

'This is me,' Jen said to him. 'These are my wobbly bits,' she said, pointing as she spoke, 'these are the stretch marks that were created by the two children we had together. Melanie, who is sensitive and clever, and Alex, who is funny and one of a kind. This is the scar I got when I was so fucked off my face on drugs I smacked my head on a shelf.' As she continued, James wondered if he should be doing the same thing, but he waited patiently for her to finish. 'I stand here in front of you with nothing to hide, and I'm all yours. I have always been since the day that we met, James. I have never looked at anyone else the way I look at you; I have never felt the same way for anyone else the way I feel for you.' There was another silence between them as Jen stood there. 'I know I hurt you last year, but I did what I thought was best at the time.'

'Jen—' James felt lost for words and racked with guilt. He took a breath and tried to clear his throat, but she interrupted him.

'No, James. I can't keep apologising. You and the kids have always been my first priority, and if anything ever happened to you …'

James moved across the room towards his wife, picking up one of the dressing-gowns that lay on the bed as he did.

'I'm not asking for forgiveness. I just need you to know this is me, all of me.'

James moved closer as he draped the gown over Jen, but she shrugged it off.

'I'm stood here in front of you naked, so you can see that I'm not hiding anything from you, I'm not someone different. I'm Jennifer Garner, your wife and the mother to your children, and I need you to accept me for everything you see right now. Will you?'

He bent down and picked up the gown again, placing it gently over her. 'Jen, you'll always be my number one, and I know I've lashed out at you recently, but I promise to accept you as you, whatever your past and wherever we go from here. Let's do it together?' He noticed Jen was shivering as she embraced him. 'I love you,' James said, kissing her forehead.

'I love you too.'

James didn't know how long he'd been sat on the bed with Jen, with his mobile phone in one hand and the other pinned underneath Jen as she cuddled in to him. Her nose started to twitch and, having watched her sleep a thousand times before, he knew she was about to wake up.

'Hey, sleepy head,' he said as he removed his arm from under her. He groaned as the blood started flowing back into his arm, which had obviously gone numb.

'You should have said something. I'd have moved,' she said, watching him trying to get his circulation back.

'No chance of that. You were snoring away.'

'Sorry, I didn't realise I'd fallen asleep.'

'You've been out for a couple of hours. You looked so beautiful and peaceful, I didn't want to wake you.'

'What about work? The kids?' Jen asked, suddenly panicked as she rushed to get out of the bed and put on the clothes that were still in a pile where she'd left them.

'It's okay. I've organised for next door to pick them both up. You know how much they love going to Jodie's.'

'But work won't be wondering where you are?' Jen said, pulling the sheet from the bed around her still naked body.

'One-handed remote access. While you've been dozy, I've been answering emails and working from my phone.' James laughed.

'You should have woken me.' A heavy silence suddenly cloaked them, neither of them wanting to address the elephant in the room.

'Jen, will you promise to always come back to me and the kids?'

Jen looked at him quizzically. 'I don't understand, James.'

'I know we need to put what happened last year behind us, and I'm trying.' James sat on the edge of the bed and looked at the wall. He had rehearsed what he was going to say to her a million times, so he took a deep breath and tried again. 'What I mean is, when you go off saving the world, will you promise you'll always come back to me and the kids?'

'But I'm not going anywhere.' Jen moved to sit next to him as she did up her bra.

'Jen, I don't want to wake up one morning and for you to have just gone again—'

'James.' Jen interrupted him. 'I'm not going anywhere, though.'

'I've been looking through the news reports. I heard what the DI said. This little boy has been asking for you. He obviously needs your help. If it *was* his mum who was found in the Trent, he's completely alone in the world.'

'I don't understand, James.'

'What I'm saying is go back to the DI and go and visit this boy. Just promise me you'll always come back to us.'

Jen looked at him, clearly surprised. 'But what you said—'

'That doesn't matter any more. Just promise.'

'I will always come home to you. Who else will put

up with my obsessive cleaning and silliness?' Jen placed her hand on her husband's face and turned him towards her. 'I love you with all my heart and more, James Derek Garner.'

He turned to look at her, and her eyes sparkled as they always did. He couldn't help himself; he moved closer and began to kiss her passionately.

Chapter Eleven

Dana

I was happy in my new life, but I always stayed guarded and never let anyone get close. I had friends, but they were the people I worked with and the customers I served. Every night, I went home alone and hid in the dark, just in case someone was looking for me, but as time passed and I followed Mr Crawford's court case, I started to relax a bit, knowing I was at least safe from him. I was always kind to the working girls on the streets because, like me, they probably hadn't chosen that life. When I could, I would sneak them leftovers from the café. Thinking back, I wonder whether that was what led to my downfall.

I was so happy but then, one day, someone walked into the café and, as soon as I locked eyes with him, I knew I was in trouble. At first, he would come into the café every day at the same time and sit in the exact same seat next to the window. He was always polite and charming. Some of the girls even fancied him but, whenever I served him, there was always something about him that I didn't trust. Nobody else would listen to me. They all carried on flirting with him and he lapped it up, making sure everyone dropped their guard around him. Even the owners loved him – he was their favourite regular. Then he turned his attention to me, but I wasn't stupid. He'd call me his favourite and always ask for me to wait on him. Then he vanished, but I knew I shouldn't celebrate that he'd gone. Maybe he hadn't recognised me? But thinking back now, I'd already realised that he had. This was just all part of his game.

It was one of the other's birthdays when it all

happened. They had all been pleading with me to go to the pub with them after work one summer's evening. I'd tried every excuse but, as soon as the shutters came down, they hooked arms with me and I found myself in this pub. The music was so loud I couldn't even hear myself think. I kept telling them I had to head home and I was only going to have one drink, but time ran away with me, and when I finally managed to escape their cajoling it was dark outside. I was afraid.

I walked back to my flat the long way as I tried to figure out whether I was being followed or not. I'd seen them do it on the crime TV programmes I devoured, so it wasn't hard. It felt like it took me forever to get to my flat, and the fact it was dark didn't help. I thought every shadow was somebody waiting to pounce. But I arrived home safely … well, I thought I had. As soon as I walked into my flat, I could smell cigarette smoke. I tried to kid myself it was because I'd been in a smoky pub, but then someone grabbed me from behind. As they placed their gloved hand over my mouth, they told me not to scream or they'd kill me. Then he whispered those words into my ear that still wake me in the night, 'Hello, Dana. I've been looking for you.' I knew I was in so much trouble, I knew there was no way out for me, I knew no one would come looking for me. I hoped this would be the end, but it wasn't. I owed them money, and they were going to make me pay.

Chapter Twelve

DI Chris Jackson

Chris drove to pick Jen up so that they could both make their way to Radford to meet the boy at his emergency foster home. He couldn't believe that just six months ago he had been tracking this woman through Nottingham with a promise to bring her home to her family. Though he hadn't quite succeeded last time, at least he knew exactly where she was now and could make sure she got home. She didn't seem very chatty and just sat watching the world go by as Chris drove to their destination. He wanted to ask about Hannah and whether she had said anything about him, but he decided against it. Jen and Hannah both lived lives so different from each other. Did Jen even know that he was seeing Hannah?

'Have you seen much of Hannah?' Jen suddenly asked, as if reading his thoughts.

'Every now and again. I sometimes come home from a busy day at work and find her at my flat.' Chris didn't think he needed to add the rest of the sordid details. Hannah had probably told her as much anyway.

'You guys making a go of things?'

Chris wasn't sure how to answer this one. He hadn't considered whether what he and Hannah got up to was classed as "making a go of things" or whether they were just friends with benefits. Chris laughed to himself, hoping that Jen wouldn't press any further, and they soon fell back into the same uncomfortable silence.

'You sure about this?' he asked, turning towards Jen as they pulled up outside 3 Dovecote Close and applied the handbrake. He wondered why Jen seemed so nervous and withdrawn. Wasn't she supposed to be motivated and determined? For some reason, he had expected her to be more like Hannah. Chris got out of the car and walked around to the passenger side to open the door for Jen, although she didn't seem to be moving anywhere in a hurry.

'We can go back, you know? You don't have to do this.' He attempted to reassure her.

'I do,' Jen said as she climbed out of the car and puller her mobile phone from her back pocket. Chris waited for her as she typed a message out before he walked up towards the front door and knocked the signature "policeman" knock.

'Detective,' Jill said as she answered the door moments later.

'Thanks for arranging this for us. This is my colleague, Jen Garner.'

Jen held out her hand and shook Jill's.

'He's just up in his room. Paula, his foster mum, has told him that you'll be coming to visit.'

'Has he asked anything about his mother?' Chris asked as they stepped into the brightly coloured hallway.

'Not that I know of. He seems more concerned about finding this Lisa Carter person. Did you have any luck locating her since our last meeting?'

'I can assure you my team are working on it as we speak.'

Jill opened one of the doors and beckoned them through to a more neutrally decorated front room with yellow throw-covered sofas, worn armchairs and a large television fixed to the furthest wall.

'Can I get either of you a drink?' Jill asked as Chris and Jen took a seat on one of the sofas.

'Coffee, please,' Chris answered, already looking

forward to his next caffeine hit. His headache had started to come back, and he found himself reconsidering whether it really was all down to stress.

'I'm good, thanks.' Jen muttered her first sentence since arriving.

'I'll get Paula to call him down,' Jill said as she left them alone momentarily. They both sat in silence as they heard slow footsteps coming down the stairs. The door opened again, and the boy came in followed by a woman who must have been Paula. Jill brought up the rear, armed with mugs of coffee. The child didn't even acknowledge Chris and Jen as he sat himself on the floor in the middle of the room.

'These nice people have come to see you,' Jill explained. 'They want to ask you about Lisa Carter.'

'My mum told me I needed to find her,' the boy whimpered.

Chris got down on to the floor, making sure he was at the same level as the child, who finally glanced up at him before swiftly looking back at the floor again. 'Do you know where your mum is? She must be missing you?' Chris asked, making sure to keep his voice even and quiet. He didn't care that "Lisa Carter" was in the room, hiding behind her own fake identity.

'I don't know. She told me to ask everyone about Lisa Carter until I found her.'

'Okay. Well, I'm here to help you find her,' Chris said, remaining on the floor. 'Do you like playing with cars?' The boy didn't answer. 'Back where I work, we have cars with blue flashing lights on and they go really fast. Would you like a ride in one?' The boy still remained silent as he looked everywhere but at Chris. 'How about next time I see you, I take you out in one of my special cars?' Chris looked over at Jen, willing her to do something but, like the boy, she remained silent, seemingly lost in her own thoughts. 'Do you know where you were living before you came here?' Chris probed as the boy suddenly burst into tears.

'I need to find Lisa. Mum told me I must find Lisa Carter and not speak to anyone else.'

'It's okay, little man. I'm here to help you find her,' Chris said as he put his arm around the crying child. He wondered how this wasn't breaking Jen's heart. *Undercover detective with an ice-cold heart through and through*, he thought grimly.

'This is pretty much all we can get out of him,' Paula spoke now. 'He either sits down here and stares at the floor, or in his room doing the same.' Chris nodded his acknowledgement. 'He has no interest in anything other than this Lisa Carter.'

'I understand,' Chris said as he heaved himself off the floor and back onto the sofa next to Jen. 'Has there been any progress in getting him in to see a child psychiatrist?'

'Sadly we're still waiting for a proper assessment. We were hoping this Lisa Carter would be found quickly or his mother would appear, but he will be undergoing further tests,' Jill explained. 'We think this Lisa holds the key to everything, so anything you can do to help in locating her would really help,' she added.

Jen fidgeted on the sofa, and Chris wondered if she was finally about to do or say something.

'Can I use your bathroom?' she asked suddenly, getting up.

Jen Garner

Jen left the room, carefully following the directions up the stairs towards the bathroom. She had this crazy idea in her head that she could go into the child's room and look for clues. She suddenly felt so unsure how she should play this. She thought that she'd put all of this behind her, but her demons still seemed to be chasing her. So much for thinking she could go back to a nice, settled life with her family.

She needed to buck up her ideas. She couldn't leave this child, sat too scared to say anything unless he knew he was talking to Lisa Carter. If it was either Alex or Melanie, she'd have hoped someone would help.

Washing her hands, she left the bathroom and returned down the stairs. She could hear the adults in the living room continuing to quietly talk amongst themselves about the boy.

'Sorry about that,' Jen said, re-entering the room. 'Is it possible that Chris and I could have a moment alone with the child?' She was unsure how Jill or Paula would react if she revealed her true identity. Plus, it was supposed to be a secret that she was now failing to keep.

'Yeah, of course. Is there anything you need from me?' Paula asked, standing up.

'No. I think we're good. If you could give us five, ten minutes, then we'll be out of your hair,' Chris responded.

'I'll just be in the kitchen.' Paula opened the door.

'Detective,' Jill acknowledged as she followed Paula from the room.

Then there was just the three of them. As Jen lowered herself to the floor next to the child, she could sense Chris looking at her with expectation.

'Hello,' she whispered as she took his hands. 'I hear you've been looking for me,' she continued as he lifted his gaze from the floor and looked at her, like he was gazing into her soul. 'My name is Lisa.' As Jen spoke, the boy moved from his position and stood up in front of her. 'I'm

Lisa Carter,' she said again, slower this time, at which point the boy threw his arms around her neck and began to cry.

'Hey, little man, it's okay. There's no need to cry. You've found me, I'm here.' Jen felt her shoulder become increasingly damp from the boy's tears.

Jen remained on the floor with the child until he stopped sobbing. When he finally did, she noticed Chris holding out a hanky for the boy's snotty face.

'Do you want me to leave you two alone?' Chris asked.

'No, please stay,' Jen said quickly. If Chris left the room, there was no way she'd be able to stop the flood of tears that were building behind her eyes.

The boy pulled away from Jen, wiping his face.

'What's your name?' Jen asked him.

'Mikel,' he responded softly.

'Well, Mikel, this is my friend Chris. He's the one who said he'd take you out in one of his cars.'

The boy looked up at Chris.

'Nice to meet you, Mikel.'

Mikel nodded his response.

'Mikel,' Jen said as she changed her position. 'Mikel, do you know why you were looking for me?'

'Mum said you'd have the answers and be able to protect me.'

Jen could feel her heart breaking. 'Protect you from what, honey?' she asked, looking up towards Chris for some direction

'The bad men.'

'Do you know who these bad men are?'

'No, but they were always shouting and hurting my mummy.' Tears began to trickle down Mikel's face again.

'Oh, sweetie. Do you know where your mummy is now?'

'No, she brought me to the big town and told me to ask everyone if they knew where you were.'

'Well, you've found me now.'

'She said I wasn't allowed to talk to anyone until I found you. I tried, I really did, but I had to talk when the policeman came and started asking me questions.'

'You did the right thing, Mikel, and you've found me now, so we're good, right?'

'Mummy said you'd know what to do ... she said you'd have the answers.'

Jen quietly wished that she did know what to do and had the answers Mikel was looking for.

'Do you know where my mummy is?' Mikel asked.

'You know my friend Chris?' Jen pointed to Chris.

'The man who is going to take me in one of his cars.'

'Yes, well, Chris and his friends are looking after your mummy, okay?'

'Is he going to keep the bad men away?'

'Yes, he is. Your mummy is safe with Chris' friends.'

'When can I see her again? I did what she asked. I found you.'

'Soon, I promise, but how about you stay here in this nice house with all these toys for now, okay?'

'Okay. I didn't have many toys before.'

'Well, there you go then. I'm sure no one will mind you playing with these toys.'

'Okay.' Mikel seemed to be happier with that compromise, and Jen noticed a change in his mood. He seemed more content now he had found who he was looking for. *Even if Lisa Carter no longer exists*, she thought.

'What shall we play with then?' Jen asked, aiming to relax Mikel before she or Chris asked any further questions.

'I'm just going to speak to Jill and Paula and see if they can tell me anything else,' Chris said, getting up from the chair. 'You two going to be okay?'

Jen looked up and smiled at Chris. She didn't trust herself not to break down in tears if she spoke.

DI Chris Jackson

'Everything okay in there?' Jill asked as Chris walked into the kitchen.

'Thanks for that,' Chris said, noticing Paula holding out a cup of what looked like coffee.

'Did you manage to make any progress in finding out who this Lisa Carter is?' Jill pressed.

'I think we did. He also told myself and my colleague his name is Mikel, so I think we can assume he is our missing child.'

'Has there been any news on the DNA results?' Jill asked.

'Not as yet. I'll chase them as soon as I get back to the office. Can I just ask what the plan is for Mikel? How long are you planning to keep him here?'

'He's been here almost a week now, so we usually look to move them on. Paula is only really an emergency shelter.'

'Okay, any idea where he's likely to be placed?' Chris asked, concerned he was about to lose his best potential witness.

'I'm afraid not. It depends where we can find him a home.'

'Is there no chance he can stay here? It would be ideal to keep him close until we locate Lisa Carter, and I have a feeling he's going to be key in finding out about his mother's death.'

'I can speak to my supervisors.'

'Thank you, Jill. That would be great.'

'Did you manage to find out anything else from Mikel?' Paula asked. 'I'm really worried about him. He's so concerned about finding Lisa Carter that he isn't eating properly and just stares at the floor whenever I try to interact with him.'

'My colleague and I think we have made some progress so, without going into it all, I hope he'll be a bit more responsive now he knows we're looking for Lisa Carter for him,' Chris lied. Of course, there was a chance Mikel would go announcing to the world that Lisa Carter had just been there, but that was a risk he was happy to take.

Jill was looking at him with a curious expression on her face. 'Who is Lisa Carter, Chris?'

'In all honesty, Jill, it's all rather complicated. I'm not even sure myself.'

'Okay, I'll drop it for now. I understand.' Jill held her hands up.

Chris doubted she did, but he was grateful she didn't press the issue.

As soon as Jen put on her seat belt and he turned on the engine she started sobbing.

'Jen?' Chris asked, concerned. He'd seen many women cry in his time in the police force but not one that he'd been working with. 'Do you want to wait a while before I drive us back?' When no response came, Chris decided to do the gentlemanly thing and turn the engine off. He felt it would be best to let her get it all out of her system before he tried to talk to her, and he placed a protective hand on her arm to try to comfort her.

'I'm so sorry,' Jen said, gulping in air.

'You've got nothing to be sorry for,' Chris said, trying

to reassure her. 'You've got no hope of a hanky though, as mine's wet from Mikel's tears and snot.'

Jen laughed momentarily before she went back to trying to calm herself down. 'It's okay. I'm sure I've got some tissue somewhere in my pockets.'

'I don't know where you want me to take you. You can come back to the office for a debrief, or I can take you home and we can debrief tomorrow. Whatever's best for you,' Chris said as he looked at the clock on his dashboard. Then he looked back at her face and made the decision himself. 'Let's get you home in time to pick those adorable kids up from school.'

'Please,' Jen whimpered as Chris put the car in gear and headed back towards Long Eaton and her home. Mikel wasn't going anywhere tonight. He was comfortably settled now he knew he'd found Lisa Carter. Any debriefings could wait until morning.

Chapter Thirteen

Jen Garner

Jen stood staring out of the window as she absentmindedly washed the pots in the sink. She couldn't stop thinking about Mikel and the life he must have led. She knew that she would do anything for her children, but she had been lucky – everything had been pretty much plain sailing. She'd hug them extra tight tonight and make sure they knew how much she really did love them.

'So, how did your first day working with our local DI go?' James asked as he came up behind her.

She jumped as he touched her. She'd been silently sobbing for Mikel, hoping no one would notice.

'Jen, are you okay?' James asked, clearly realising something was wrong.

She dropped the plate she was washing into the soap suds and turned around. She knew her eyes must be puffy and red from the tears.

'Jen, what's happened?' As he spoke, she fell into her husband's strong arms and let all her emotions pour out. 'Jennifer?'

She took an audible breath before lifting her head and looking at him. 'I'm sorry.'

'What for? You've not done anything. Is it that DI?' Jen knew James didn't like DI Jackson very much after the way he'd treated him the previous year. He was clearly looking for more of an excuse to hate him.

'No, James. It's just the case.'

James lifted Jen's face to his and wiped her tears away gently with his thumb. 'Do you want to talk about it?' he asked.

'It's just the boy ...'

'The one who was looking for you?'

'Yeah ...'

'Sit at the table. I'll make us both a drink, and you can tell me all about it.'

Jen reached over the table for the tissues before she started crying again. 'He's so alone, James,' she explained. 'He has such a hard life, and the worst of it is his mum is dead ... and he doesn't know.'

'Okay.'

'She's lying in the Derby Morgue. From what Chris has told me, things can't have been great for him, even before she died.'

'But he's found you now, hasn't he? And you're going to go in and kick ass and save the day.'

Jen laughed at her husband's directness. If only things could be that easy. She felt herself turning serious again. 'I keep thinking about last year ... the kids and how I would do anything for them. I bet Dana, the boy's mum, would have done anything for him ... but she's ended up in the morgue.'

'Jen, I love you and the kids adore you.'

'But this is it. Dana wasn't so lucky.' Jen had just managed to calm herself down, but now the tears began again. Clearly unsure what to do, James reached across the table and held her hands in his.

'Jennifer Garner, I love you with my whole heart. I promise you, whatever happens, I will always be here for you and the kids.'

'James—'

'Now, come on, you know what our two are like. They'll be in here looking for us soon.'

Jen laughed again, wiping away her tears. Her fingers came away black from the smudged mascara that she'd stupidly reapplied when she'd got back home, wrongly assuming she'd got all the crying out of her system. She stood up and moved around the table to James, sat on his knee and fell back into his arms again.

'Mum, Dad!' Melanie excitedly ran into the kitchen. 'Uncle Max is here.'

'*What*?' Jen couldn't believe her ears. She wasn't expecting him, was she?

Just then the doorbell rang, and the kids raced to answer it. Jen hurried to get there before they did. 'Max?'

'How are my two favourite people?' Max asked as Melanie and Alex pushed past their mum.

'How come you've come to see us?' Melanie asked excitedly.

'Well, it's been such a long time since I saw you both, I decided it was time to pay a visit.'

'You'd better come in then,' Jen said, stepping out of the way to let Max into the house. As he passed, he embraced her and kissed her on the cheek.

'I hope you don't mind me showing up like this?'

'No, no, of course not, come in. James and I are just in the kitchen.'

'I hope everything's okay?' Max asked, obviously noticing the smudges under her eyes.

'Yeah … we're good. The kids are happy you're here, so you can't really leave now you've been spotted.'

Max laughed as Alex grabbed hold of his hand and led him towards the living room.

'Let the poor man get through the door,' James said, popping his head out of the kitchen. 'Drink, Max?' he asked.

'Please.'

As promised, Max had become a regular feature in their lives. He was the closest thing to family Jen had. When she'd left last year, she'd promised him things would be different – and they were.

Max settled down on the sofa with the kids bouncing next to him excitedly.

'Has the DI or someone contacted you?' Jen asked. She couldn't wait. She needed to know if he was here because of the case.

'No? Why would they?'

'I'll talk to you later about it,' Jen said quickly, noticing the kids were listening in.

'Okay. I've left Hannah in charge.'

'We can all sleep safely tonight then.' Jen laughed.

'Uncle Max,' Alex chimed in. 'Tell us one of your stories.'

Max was always full of stories, mostly about their mum, and they lapped it up.

'Drinks are served,' James said, walking into the front room with a full set of mugs balanced on a tray. 'You've just missed dinner, I'm afraid.'

'Not to worry. I grabbed something on the way.' Max smiled.

'Will you be staying?' Jen asked. 'I can sort out one of the kids' rooms and they can share.'

'Yeah! Please! Uncle Max, you can have my room,' Melanie squealed.

'Calm down, you two,' James warned.

'I'd love to stay, if that's okay with you both? Don't worry about sorting the kids' rooms, though. I don't mind crashing on the sofa.'

Jen had forgotten that Max hardly slept when she'd made the suggestion. Thinking about it, she had no idea what state the kids' rooms were in anyway, so maybe it was a good job.

'As long as you don't mind?' Max asked again. 'I'd

hoped to get away earlier and book a hotel, but you know how it is.'

'You're always welcome here.'

'Right, Melanie, Alex, drink your hot chocolates, and then it's time for bed. You've both got school tomorrow,' James said, taking a seat across from the sofa.

'But, Dad—'

'Max will still be here tomorrow.'

'How about I pick you both up from school and take you out for dinner somewhere?' Max said quickly, clearly trying to keep the peace.

'Yeah … okay.'

'Only if it's okay with your mum, of course?' Max looked at Jen.

'Mum, can we?' The kids both asked in unison.

'I don't see why not,' Jen replied as the kids started dancing around the room in excitement. 'Now, let's get those drinks drunk and teeth cleaned ready for bed.'

Having managed to milk it for another hour, the kids were finally in bed and Jen came back downstairs.

'Sorry. I think I might have hyped them up too much.' Max turned and apologised to James.

'Nah, don't worry about it. You know they both adore you.'

Max laughed. Jen knew he had dealt with many criminals and terrorists in his time, but two excitable children were a whole different kettle of fish. Jen was so glad that Max had decided to become a more permanent feature. The kids were always so excited to see him, and he'd become a prominent figure in their lives, settling happily into the role of "Uncle Max".

'Phew.' Jen felt exhausted. 'Do we still have that bottle of white, James?'

'I can have a look in the shed. Max, would you like to share a bottle with us?' James asked, getting up.

'I'll go,' Jen offered.

'No, you stay here. You can fill Max in on the boy.'

Max looked over at Jen quizzically, and she sighed. She'd wanted to leave discussing Mikel for as long as possible, just wanting to savour the fact that Max was here to see the family.

'I guess I'd better tell you about it,' Jen said as she moved to sit in her chair.

'Had I better go and get my laptop?' Max asked.

'Maybe. James, will you give Max a hand with his bags before you get the wine?'

'I can manage,' Max responded as he left Jen sat in the living room. She hadn't expected him to appear, but now he was here she really didn't want to make it about work.

'So, tell me about this boy,' Max said, once he'd returned to the sofa and booted up his laptop.

'The local DI contacted me a couple of days ago about a child who'd been found walking around Nottingham ... asking for Lisa Carter.'

'Ah, the famous DI Jackson that I've accidentally heard so much about,' Max said, raising his eyebrows.

'Is Hannah smitten?'

'I've unwittingly walked into so many conversations that I wished I hadn't. I pretend that I don't hear anything but, you know, she and Sam are always gossiping. I feel like I know the man better than his mother probably does.'

They both laughed as James returned with the wine and looked at them both in confusion. As Jen recovered enough to take a glass from James, she let herself relax. She had to admit, it felt kind of nice having her two favourite men in the same room and getting on – which was a bonus.

'So, tell me more about the boy?' Max asked, once the laughter had died down.

'Do you want me to leave?' James asked, standing up.

'No, James, please stay.' Jen looked at him pleadingly. 'I don't want to keep anything from you any more.'

'Max?' James checked.

'You can stay, as far as I'm concerned.'

'So, the boy, Mikel ...' Jen began again. 'The local force pulled his mum out of the River Trent earlier this week. They think that she'd gone in the same day as Mikel was found in Nottingham asking for Lisa.'

'Right.'

'The DI came to see us in the hope that I would go and see Mikel as Lisa Carter.'

'Did you have any luck?'

'Yes. He had hardly been speaking to anyone. But once I told him I was Lisa Carter, he broke down in tears telling me that his mum had told him to find me. When I asked him more about his life, he told me that his mum was always getting hurt and shouted at by bad men.' Jen looked over towards where Max was sitting.

'So, what are your thoughts?'

'I don't know, Max. I don't understand where Lisa Carter comes into all of this.'

'James?' Max turned to him, and James almost jumped at being asked his opinion.

'You're asking the wrong person. I'm just here to provide the comfort.'

'How much has the DI said that they know about his mum?' Max looked back at her.

'Not much. It was hard going seeing Mikel, so Chris brought me home. We're going to debrief first thing tomorrow.'

'Fancy some company? I have to admit it concerns me that, over ten years down the line, someone is looking for you. Even if it is a child.'

'Then you can see the DI in action too.'

'Hopefully not in the way Hannah has so graphically described.'

'I don't know, Max. I suppose you could ask him?' They all laughed and the tense atmosphere that had surrounded them suddenly lifted.

It was nice having Max there. They talked for hours over the bottle of wine while Max recounted tales of Jen's glory days to James, who seemed to be full of questions and amazed at the things his wife had been involved in. Once the bottle was empty, James went back to the shed for more. As he returned and topped up their glasses, he said, 'You never finished telling me the story about the time Jen split her trousers moments before meeting the Prime Minister.'

Chapter Fourteen

Dana

After he had beaten me and raped me repeatedly, he laughed at me; he laughed at me crying silent tears as I lay all crumpled on the floor like a dying animal. I knew this would happen if I ever got caught but I'd believed, with Mr Crawford locked up in jail, that I'd be safe. He trashed my flat, looking for the drugs, as I pleaded with him to stop, telling him they weren't there and that I had sold them all on. When he asked where the money was, I told him it was gone, but he didn't believe me. He told me I was going to have to pay back every single penny plus interest. I told him I would. I'd go to the café and get extra hours and pay every single penny back. He laughed again and dragged me up off the floor, told me I was coming with him, and if I dared try to escape he'd make sure I didn't live to face another day. I was in so much pain as we began the descent down the stairs from my flat. Why couldn't he have just left me there to die? He bundled me into a black cab and, when we were away from the city, he forced me into the boot of a waiting car, telling me I didn't deserve a seat. He had cut tiny holes in the boot so I could still breathe, and he told me to stay quiet. With every speed bump and pothole we drove over, I was reminded of the pain I was in. I don't know if I lost consciousness or fell asleep, but when I woke up I knew we were in the back streets of London. I could smell it. I was bundled out of the car and pushed into a house where I was met by the house madam. She was a cold woman with a fake smile and a face plastered with make-up. Her eyes bored into me as I was presented to her. I couldn't tell what they were saying to each other, but I knew she was mad. She kept shouting at him, asking how I was meant to work in the state he had brought me in.

He pushed me down onto the floor and laughed, telling the house madam that he would be back to check on me and collect my earnings. I was hardly able to move without the pain shooting through me, so I don't know how he expected me to work. No one would want sexual favours from someone whose face had been beaten to a pulp. Once he had left, slamming the door behind him, I saw a softer side to the house madam, who helped me up and supported me up the stairs. She showed me where the bathroom was, and then I was taken into the room that I would come to know as my own; where I would be made to perform the most humiliating acts on men and women alike. I had to do whatever was asked of me. I sometimes, genuinely, wished he'd have killed me that day he found me, because what I went on to suffer was much worse.

After a while, I didn't count the days any more, I didn't watch the sun come up, I didn't even count the punters. I just existed from one humiliation to the next. I was worthless. I doubted I would ever pay the debt off that I owed to Mr Crawford. I shouldn't have run when I did. I should have handed myself in to that officer, because maybe, somehow, she could have helped me and I would have been finally free of George and his men. Maybe I would be living somewhere else with a new identity. But I'd been caught, and now I was back in the situation I'd wanted so much to leave behind.

Chapter Fifteen

DI Chris Jackson

Chris had the sudden feeling of *déjà vu* when he was woken early by the sound of his mobile phone ringing. Why did this always happen when he got involved with the Garners?

'DI Chris Jackson.' He answered his phone in the most cheery voice he could muster. If he was about to be told that James Garner need bailing out again, he was going to hang up.

'Sorry to disturb you at this time of night, sir, but there's been a fire.'

'Where?' Chris tried to sound like he was interested, but he longed to be back asleep.

'3 Dovecote Close, sir.'

Shit. That's where Mikel was staying. Chris sat up suddenly 'Did everyone get out of the house okay?'

'Yes, sir, all present and accounted for. The owner of the house, a Paula Seamoor, asked me to get hold of you.'

'Can you let the officer in charge know that I'm on my way?'

'Will do, sir.'

With that, Chris was out of bed and on his way, out of his flat and driving towards Radford and the emergency shelter that housed Mikel and Paula. As he drove, all sorts of scenarios ran through his head. Had they phoned social services? Did he need to ring Jen? *No, Jen was better left out of this*, he decided. It would have just been some faulty wiring or something, that's all.

Chris pulled onto Dovecote Close and found himself unable to get anywhere near the scene. The entrance to the street was being blocked by what Chris guessed was a second fire engine. He noticed several firefighters talking in a huddle on the grass verge. As he got out of his car, he had to stop himself choking on the thick, acrid smoke that filled the air.

'Detective Inspector Jackson.' Chris flashed his card at one of the firefighters. 'Who's in charge here?'

'Watch Manager Teddington, sir. He's just talking with the fire investigation officers.'

That's when Chris caught sight of Paula running towards him.

'He's gone … Mikel's gone!' she shouted. 'I left him sat in the ambulance. I turned my back, and he was gone. They said he left with his father, but that can't be possible.' Paula appeared breathless with panic.

'Okay. Don't worry, Paula. He can't have gone far.' Chris didn't want to panic Paula further, because there was no way Mikel would have gone off on his own. When Chris had left him earlier that day, he was content that he'd found Lisa Carter. So why disappear now? Unless … no, he couldn't think like that. He spotted a uniformed officer and walked over. 'DI Jackson.' Chris introduced himself. 'I have a small boy missing. He's around the age of six and he goes by the name of Mikel. I want as many officers as possible on the scene. I'm also going to need someone to contact my partner Detective Ryan.'

The officer looked at Chris, clearly confused for a moment as to why this person was issuing orders to him, then he sprang into action, calling for all available back-up.

'Paula, have you contacted Jill or someone at social services?' Chris asked as he turned back towards her.

'My phone is still inside. You were the first person I thought of once we were out of the house.'

'Here, take this,' Chris said, handing her his phone, then he noticed a second police officer. 'Officer! I need someone to contact social services. Then I need you to speak to this lady and get a full description as to what Mikel, the missing child, was wearing and get it circulated to all teams in the area.'

'Sir.'

'Paula, this officer is going to sort you out. I'm just going to find the watch manager and see if I can work out what's happened.'

'Thank you so much, Inspector.'

'I'm looking for Watch Manager Teddington.' Chris approached another group of firefighters who had begun to roll the hose back up.

'That's me.' A tall fire officer walked over and shook Chris' hand.

'Detective Inspector Jackson. Do we know what's happened? Or is it too early to tell?'

'One of my guys thinks it's arson – petrol bomb through the letter box. The occupants were lucky to have an automatic fire alarm fitted. My guys were dispatched as soon as the call came in.'

'I've just also been informed we have a small boy missing,' Chris added. 'Are you sure there's no one left in the house?'

'One of my team has just been back in and cleared the house. No one is going in or out until we've managed to do a site inspection.'

'This may be nothing, but I need you to send one of your pumps to an address in Long Eaton. I've just got a really bad feeling that this is a targeted attack.'

'I'll call in and get the Long Eaton team sent over. Is everything okay, Detective?'

'I really do hope so,' Chris said as he looked up at the

smoke-filled sky, hoping that Jen hadn't done anything silly and that her house wasn't next to be targeted. 'I've instructed one of the officers to call for back-up and get a search started for the boy,' Chris told the watch manager.

'Until we've cleared the house, it's a no-go area.'

'Understood.' Chris walked back towards the officer he had first spoken to, but then he spotted one of his own, Sergeant Wes Curtis – he was one of the good guys who had requested to speak to Chris after he'd been called out to the Garner household when Jen was originally reported missing. 'Wes, I need you and Officer Haywood to get over to the Garner household and check everything is okay.'

'Will do, boss. What's going on?'

'The firefighters think this incident might be arson, and the last thing we need is that house going up too.'

'On our way,' Wes said, jumping back into his car. 'I'll call control and get them to remind me of the address.'

'Sir, I've called in everyone I can.' The officer he'd initially spoken to appeared next to him.

'Thank you, Officer …?'

'Hunt, sir.'

Just then he saw Julie's car pull up, and he felt a sudden wave of relief. 'Gather everyone together. I want a coordinated search of the area. If need be, I want everyone in this area woken up and their sheds checked. No one is leaving here until we find the boy.'

'Do we have a photo, sir?'

'I'm just trying to source one as we speak.'

'Boss, what's going on?' Julie asked as she approached. 'They said on the phone there'd been a house fire. Then I've just heard on the radio something about a missing boy.'

'I'm so glad you're here,' Chris said, knowing that he

could now delegate some of this mess to her. 'There's been a suspected arson at the house where Mikel has been staying, and now he seems to have vanished.'

'Woah ... okay, what do you need me to do?'

'Are you happy to coordinate the search? I'll go over and speak to the paramedics.'

'On it,' Julie said and immediately began issuing orders to the gathered group of police officers. 'Right, I need four of you to start knocking on doors – though I can't imagine anyone still being in their homes with all this going on.'

'Inspector.' Chris turned round to see Paula, suddenly remembering that he'd given her his phone.

'I've managed to get through to someone at the office, and they're getting hold of Jill as we speak. Is there anything I can do to help?'

'Are you able to go over the circumstances that led to Mikel's disappearance with me?'

'After I got myself and Mikel out of the house, we were sat being checked over by the paramedics. I was being asked questions about the house and whether there was anything they should be aware of before the fire service went back in. I told Mikel to stay put while I just pointed something out. When I returned, he'd gone.'

'And how did Mikel seem at the time?'

'He was a bit frightened, if I'm honest – then again, I was too, being woken up by a high-pitched alarm and smoke.'

'And when you were both in the ambulance?'

'He had calmed down a lot, or I wouldn't have left him. Plus, they'd given us both a blanket, so he was warm.'

'So, what happened when you left him?'

'He said he was happy to stay with the paramedic. I told him I'd be back in a couple of minutes ...' She looked at Chris as the tears silently trickled down her face.

'Thank you, Paula. Can I ask if you'd wait on the grass verge with the others so I know where you are if I need you?'

'Please will you let me know as soon as you find anything out?'

'Of course.'

'Boss.' Chris hadn't noticed Julie approaching. 'I've coordinated the officers. Several of them have gone into the back fields. I've spoken to the watch manager, and he's happy for those who live on the Close to return to their homes. I've asked several officers to assist them and run a quick sweep.'

'Thanks, Julie. Have you heard anything from Wes on the radio?'

'Not yet, but I can chase him up if need be.'

'Don't worry. I'm sure he and Nikki are more than capable of handling the Garners. If there'd been a fire, we'd have heard by now.'

Jen Garner

Jen wasn't sure what had woken her first; the flashing lights or the banging on the front door.

'What the fuck?' James grunted as he got out of bed. 'Who on earth is knocking on the door at this time in the morning?' he groaned sleepily as he made his way downstairs.

Jen instinctively went to check on the kids, even though their rooms were at the back of the house and they slept through almost everything. She still needed to make sure that the commotion hadn't woken them.

Once she'd returned to her room, she heard further voices from below. Quickly, she grabbed some clothes and ran downstairs to find James in conversation with a police officer and somebody else who appeared to be a firefighter.

'What's happened?' she asked, dreading the answer.

'Ah look, here's Mrs Garner now. Unless you need anything more from me, I'm going back to bed,' James muttered as he turned away from the door and headed back towards the stairs.

'Sorry about my husband. He likes his sleep and is up in a couple of hours for work. What can I help you with?' Jen asked.

'I'm Sergeant Curtis and this is Crew Manager Sheldon from the Long Eaton Fire Station. May we come in?'

'Yeah, yeah,' Jen said, taking a step back. 'You might have to come through the kitchen. We have guests using the living room.'

'It's okay, Jen. They can come in here,' Jen heard Max shout. *Of course he was awake*. If he'd managed to doze off, the commotion outside would have more than certainly woken him up.

She turned back to the two men on the doorstep. 'Can you do me a favour? Is it possible you can switch the flashing lights off, please? The last thing I need is the kids waking up too.'

'Of course, Mrs Garner. Now we know there's no incident,' the crew manager said, and then he turned his attention to talking into his radio.

Incident? Jen thought to herself. Who'd called the fire brigade in the first place? It certainly hadn't been her, and she very much doubted Max would have either.

'Can I ask what this is about?' Jen pressed, inviting the officers into the living room and turning off whatever Max had been watching.

'DI Jackson asked that we come and check on you.

An automatic fire alarm was triggered at an address in Radford earlier this morning, and there were some concerns for your welfare.'

'In that case, you can thank DI Jackson very much, but you can see we're all well.'

'Mind if I take a look around the house?' the police officer asked.

'Yes, I do mind! Both my kids are, hopefully, still fast asleep, and the last thing they need is you waking them up.'

'Have you been out anywhere in the last couple of hours?'

'No, I can pretty much guarantee I was in bed with my husband asleep.'

'Can anyone verify this?'

'I can,' Max piped up. 'I've been here all evening.'

'Thank you, sir. Can I take your name?'

'Detective Chief Inspector Max Carver. My ID is in my car if you need me to get it.'

Sergeant Curtis looked suitably taken aback. 'I'm sorry to wake you, sir. There will be no need for your ID.'

'I'd like to check the perimeter of the property if that's okay with you, Mrs Garner?' The crew manager said, having finished with his radio. 'I don't think that will disturb the kids.'

'Yeah, whatever. I don't understand what this is all about, though. Why is Chris so worried about us?'

'There's been a suspected arson at a house in Radford, and a small boy has been reported missing,' Sergeant Curtis replied.

'*Mikel*?' Jen didn't want to believe what she was hearing.

'DI Jackson wanted to check he wasn't with you.'

'Mikel is missing?' she asked again, louder this time.

'The child had been receiving treatment from the paramedics and then vanished,' Sergeant Curtis explained.

'Oh god.' Jen took an audible breath in as she realised how serious the situation was.

'We have search teams swarming all over the area as we speak. Hopefully, we should have him home in time for his breakfast.'

Chapter Sixteen

DI Chris Jackson

As the sun began to rise over Radford, Chris felt exhausted and no doubt looked it too. He vaguely tried to work out if he'd always felt this tired at the end of a long shift. What was wrong with him? The only thing spurring him on was the need to find out what an earth had happened to the six-year-old boy who hadn't been seen since early that morning.

He had spoken to the paramedics, who had informed him that a man had approached who they'd wrongly assumed was the boy's father by the way Mikel had reacted to him. Apparently, Mikel had even called him "Dad". They hadn't thought to question him and had let them go off together. Paula had admitted to him that it wasn't widely known that her house was an emergency shelter, so perhaps it wasn't the paramedics' fault they'd made the mistake.

Though Watch Manager Teddington stayed on site, many of the other fire teams had returned to their stations. The Garner household had been cleared with no sign of Mikel there either. Chris requested that a police car be positioned outside the Garner house just in case Mikel turned up there, but he doubted it, unless whoever had him was going after Lisa Carter next – although wasn't her former identity still a secret?

Chris was awaiting further instructions regarding social services' procedure, which would no doubt include a missing person's report being logged.

'There's a Maccy D's close by. Can I get anyone

anything?' Chris asked as he approached Julie and the team from social services.

'Yes please, boss! I'm feeling rather peckish.'

'Jill, Paula?' Chris asked, making sure he wasn't excluding anyone.

'I'm good, thank you,' Paula replied 'Hopefully they'll clear the house soon, and I'll be able to get in and get some windows open.'

'Jill?'

'I'm okay. Thanks though, Chris.'

'Just you and me then, Julie,' Chris said as he turned to leave. Before they both headed out to the car, he made sure to leave an officer on the scene in case Mikel made a magic return.

'Where do you think he's gone?' Julie looked towards Chris as they turned in to the drive-through.

'I genuinely have no idea. It just all seems a bit strange to me. I don't know if you heard the fire crew talking, but they suspect arson. Can't confirm anything till the dogs have been in for a sniff and they've run a few tests.'

'But why?'

'In all honesty, I don't know. There weren't many of us that knew about Mikel's existence in the first place,' Chris said as he pulled up to the window and began to order breakfast.

Julie began to fish around for some money as they moved along to the next window.

'My treat,' Chris told her, pulling out his card. 'I took Jen Garner with me to meet him after she turned up in my office yesterday, having, um … worked … with Lisa Carter in the past.' Chris glanced at Julie to see if she'd noticed his hesitation.

'What was she like, after her meeting with him?'

96

'Heartbroken I think is the best way to describe it. I took her home, and we agreed to meet up today for a debrief, though it looks like I might be at the crime scene for a while yet.'

'But was she heartbroken enough to come and take him?'

'I don't know. What would she have to gain from it?'

'Giving the child a better life?'

'Isn't that what the adoption process is for?'

Julie looked thoughtful. 'Has she agreed to help with the case?'

'I think her curiosity means she'll have to. Anyway, she has an alibi. Apparently, she had a friend staying, and there'll be her husband, of course.'

'Topping up on the caffeine, I see,' Julie said as she noticed the large coffee Chris had ordered.

'Yeah. I've not got the time to deal with another caffeine withdrawal headache.'

'Would you take her back? Jen, I mean, if she was your wife, after everything last year?' Julie asked as Chris started to head back to the scene.

'I don't know. Though we worked the case, we were never told the ins and outs of it. If you remember, we were convinced her husband was involved, along with his friend, Harry.'

'James didn't help himself, though.'

'I couldn't agree more, but I don't know … I hope for the kids' sake they can sort stuff out.'

'And now she wants to be involved in this case, that strangely seems related to this Lisa Carter. You spoken to Hannah much about it all?'

'No, not really. Hannah wasn't with the service in Jen's heyday. She joined some years after. It's a difficult one, anyway,' Chris continued. 'With Hannah, I don't want to press her too much about work-related things, because I'm sure some of the stories she could tell would stop anyone sleeping at night.'

'You ever considered it? You know, joining the Met?' Julie asked.

'I used to think all I wanted was a police career and to go the furthest I could, but ... things have changed.'

'In what way?'

'The politics of policing. Soon they'll have me shackled to a desk and I won't be able to go out for cases at all – anyway, who would run the team?'

Julie took a bite from her breakfast muffin. 'And you wonder why I don't want to progress any further. Anyway, what's the plan, Inspector?'

'Plan? More coffee!'

'Other than more coffee?'

'I guess one of us needs to head into the office and round up the troops, though I'm not sure how well we're going to do with our depleted team. Don't suppose you've heard from Sally at all? I do miss the smell of Coco Mademoiselle in the mornings.'

'From the sounds of it, everything is fine, and she's really enjoying the change in scenery.'

'I'm glad to hear.' Chris replied as he ran through things he needed to do that day in his head. 'Julie, are you happy staying on the site, just in case Mikel turns up or there are any further developments?'

'Yeah, that's fine, boss. I'll also keep an eye on Paula as we don't want her disappearing too. You going to contact Jen?'

'I think I'll leave her till I've had a chance to figure things out more.'

The fire engine had long gone, the police officers sat in front of her drive had changed over, and Jen was sat sipping a cup of tea, wrapped in one of the throws from the sofa. Max had been his usual self, just sitting there quietly, waiting for Jen to break the silence that hung between them. Jen was acutely aware of the ticking of the clock on the mantelpiece, as time marched on and the world continued turning. She knew it was only a matter of minutes before James was up and off to work, followed by the kids heading off to school. When would everything just stop for a moment? When could she get off the crazy runaway train she felt like she was back on again?

'I don't know what to think, Max.'

'About what?'

'Mikel, his mum, the bloody Lisa Carter woman ... and I guess those men outside in their shiny police car.'

'What was Mikel like when you met him?'

'As soon as I revealed I was Lisa, he hugged me and told me his mum had told him to find me and that I was going to help them. All he wanted was his mum.'

'So, he doesn't know she's dead?'

'I don't think so, which makes it all the more heartbreaking.'

'And our favourite DI?'

'We didn't really talk on the way back. Surprisingly, for a man, he noticed how upset I was and said we'd talk tomorrow ... which I guess is today now – but he's probably got a whole load more stuff on his mind with the fire as well.'

'This will be a good first case for Hannah,' Max said absentmindedly.

'Is she definitely going to be replacing you then?' Jen

quizzed, totally forgetting where the conversation had originally been heading.

'Yes, if the powers that be see fit.'

'Does she know?'

'Yes, we've had long conversations about it all.'

'Shame I can't turn back the clock.' Jen spoke without thinking.

'Jen, I've always said there'd be a place for you on the team—'

'I made my choices, Max.' She cut him off. 'If I came back, who would look after grumpy upstairs, and the kids? *Anyway* – Mikel?' Jen wanted to change the subject quickly before he pressed the issue any further.

'You need to work out why he was looking for Lisa Carter and not, say, Hannah or myself.'

'He's far too young to have known about me back in the day.'

'So, what about his mother?'

'See, I think that's where the answers to this mess lie – with his mum. But she's lying in the Derby Morgue.'

'We need to figure out where your paths crossed.'

'I just feel like I don't have the energy for this any more. Does that sound bad, Max?'

'Not at all, but think of it this way: every time you think you're done with the service, you get pulled back in. When you first left, you were in a new relationship with James and everything was amazing. Last year you were dragged back into something that you had no control over, and now ...' Max heard the noises from upstairs pending James' arrival and clearly decided to make a quick exit. 'I'm going to see if the guys outside fancy a hot drink.'

It played on her mind as the early morning chaos began. She worried that she really didn't feel like she couldn't handle opening the can of worms that Mikel's case would lead to. She hadn't exactly come out of it unscathed last time. James had lost a best friend, and she'd almost lost her marriage. Was just leaving Chris to do his job the answer? She needed to decide because, what with the suspected arson and Mikel's disappearance, she could tell danger was afoot.

As the day began, she did what she always did and turned on autopilot: James' lunch made, kiss, out to work. Kids' breakfast made, then washed, changed and off to school. She only stopped when Melanie and Alex suddenly declared they wanted "Uncle Max" to take them to school. She wasn't sure how the other mums at the school gates would react to Max. There'd be talk about who the mystery older gentleman was with the Garner kids. She laughed thinking about it. Maybe she needed a run – maybe that would help her figure stuff out. Or maybe she just needed more sleep and chocolate ...

Chapter Seventeen

DI Chris Jackson

Chris greeted his colleagues as he entered the incident room. Since leaving Julie, he'd slipped home for a quick shower and a handful of hair gel before feeding the cat and heading in to continue his day. As far as he knew, there'd been no sightings of Mikel or the bloke who'd claimed to be his dad, and a thorough search was being conducted of the area. It was almost like they'd disappeared into thin air.

'I'm going to grab my tie, and then I'll be with you all,' Chris told his team.

'Boss,' Officer Haywood shouted after him as he headed back to his office. 'There are two people waiting downstairs to see you.'

'Any idea who they are? And what they're after?'

'I could've sworn one was Jennifer Garner, but the other one ... I'm not too sure.'

'Thanks. I'll head down shortly.'

Who on earth had she brought with her? No doubt she was here because of the early morning wake-up call – and the police car that, as far as Chris knew, was still stationed outside her house. Grabbing his tie, he logged on to the computer, making sure there had been nothing important come through on his emails, and then headed down to reception to greet his unexpected visitors.

'Jennifer,' Chris greeted her, looking curiously over towards Max, who he hadn't seen since last year.

'DI Jackson, this is Max Carver. We used to work together.'

'Nice to see you again, Max.'

Jen looked over towards Max, clearly surprised.

She didn't realise they'd met before?

'Detective Jackson, I've heard a lot about you.'

Chris noticed Jen's mouth twitching as Max spoke and realised that most of the stuff he'd heard had probably come from Hannah. 'All good things, I hope. Now, what can I do for you both?' Chris asked, keen to move the conversation out of the reception area, just in case.

'Max and I would like to speak to you about Mikel – and our early morning wake-up call.'

'Let's take this meeting somewhere private.' Chris nodded at the officer on reception, and they were buzzed through. 'I'll get you all signed in from my office,' he told them, grabbing a couple of lanyards from behind the desk. As they walked through the station, Chris realised Jen was getting attention.

'You a local celebrity around here, Jen?' Max asked, obviously noticing people staring at her.

'Possibly. The officer on reception always does a double take when I come and visit.'

On entering his office, Chris hastily moved some things aside so his guests could sit down. 'Now, how can I help you both?' he asked, once they were all settled.

'We were hoping for some kind of update. Any news on Mikel?' Jen asked.

'Well, I got a call at 3 a.m. this morning regarding the house Mikel was staying in with Paula. The officer informed me that the house was on fire and that Paula had asked for me to be contacted. So, I rushed down there and, almost on arrival, Paula came running over to tell me that the boy had disappeared.'

'Did anyone see what happened?' Max questioned.

'According to the statement from the paramedic, Paula had left briefly to speak to Watch Manager Teddington.

A man approached the ambulance and, from Mikel's reaction, the paramedics were led to believe that he was Mikel's father. So, they let him go ...'

'So, we've got a missing boy. How does all of this fit in with the wake-up call this morning?' Max continued.

'Watch Manager Teddington confided in me that his officers suspected arson. With Mikel finally opening up after finding Lisa Carter, I was worried the child would either go and find you, or the Garner household would be the next to go up in smoke.'

'Always me.' Jen rolled her eyes.

'So, where does all this sit in the bigger picture?' Max asked.

'This is where it gets a little more complicated. I'm sure Jen has filled you in?'

'She has.' Max looked thoughtful. 'Do we think Mikel has been snatched and the fire was just a ploy to get him out of the house?'

'If I'm honest with you, it has crossed my mind. We have too many incidents that, individually, might not mean anything. But when they're all put together ...'

'So, where are you up to with the investigation?' Max pressed.

'The team and I, with the help of social services, were beginning to piece together Dana and Mikel's life,' Chris answered with a degree of confidence.

'And Jen?'

'The team aren't unaware of Jen's other identity but, when I realised who Mikel was asking for, I approached Jen for help in breaking the deadlock.'

'And here I am,' Jen chimed in.

'Just to let you know, I've had the results back from the DNA test, and the boy is definitely Dana's son. In a way, this makes his disappearance even more concerning, given what we know about her past.' Chris looked over towards Max. 'Are we going to have an issue with jurisdiction?' Chris had to ask; he didn't want his team losing another case to Max's team.

'Hmm, I don't know,' Max answered, which didn't exactly fill Chris with confidence.

'I can take you to meet my team now if you like, and they can fill you in on where we are with Dana and Mikel's life. Julie, my partner, is still at the crime scene, keeping on top of what's going on there.'

'Okay. I need to ring and speak to Hannah and set things in motion our end,' Max said.

Upon hearing Hannah's name, Chris felt his heart miss a beat. He realised she was never far from his mind, despite everything going on.

'Max, can I suggest you hold fire on calling the team? Let's see what Chris has got and what plan his team have regarding Mikel before we set in motion something that will be harder to stop than start,' Jen suggested.

Chris reached down into his drawer and pulled out two ID passes, handing them to Jen and Max. Then he led them through to the incident room to meet his depleted team.

'Before we meet them all,' Chris warned them, 'can I just assure you both that if we need more detectives on the case, I have been promised extras.'

'It's okay, Chris. I understand about police cuts and budgeting.' Jen winked at him as they entered the incident room, where his team looked to be working away.

'Can I have your attention for a moment?' Chris raised his voice slightly to make sure they were listening. 'As I'm sure many of you know, this is Jen Garner. She and her colleague, Max Carver, have come to help us with our case concerning Mikel and Dana.'

The room went silent, presumably as they all tried to work out why Jen had suddenly inserted herself into the case. 'I've had the team look into certain aspects of Dana's life prior to ending up in the Trent,' Chris explained, leading Max and Jen further into the room.

Jen Garner

Jen couldn't help but feel a wave of discomfort as she imagined the officers judging her for last year's events. She almost felt like she had to explain to them the whys and wherefores, but then she realised she was being silly; there was no need to justify herself to them. She'd done what she'd had to do for the sake of her family and Chloe.

'Do we have any news on the cause of the fire?' she asked Chris, trying to ignore her paranoia.

'I was just messaging Julie now. She's going to conference call in the next ten minutes.'

'You said Dana's body was still at the morgue? I think I'd like to visit and speak to the pathologist,' Jen said with a glance over towards Max.

'I'm not sure how much more she'll be able to tell you, other than what's in the reports.'

'Still, I'd like to meet the pathologist who performed the autopsy.'

'I'll phone her and see if we can organise something.'

Jen was aware that the team had fallen into an uncomfortable silence around her.

'Greg, do you want to start us off on what we've found out about Dana and Mikel's life?' Chris broke the silence.

Jen and Max sat as Chris' team filled them in on everything they knew so far about the unfortunate events surrounding the lives of the mother and son.

'So, there's three years we have nothing for?' Jen asked in disbelief.

'Afraid so. They seemed to disappear into thin air,' Greg replied with a frustrated sigh.

Jen was aware of Max shifting in his seat beside her. 'Jen, can I have a word?' he interrupted.

'Can we use your office?' Jen asked Chris, aware she was disrupting the state of play.

'Yeah, of course. Is there anything I can help you with?'

'No, Max and I just want a chat.'

'Okay, I'll show you the way back.'

'No, it's good. I think I remember the way,' Jen replied as she and Max made to leave the room.

'What's going on there?' she overheard one of the team ask, as they walked away.

Max followed Jen into Chris' office, closing the door behind them. 'Jen, you are getting incredibly involved in this investigation,' he said as soon as they were alone.

'I know, Max, but I just feel like I have to ... especially now Mikel is missing as well.'

'What happened to leaving this all behind?'

'I know, but I hate to say it ... I sort of miss it all.'

'And James and the children? As much as I want you back, you know yourself that we live in a dangerous world to bring children into.'

Jen hadn't really thought about her return to the service properly since the previous year. There was no way she could change her name and expect that no one would get hurt this time. Yet, here she was, sat in her local police station with the local policing team and, seemingly, there was no escape.

'What about you and Hannah, though?'

'Jen, you can't have the best of both worlds! I'm here

with you in Long Eaton to see the kids, not to solve murders.'

Jen gave him a vague smile, trying to work out what to say next. 'This kid knows who I am. I can't let it drop now. If we go into that meeting room and declare we're taking the case off the team, Chris won't just stand by and let it happen. You remember what he was like last year?'

Max just looked at her, and she knew what he was thinking – his brightest star, still refusing to let anything drop. 'Someone needs to pick those kids up. Remember they were promised dinner out by Uncle Max?' he reminded her.

'Yeah.' Jen sighed in defeat. 'I'll grab our things, and we can head off.'

Max laughed. Both of them knew this wasn't the end of the matter. 'I'll go and get the kids from school. Just send James a message and tell him that's what I'm doing,' he said with a sigh.

Jen almost ran and hugged him.

'But I want you home at a reasonable time, to put the kids to bed at least. Then I want a debrief for both myself and your husband before bed, okay?'

'Thanks, Max.'

'Don't let me down, Jen. I know exactly what you're like with your superhero antics.'

Jen smiled at Max. He really did know her far too well.

DI Chris Jackson

'Julie, you're on speaker phone.'

The team had arranged themselves around the meeting table, along with their newest recruit once Jen returned from the office without Max. Chris could tell that Jen was nervous as her eyes began darting around the room.

'Afternoon, boss,' Julie responded.

'Julie, we've been joined by Jen Garner. She's come to help us for the time being with this case.'

'Hi,' Jen chimed in.

'Let's get on. How are things looking your end?' Chris continued.

'The fire investigation team have just finished their assessment of the scene, and I have the preliminary findings from them. As far as I'm aware, Mikel is still missing. Nothing has been flagged during the searches of the surrounding area.'

'Okay. Shall we start with the fire and move on to Mikel afterwards? Everyone in agreement?' Chris asked his team, who were sat eagerly awaiting instruction.

Julie began speaking again. 'So, the fire investigation team say that the fire is likely to have been caused by arson. Paula and Mikel were both very lucky to have escaped unharmed. If it hadn't been for the fire alarm, it might have been a different story.'

'Any ideas on accelerant used?' Greg cut in.

'They aren't a hundred per cent certain till the test results come back, but we suspect petrol. A Molotov cocktail, basically.'

'Greg, will you get hold of all the petrol stations in the area?' Chris instructed.

'Sir.'

'They expect that the substance was posted through the letter box,' Julie explained.

'Did the investigation team give any further hints as to their findings?' Chris asked.

'Afraid not, boss. It will all be in their report, so I'm told.'

'Fine.'

'Is it too early to assume that the fire was started to get Mikel out of the house?' Jen suddenly piped up.

'I don't think we can rule that out at this stage,' Chris responded. 'Any further information regarding Mikel?'

'Jill and Paula, along with the paramedic who released Mikel to the person they thought was his father, left with a DI Holman.'

'Okay. I'll contact the DI and see where they are with Mikel's disappearance.'

'To be honest, boss, it's sort of like he's disappeared into thin air.'

'Do you want to make your way back in, Julie? We'll make a start on what we've got.'

'Not a problem, I'll be back in the next hour. Boss, can I just add that Jill and Paula were very friendly with DI Holman, which might be why they chose to leave with her and completely ignored my presence.'

'Right. Okay. Get yourself back. We'll catch up once you're here.'

Julie hung up and Chris looked around at his team, although his mind was whirring. *Why hadn't DI Holman been contacted first thing if they were so pally with social services? Why ring and wake him up?* 'What are everyone's thoughts?' he asked.

'I think Jen is right that the fire was started deliberately in order to get Mikel away from the house. But what I'm struggling with is the why,' Trudie spoke up.

'Anyone else?' Chris looked around the room.

'Do we need to start treating Dana's death and Mikel's disappearance as one case?' Trudie questioned again.

'Do you think there might be a connection, Jen?' Chris turned to her.

'Erm, sorry, my mind was elsewhere.' Jen appeared to snap herself out of her own thoughts. 'Possibly. I was looking over the timeline on your incident board earlier. When Dana disappeared with Mikel from their lodgings, what's not to say they left with the same person who's just taken Mikel?'

'Then why not leave Mikel there rather than to fend for himself on the street?' Trudie asked.

'I don't know ... maybe she ran?'

Chris let Jen's answer hang in the air for a while before carrying on. 'Let's think back to what we know about Mikel's arrival into Nottingham. We know that Mikel was walking around Nottingham asking for Lisa Carter at approximately the same time Dr Walsh believes Dana entered the Trent.' Chris stole a glance at Jen who seemed to look uncomfortable and out of place, picking up the pen that was in front of her and then putting it down again.

'Maybe this Lisa Carter person has got something to do with his disappearance?' Colin suggested.

'Guys, trust me when I say Lisa Carter has nothing to do with Mikel's disappearance.' Chris jumped in before anyone else had a chance to comment; they needed to continue to keep Jen's second identity secret, at least for now.

'But we don't even know who this person is, boss.'

'This is not open for debate. Lisa Carter has nothing to do with Mikel's disappearance.' Chris raised his voice over the heated conversations that were beginning to start up around him. He made a decision and continued. 'Social services located Lisa, and Mikel has had a meeting with her. We are confident that everything with Lisa is above board.'

'Do we know why Mikel was asking for Lisa?' Trudie asked.

'From what I understand, Mikel had been told by his mother that Lisa would be able to save them.'

'Hang on! Save them from what?' Colin butted in.

'This is where the trail goes cold,' Chris admitted.

'I think we can safely say,' Jen spoke up, 'that it was from whoever torched the house and then took Mikel from the ambulance.'

'So, this all comes back to Dana and those missing three years,' Colin concluded.

'I think we need to come up with a plan of action based on what we know so far,' Chris said. 'Greg, are you okay contacting all the petrol stations in the area, like I said? The fire report should be able to nail down the brand, but we can get ahead of the game and see if we can find anything out first.'

'Not a problem, boss.'

'Colin, can you see if any of the witness statements are available on the system? Also, see if we have an artist's impression of the man who took Mikel.'

'Boss.'

'Trudie, will you do your stuff on social media?'

'Of course.'

'Jen and I will try and locate DI Holman and let her know where we are with things. There isn't much point in duplicating work. Let's get to it, team.'

Everyone got up from around the table and headed towards their office to begin the task at hand.

Jen left her seat and followed Chris into his office, closing the door behind them. 'Thanks for that.'

'You don't make things easy.'

'Yeah, I know ...'

Chapter Eighteen

Jen Garner

Jen climbed out of her car and couldn't help but feel the buzz of the last twelve hours. She walked up the drive, already hearing the sounds of excitement and squeals of happiness coming from the house. Turning her key in the lock, she waited for the kids to run and greet her ... but there was nothing. They were too busy having fun to even notice she was home. *At least that means I'll be able to have a wee in peace*, she thought with a smile. She wasn't even usually afforded that luxury around here.

Jen was just watching Max playing with the kids when the familiar scent of her husband's aftershave hit her senses.

'How long have you been stood there for?' James asked as he kissed her neck.

'Not long. I just enjoy watching them having fun.'

'They were both full of excitement about him picking them up when I got home.'

'Guessing school was okay?'

'As far as I know.' James wrapped his arms round her waist. 'Let's sneak off for a bit, go and hide in the conservatory and leave them to it.'

Jen laughed. 'Foreplay in the conservatory? I'm a lucky girl.'

'Well, if that's what you want,' James said, sweeping her up into his arms.

It must have been the sound of the swishing air, because at that moment Alex turned round and Jen knew any chance of conservatory foreplay was off the table.

'Mummy, you're home!' he cried as James placed her

carefully back down on the floor. 'Did you have a nice day?' Alex asked her.

'Yes, I did, thank you. How was school?'

'Guess what, Mummy? Uncle Max picked us up from school.'

'Did he, now? I bet that was a nice surprise!'

'Yeah, I went and stood with Melanie as she was looking all around for Max and didn't think he was coming. She even went to tell Miss Harrington, but then I saw him!'

'Calm down, little man,' James said. 'Let your mum sit down.'

At that point, Alex went on to tell her all about his day and how Max had picked them up and taken them for dinner at some American restaurant where they'd had a massive cheeseburger. While Alex was reliving his day, Jen smiled over towards Max; he looked exhausted. Had they finally found something that would tire out her former boss? Was a few hours with the Garner children all it took?

Melanie wasn't as enthusiastic about her day but relished the fact that someone else had picked them up from school. Never mind the burger joint.

Once the excitement of the day had died down, it was time for the kids to say their goodnights and head up to bed.

'Uncle Max, will you still be here in the morning?' Melanie asked.

'Do you want me to be?'

'Yes! You can take us to school and come and meet my teacher. It's open morning.'

'Do you really want me to meet your teacher, Melanie? They might tell me things that I'll have no choice but to pass on to your mum and dad,' Max teased, clearly noticing the look of horror that crossed Jen's face.

'Right, come on you two – bed. You might have had burger and chips, but your mum and I are yet to eat,' James told them in his stern "get to bed" voice.

Once the delaying tactics were over, and the kisses goodnight distributed, Jen at last found her way into the conservatory and flopped down on one of the sofas. There was so much stuff she needed to think through, but those moments of family bliss had distracted her from the task at hand. She looked over the garden and up towards the night sky, hoping that Mikel was safe, wherever he was.

'James told me to come and tell you dinner will be ready in five,' Max said, appearing in the doorway. Jen looked up and smiled at him. She knew he was dying to know how the rest of the afternoon had gone.

'Will you be joining us?' she asked him.

'I hope so.' Max laughed. 'I may have taken them to a burger joint, but I certainly didn't partake in the evening meal.'

'I guess debrief will be over dinner.'

'Oh, I'm counting on it.'

'What's James cooked anyhow?'

'I have no idea, but it smells good.'

'Tell him I'll be there in a minute.'

Jen took a moment to look up at the sky again. Today had felt scarily good. Last year, working on Chloe's murder case, she had felt her old self creeping back in. Could it possibly be time to start thinking about going back to work? She couldn't return to her old team – the work was far too dangerous with a family in tow – but what about police work? *Detective Inspector Jennifer Garner*. She smiled to herself.

'That was lovely, James,' Max said, putting his knife and fork back onto his plate.

'Well, I thought with you taking the kids out for dinner and the wife busy at work, I had better make an effort.'

Jen laughed as she reached her hand across the table. 'More wine, Max?' she asked as she lifted the bottle to top up James' glass.

'Oh, go on then. I might need it for the main event.'

'I took the liberty of asking Alex if we could borrow his chalk board,' James said, getting up from his chair.

'Yes, and he gave me a good demonstration of how to use it. He told me at school they have interactive whiteboards, but this would have to do until Daddy installs one,' Max added as James erected the chalk board, passing his wife the box of coloured chalks.

'Come on, you two.'

'I can find my laptop if you'd prefer?' James continued to tease her.

'No, the chalk board is good.' Jen sighed.

Once the laughter and teasing were over, James cracked open a beer and offered Max one as they waited for Jen to begin.

'So …' she started, before recounting everything that had happened that afternoon.

'The fire brigade think the fire was started on purpose?' James asked almost immediately.

'Yep. When Chris arrived at the scene, they already suspected it. That was why we got our early morning wake-up call.'

'Jesus, did the family get out okay?'

'The fire alarm woke them, luckily.'

'Did the DI say anything about Mikel's disappearance?' Max asked.

'Not a lot. The whole investigation was taken over by this DI Holman for some reason. Though Chris' colleague, Julie, seemed to think Jill had a working relationship with that DI, which could explain why. A missing person's report has been filed for Mikel, and the paramedic who let Mikel go with his dad has been with a facial recognition artist. Oh, and the Nottingham team also managed to find an old arrest record for Dana when she was caught up in a raid about six years ago.'

'Surely Chris can overrule that other DI, though?' James asked. 'I'm not a great fan of the guy, don't get me wrong, but it seems silly there being two investigations.'

'Here's hoping. He was going to contact her once our meeting had finished.' She turned to Max. 'What are you thinking? You've gone quiet.'

'I'm wondering if we need to look into it.'

'Huh?' James looked confused.

'I mean "we", as in my team. Jen had already left the service six years ago. I need to be back in the office so I can look at the records,' Max explained.

'Oh, so that's my wife off abandoning us to go to London again?' James muttered. Jen shot him a dirty look.

Max ignored James' comment. 'We know that Mikel is the son of Dana, who they pulled out of the Trent. They believe she went in at the same time as Mikel was found. Correct?'

'Yep.'

'Mikel was told to ask for Lisa Carter and not speak to anyone else till he found her.'

'Which means all this leads back to me again, doesn't it?' Jen said, looking over towards her husband. 'It's kind of like whoever took him, took him before he had a chance to tell me anything more.'

'I don't want to rain on DI Jackson's parade again, but we have better resources, and we're able to speak to the street girls in London a lot easier than Chris' team,' Max said.

Jen looked over at James again. Could her marriage cope with another trip into the depths of her past? There was silence around the table before James finally spoke.

'Jen, go.'

'What?'

'Go to London and save the world. Do what you you're good at doing.'

Jen wondered if he was really drunk. 'What are you saying?'

'Come on, Jen, I saw how much you were glowing when you walked in earlier. You mean to tell me if I told you not to go, you'd stay here anyway?'

Jen didn't answer as silence fell again.

'Look, I can get Mum and Dad to take the kids for a week or so. It's almost the end of term, so it's not like they're doing anything in school anyway.'

'James …'

'I'll continue to work away in my non-air conditioned office, fixing people and equipment while you're busy being a superhero.'

'James …'

'Come on, you know yourself that your old team have better resources and better facilities than DI Jackson and his team. Go find this boy and bring him back safe.'

Jen smiled at her husband. This had all been so unexpected, but she'd be lying if she said she hadn't thought Max's team would be better at handling this mess than the local police force. James was right, but could their marriage really cope with the strain it would no doubt bring?

'So, what will it be?' Max asked.

'Listen, I know we've done it once before, but Chris seems so invested in this case. It would be wrong to rip it from under his feet again.'

'Well, as long as he knows I haven't killed you this time, and no one reports you missing, I think we're fine.'

'I mean,' Jen said, ignoring her husbands' silly remarks, 'could we not work on this together? Pooling our resources and building on the leg work Chris and his team have already done?'

'I'm not sure, Jen, but if it means I can keep my eye on you in London, and Chris and his team can work things this end, then so be it.'

Jen made eye contact with her husband and mouthed the words, 'thank you'. Maybe if she'd just done this the first time, if she'd just told him the truth when they'd met – the way Chloe had done with her boyfriend, Adam – things would have been different.

'You'd better give the DI a ring then, Jen, and tell him the plan. I'll break the bad news to Sam that we'll be needing those files again.'

Jen finally made it up to bed at around 1 a.m. She'd been so busy with all the excitement and the planning – never mind the call to Chris – that she'd hardly realised it was so late. Chris had required a lot of convincing that it was a good idea to involve Max's team, no doubt scared about having the carpet ripped from under him once again.

Jen had left the boys talking downstairs as the conversation moved on from the case. She realised now just how tired she was. Just because Max stayed up all night didn't mean she had to as well – especially if she was about to open the Lisa Carter box again.

Chapter Nineteen

Dana

I never paid attention to who my clients were; some were nicer than others, some were loving and gentle, for some I was just a rag doll to be used and abused. But then something unexpected happened ... I got pregnant.

I really don't know how it happened. They had us all on pills, which they handed out daily to us like we should be grateful for them. I started to become sick, really sick, to the point I couldn't perform. They had a doctor come and visit me, and that's when they discovered it. I was so happy to find out I had this little person growing inside of me that I had to protect. After the doctor left, the house madam had these terrible rows with someone, telling them that I couldn't continue to work in my state and that it wasn't her fault I had ended up pregnant. They tried to make me carry on, but I was continuously too ill to work which was a blessing ... because I had to protect my baby.

I didn't know what was happening when it started. The pain was so intense, I thought I might be dying. I couldn't breathe, I couldn't think, never mind suck someone's cock. I told the house madam, and a look of panic filled her face. That was when my waters broke and everything got serious. I was bundled into a car and driven away as the pain intensified. My whole body was screaming out for me to push, but I couldn't. I wasn't prepared to bring a baby into the world in the back of a dirty car. I felt like I was in that car for hours ... perhaps I was.

We pulled up outside this hospital, and I was shoved out of the car and left to make my own way to maternity. Somehow, I managed to get inside, where I gave birth to a beautiful baby boy in the hospital corridor where I'd fallen, unable to make it any further.

That should have been the happiest day of my life, but it was filled with pain, torment and tears.

I never even thought about what would happen once the baby was here; I just knew I wasn't going to let anyone take my little boy away from me. Then, one day, a bloke turned up, offering to take me home. But where was home going to be now?

I was taken to a smart-looking building and presented with a fully furnished flat, food in the cupboards and clothes in the wardrobes. He told me Jess would be over to see me as soon as she was back, and I waited to learn my fate.

I made my way through all the postnatal services, as midwives turned into health visitors who then turned into social workers. I wasn't allowed to tell them where I had come from, I wasn't allowed to tell them who the father was – the fact I didn't know who he was anyway probably helped things. I always make the mistake of trusting people who then went on to let me down, but Holly, my social worker, was different. So kind and gentle. She made me believe I could leave everything behind and be happy with Mikel. So, I began the journey of trying to forge a better life for myself.

Jess and the ginger-haired man used to visit me once a month with supplies or whatever I needed. There was one condition to all of this: I had to keep the landlord happy and give him whatever he wanted. I had escaped the brothel, but I was now someone else's sex slave. I was still somebody else's property.

Then a different girl started to visit me. She told me she was a friend of Jess', but she wasn't like her; she was so kind to me. She used to sit with me and play with Mikel, or talk to me like a friend. Whenever the landlord had been over for his rent, she used to apologise and tell me she was sorry for what I was going through. She told me that she wished that she could help me and that maybe one day I'd get out of this mess.

So these people became my only visitors: Holly, to check up on me and make sure Mikel and I were safe, Jess and the guy who brought me supplies and occasionally made me take part in their sex games, the landlord ... and then her.

Chapter Twenty

Jen Garner

Jen could hardly open her eyes when the sound of her alarm woke her. She needed to get showered, changed and packed. She crept into the en-suite from the dark bedroom, where she planned to stand under the shower until she felt human again.

She hadn't been stood under the water long when she heard the en-suite door opening. *What on earth were the kids doing up at this time in the morning, never mind in her bathroom?* She was just about to say something when the glass door of the shower opened.

'James?'

He let his dressing-gown drop to the floor and stepped in next to her. She ran her hands over his chest as their eyes met and, in that moment, she felt the old spark of electric between them. As she held his gaze, he pulled her close and kissed her neck slowly as the water ran over them both. Confined in the small space of the walk-in shower, James pushed her back, grabbing her by the waist and lifting her as she instinctively wrapped her legs around him. She let him take her weight as he slowly guided her down. She let out a moan of excitement as their bodies connected.

'James Garner, I love you more than anything in the world,' she whispered as they began to move together, under the warm shower.

The office still looked and smelt the same, and no doubt still housed the same team. They'd come back via Max's Kensington home so they could both drop stuff off and

Jen could pick up the ID she'd thought she'd never need again.

Jen spotted her old desk almost how she'd left it. She'd expected it to have been stacked high with other people's things, given everyone had assumed she wouldn't be back.

'Jen, you came back!' Sam, the PA, greeted her with the same amount of enthusiasm she always had, whatever the situation.

'Yep, I couldn't keep myself away.' Jen smiled at her.

'I have news. I did what you suggested – I enrolled onto the training course.'

'So, you're no longer Max's PA?'

'Max said I could stay on while I trained. I think he's secretly worried he'd have to type his own letters if I went.'

Jen laughed. 'That's great news anyway. We'll catch up more later. I think we have a call scheduled?'

'Yeah, of course – and I want to hear all about the dishy DI Jackson.'

'Umm, I'm pretty sure I'm not the one who's sleeping with him?'

'Yeah, but you might tell me more about him as a person ... and not just what happened when last you got him into bed.' Sam laughed.

'Do you think she's smitten?'

But Sam didn't have time to answer because, just then, Hannah herself appeared and embraced Jen.

'I didn't expect you back so soon.'

'Seems like I'm a bad penny, always turning up at the wrong time.'

'Max leaves me in charge for a week and you bring him back two days later?' Hannah laughed. 'I'll never get him to leave that seat again for at least another ten years,' she added.

'You never know your luck,' Jen responded, wondering how much Hannah really knew about Max's retirement plans. 'Anyway, I suppose I'd better go and speak to Max before this call.'

As she wandered towards Max's office, she could already see him deep in conversation on his desk phone.

'So, here we are again, Jen,' Max said as he put the phone down and adjusted his chair, muttering something about Hannah changing it again.

'Did Sam manage to locate many of my files?'

'There's now a whole special vault holding all your files,' Max joked. 'We decided it might be best to work out exactly what we're looking at before we start getting stuff out again,' he explained.

'Have you had any further thoughts on it, or did the kids wear you out that much yesterday?'

'I must admit that I did fall asleep in the chair for a couple of hours. Though by the time James left me to it, there wasn't much time to do anything else.'

'I did wonder what time he came up.'

'He's a good man. You've landed on your feet there.'

'I hate doing this to him, Max.'

'He was the one who suggested you come back here. At least he knows where you are this time, and he seems to have accepted it.'

'Yeah, here's hoping.'

'Right,' Max said as he stood up. 'Pep talk over. Let's get down to business.' Jen took the hint and followed Max into the meeting room.

DI Chris Jackson

'Morning, boss. You wanted to see me?'

Chris hadn't slept well since his late-night call from

Jen. His mind was all over the place. He didn't trust Max as far as he could throw him, but if working with his team would bring Mikel home and Dana's killer to justice, then so be it.

'Yes, sorry, take a seat. Can I get you a coffee or something?'

'Will I need one?' Julie asked quizzically.

'That depends really.'

'Then maybe you'd better get the whisky out from your drawer.'

'Whisky? I don't know what you're talking about.' Chris laughed. 'It's too early for whisky.'

'I'll wait a bit then.'

'Julie, I don't know how much you remember from last year, or how much you worked out, but … Jen Garner and Lisa Carter are the same person.'

'Seriously?' Chris watched as things started to add up in Julie's head. 'I guess it all makes sense though, with the case being closed so suddenly once we had Harry locked up. So, Hannah knew that Jen was Lisa when she came up?'

'Yes …' Chris got lost in his thoughts for a moment, remembering the previous year. 'Anyway, the long and short of it is that Jen has suggested we work a joint investigation. I suspect it was a matter of realising we could work together, or they could take the case away but have me on their backs.'

'They seem to have you all figured out.' Julie smirked.

'So, I'm waiting on a conference call from them about our next move.'

'And you wanted me to come and join in on the fun?'

'Yeah, something like that. My top detective on my side at least.'

'Are you going to reveal all to the team?'

126

'I'm undecided. I feel that it would be best for Jen's safety if people didn't know she was Lisa. But I hate lying to you guys.'

'Tough decision there, boss.'

'I think I'm going to wait and see how it all plays out.'

They were both distracted when Chris' office phone began to ring.

'Here we go then,' Chris said, picking it up.

'Detective Inspector Jackson … Let me put you on speaker phone.'

Chris reached over and pressed the button so Julie could listen in. 'Just to let you know, I have my detective sergeant, Julie Ryan, here with me.'

'Morning, Julie.' The voice on the other end responded.

'Sir.'

'So, let's kick things off then. Here in London we have myself – Max Carver – Detective Hannah Littlefair and Jennifer Garner, who I trust you both know well. There's also Sam, my PA and detective-in-training. I've also asked Angela Currant from the sexual exploitation team to join us. Hopefully she'll be able to give us some insight into what we're up against.'

'Morning all,' Chris responded, wishing he could see them.

'Chris, do you want to start us off?' Max asked.

'Okay, Dana Antwar is our victim …' Chris went on to explain about finding the body in the Trent and the events that followed.

'Angela, was Dana on your radar? I know you work very closely with a lot of the street girls in London,' Max asked.

'There are so many working girls out there. I'm afraid Dana herself wasn't on my radar. I have asked my colleagues, and I'm waiting to hear back from them all.'

'Does anyone know where this fits in with Jen's timeline since she left us the first time?' Max continued.

'We understand that Dana fell pregnant the September after she was last arrested, and Mikel was born in June,' Julie interrupted.

'Jen, did you have any thoughts on whether you and Dana crossed paths at any point?' Hannah asked.

'I was pregnant with Alex in the same year, but I don't think she was in any of my new baby groups,' Jen responded.

'I think we really need to find out how she knew you, then we might have some clue who could have taken Mikel.'

'But she didn't know me as Jen. Mikel asked for Lisa Carter,' Jen reminded Hannah.

'Which leads me back to thinking she must have known you before you ran off into the sunset.'

'Angela, when she was arrested in the drugs raid, wouldn't she have been referred to your team?' Max asked.

'I would have thought so. I need to go back to the office and look into this further, because a quick search before I came over didn't bring anything up,' Angela explained.

'So, how does Mikel come into all of this, other than asking for Lisa?' Sam asked.

'I spoke at length with the social worker who was linked with Dana after the birth of her son—' Chris began, but then he was interrupted.

'So, we lose Mikel for three years until he finds his way to Nottingham?' Sam interjected.

'In the brief chat I managed to have with Mikel, he confirmed that his mother brought him to Nottingham and told him to find Lisa,' Jen clarified.

'How did they know you were in Nottingham, though?

There has to be some crossover somewhere.' Max sounded frustrated.

'I assume Mikel is still missing?' Jen asked.

'I haven't spoken to my team for developments yet, but it certainly seems that way.'

'So, Dana and her son came to Nottingham to look for Lisa. But instead of finding her, Dana ends up in the Trent and Mikel in an emergency foster home,' Sam concluded abruptly.

'That about sums it up.' Chris sighed.

'Is it worth me and Jen going to King's Cross station tonight and showing Dana's photo around to see if anyone recognises her?'

'Might be an idea, Hannah. Angela?' Max asked.

'I don't see it being an issue. We haven't got anyone working undercover in that area, so you shouldn't come across any problems.'

'Chris, any thoughts?'

'Fine by us,' Chris responded, as his mind lapsed into thinking about Hannah.

'Chris, what can you remember about your conversations with Dana's social worker?'

'Holly Lord,' Chris corrected.

'What can you remember about your conversation with Ms Lord?' Max began again in frustration. 'Had Dana disclosed much about her past and how she found herself in the UK to start with?'

'When she applied for asylum, and also from her conversations with Ms Lord, we know that she had been brought over from Iraq, having been promised a better life. She also disclosed that she was scared of her former pimp.'

'Did Ms Lord get any names from Dana?'

'Afraid not. If I remember rightly, she didn't like talking

about her past and didn't disclose much, which her file's notes pretty much back up.'

'So, that's another angle we can look at – who trafficked her over? What cases that you worked on in the past involved trafficking, Jen?'

'Other than the obvious, I'd need to have a think and a search on the system.'

'The obvious being?' Chris asked, wishing again he could see the facial expressions of the people on the other end of the conference call.

'George Crawford. His daughter is Jessica Adams, who was Harry Greenidge's girlfriend,' Jen explained.

'I'm sure you're aware of how they both fit into the picture?' Max questioned.

'Yes, I spoke to Harry last year. He came across as a cocky shit in the interview room if I remember rightly.'

'But he saw the light during his court case.' Jen seemed to be almost defending him.

'I'm glad to hear it.' Chris wasn't completely convinced.

'Would it not make sense that Dana is connected to the Crawfords?' Hannah suddenly asked.

'How so?' Max enquired.

'Well, look at the timings for one. Jen was back here last autumn, and Dana appears, what, six months later? We shut down Jessica's operation for a start.'

'Then why did she end up in the Trent? She could have quite easily walked around Nottingham asking for me,' Jen piped up.

'How do we know she didn't? We only know about Mikel because people get concerned about a six-year-old walking the streets; a washed up thirty-something, they'd probably avoid.'

'Good point. But who has Mikel now and why?' Jen sighed.

'There are too many strands to this. I think we need to narrow it down and look at one thing at a time,' Max suggested, much to Chris' relief as he struggled to keep up with what was going on. 'Hannah, you and Jen go ahead and make arrangements to visit King's Cross.'

'Do we have a recent photo of Dana we can take with us?' Hannah asked.

'She'd have probably had a photo taken for her asylum application,' Julie suggested.

'Good idea. I'll have a look now.'

'Chris, can you and your team find out if there's any further information come through regarding the fire at the emergency shelter and Mikel's disappearance?' Max instructed.

'Okay. Is there anything else you need us to look into?'

'No. You guys can just continue your investigations your end and keep in contact. If we need anything, I'll let you know. Oh, and I'll get Sam to check her spreadsheets for anything related to Dana or Mikel.'

'George Crawford's incoming and outgoing mail and the visitor logs?' Sam questioned.

'The whole lot, please.'

'Okay, boss.'

'Everyone happy?' Max asked. 'We'll speak to you later, Detective,' Max said when he seemed satisfied nobody had any further questions. Then he promptly ended the call.

Chapter Twenty-One

DI Chris Jackson

Chris stared into the middle distance, trying to work out how he was going to play this – though his thoughts were all of Hannah dressed up for a night out. 'What do you think?' he asked as he finally broke free from his imaginings and turned to look at Julie.

'They get all the fun while we do all the paperwork?' Julie muttered.

'I think you've just summed it up!'

'I'll go and get us a coffee,' Julie said, obviously noticing his thoughtful expression.

'Thanks. You might want to rally the team as well.' He nodded towards the office. *What would be their reaction to the news they were working with the London lot?*

He was about to find out as he traipsed into the incident room and greeted them. He'd made sure he had two paracetamol in his back pocket for his insane headache.

'Morning, boss,' Trudie greeted him. 'You okay? You don't look so good.'

'Yeah, just tired.' He sat in the chair reserved for him at the top of the room as Julie handed him a steaming coffee. 'Right, what have you got for me?'

'I'm having big problems trying to get anything from DI Holman,' Colin began. 'I know she's based in Radford, and we're all part of the same policing team, but it's kinda like she's become territorial.'

'What makes you say that?'

'I keep ringing and emailing, asking for copies of statements, but nothing seems to materialise.'

'Do you think that the officers just haven't entered them into the system yet?'

'Maybe, but it's been a whole twenty-four hours since the fire now! And there's still no incident reports, witness statements or even a missing person's report for Mikel on the system.'

'We know that Mikel was taken, so I agree that you'd have thought there would be more of a song and dance about it. I'll give her a ring once I'm back in my office and see what the hold-up is.' Chris ran his hands through his hair, unsure how he was going to get through the day whilst he was completely shattered and with the headache from hell. He tried to rally himself. 'Greg, petrol stations?'

'I've visited all the ones in the local area to the house and collected CCTV but, as we have no clue when the person collected the petrol or what the brand of petrol was, we're at a bit of a dead end.'

'Noted. Anyone got anything at all on Dana or Mikel? Have we managed to get anything from the landlord yet?'

'No, boss. He isn't taking my calls, I might have a trip up to his office after this meeting, see if I can unearth anything,' Trudie responded.

'I know this is a long shot, but why not have a search online and see if he pings on anything? You know, people complaining about their landlord, that sort of thing?'

'Got it, boss.'

'Something else that's bugging me, boss.' Colin looked up from his computer. 'There's been no media attention about the fire either. *Nottingham Today* are usually always on the ball to the point that they're annoying!'

'Julie, would you mind giving the press office a call and finding out why nothing has been released to the media regarding the fire? Might also be an idea to give the

Nottinghamshire Fire and Rescue press office a call and ask the same.'

As Chris shifted in his seat, he could feel the contents of his back pocket reminding him to not finish his drink before taking the pills. He wondered about the progress Jen would be making in London with Hannah. He was already fully aware of what Hannah looked like dressed up to the nines; it was just a shame he was in Long Eaton and unable to experience it for himself. The thought of possibly working with Hannah again filled him with the kind of feeling he had recently forgotten – the excitement and sense of longing to see her again.

'If anyone needs me, I'll be back in my office trying to get hold of DI Holman,' Chris said as he got up, took the pain relief and headed out of the incident room, leaving his team busy with their tasks.

Chris had been sat at his desk for a while with a phone in one hand and a coffee in another. He had been put on hold while they searched for DI Holman's location. As he debated his choice for lunch, the phone was finally answered.

'Detective Inspector Holman.'

'Afternoon, DI Chris Jackson here. I'm just calling regarding the investigation into the suspected arson at 3 Dovecote Close.'

'Afternoon, Chris. Good to finally get to speak to you. I've heard a lot about you and your team.'

'All good, I hope,' Chris said warily, hoping he wasn't about to be asked about last year's drug haul.

'Naturally. How can I help you?'

'My team and I are struggling to access any information regarding the fire.'

'Oh, what aspects?'

'There doesn't seem to be anything on the system at all.'

'That's a bit strange. Let me contact the IT department. I'm almost a hundred per cent sure stuff had been uploaded by my officers.'

'I also wanted to query with you why there's no missing person's report on the system that we can access regarding Mikel's disappearance?'

'We've decided to hold off, just in case the kid returned.'

'Returned?' Chris couldn't believe what he was hearing 'What do you mean returned?' he asked, on the verge of raising his voice.

'Yes, returned to the city centre where he was found, or the scene of the fire.'

'Isn't that a bit of a strange decision, given the ambulance driver says Mikel left with somebody he thought was his father?'

'My point exactly, Inspector. If Mikel left with his father, no crime has been committed.'

'But if he didn't? Plus, I'm pretty sure his father was listed as unknown. There's also the fact that his mother was pulled out of the Trent at the beginning of this week.' Chris struggled to understand the other DI's complacency. 'Okay, so what about the arson?' he carried on, determining he'd probably need *another* strong cup of coffee after the call finished to calm himself down.

'Ms Seamoor's house was used as an emergency foster home. We have no proof it was someone connected to Mikel who started the fire. As you would expect, Ms Seamoor has dealt with plenty of angry parents in her time.'

'None of them have set fire to her house before now, though,' Chris replied sarcastically.

'You would be amazed at the lengths some parents will go to, Inspector. I have worked with Jill for years on such cases.'

'With all due respect—' Chris could feel himself getting more and more frustrated by the second. He looked around his office for inspiration, and that's when he saw Trudie frantically trying to get his attention from his doorway. 'DI Holman, could you please contact your IT department and chase where these missing witness statements have vanished to, and let me know the outcome?'

'Will do, Detective Jackson.' And with that, she put the phone down. He let out a long sigh. Where was this woman coming from? She was a detective inspector like himself, yet she seemed to be taking the easy way out of the situation. The problem was he wasn't exactly sure what he could do about it at the moment. Chris realised that Trudie was now in his office and was stood in front of his desk fidgeting, clearly desperate to talk to him.

'Sorry, boss. We've just hit on something with the landlord.'

'Now that's a bit of news I'm pleased to hear. Tell me more,' Chris said, getting up from his desk as his vision momentarily blurred. 'Bloody painkiller side effects,' he muttered under his breath as he followed Trudie into the incident room. 'So, what we got?' Chris asked as he sat down heavily on the chair next to Trudie's computer.

'Right, well, I did a quick Google search on our landlord, Gordon Parks, and came across something one of his past tenants had written on a university accommodation letting page.'

'Okay, so you mean something like Rightmove?'

'Sort of, boss. Students can leave reviews on property lettings so that other students can make informed decisions before they start renting.'

'So more like those review sites for products?'

'Exactly. So, somebody called "Notts Gal" wrote a comment about the creepy landlord at Regatta House.

Apparently, he told her that if she ever couldn't afford rent, she could pay in other ways.'

'Other ways, meaning sexual acts?'

'That's the impression I got.'

'Do we know who "Notts Gal" is?'

'Julie is on the phone to the university as we speak.'

'Have you found any further posts about the landlord?'

'Not that I've come across yet. This was the first one I hit upon.'

Chris turned to the rest of the team. 'Colin will you do a criminal record check on this landlord, Mr Gordon Parks?'

Trudie was looking thoughtful. 'I'm just wondering, boss, if Dana was paying for her rent in umm ... "other ways" ... too?'

'I can see where you're coming from.'

'If you think about it, ever since Greg and I went to visit him when we first started investigating Dana, he's been promising to show us receipts for this rent paid a year in advance but, as yet, nothing has materialised.'

'I've got something!' Colin shouted, cutting into the conversation. 'Our Mr Parks has been arrested several times for kerb crawling.'

Chris sprang into action. 'Trudie, Greg, go back to see Mr Parks and try to chase up these receipts or records for the rent received. Don't mention anything about what we now know until I've got something more concrete.'

Trudie and Greg nodded their agreement and headed quickly out of the incident room.

'Boss, that could be the reason why Dana left in the first place.'

'Quite possibly, Colin, but it still doesn't account for the next three years. Julie, you getting anywhere?' Chris shouted across to where Julie was sat with the phone held to her ear against her shoulder as she tried to make notes at the same time.

'The accommodation team are just looking into it, boss,' she called over.

'Colin are you happy to keep searching the web for anything else written about our Mr Parks? I just need to go and make a call.'

'Of course, boss.'

Chris got up from the seat, hoping he could get to his office before he had another loss of vision. Maybe it really was time for another doctor's appointment.

Sitting at his desk again, his thoughts quickly turned to Hannah and Jen's trip to the darkest depths of London. He needed to report back to them what his team had just discovered, but he reasoned that maybe it was best to wait till they had something more concrete rather than relying on hearsay from an internet forum. There was one person he had to speak to, though, before the business with the landlord was confirmed either way.

'Nottingham Social Services. Holly Lord speaking.'

'Hi there, it's Chris Jackson.'

'Good afternoon. I wasn't expecting to hear from you guys so soon.'

'I wondered if I could pick your brains about something that has come up about Dana?'

'Of course, fire away.'

'We've had some information come to our attention about the landlord at Regatta House.'

'Oh?'

Chris realised he wasn't quite sure how he was going to break the news to the social worker. 'Holly ... we have reason to believe that Dana may have been paying for her rent using sexual favours.' Chris waited for a couple of seconds for Holly to respond before continuing.

'I understand that, if this is the case, there'll be a whole protocol that will need following your end. I just wanted to give you the heads up, to be honest.'

'Right. Thank you, Chris.'

'Did you ever notice anything odd about the landlord, or did you never really see him?'

'The times I saw him, he seemed like an okay guy. I didn't really have any cause to suspect that anything was going on between him and Dana.'

'We're not a hundred per cent certain. We're at the inquiry stage at the moment.'

'Well, thank you for letting me know.'

'Not a problem. Could I ask you to keep the information to yourself for the time being?'

'Of course. It will only lead to more paperwork, so I'll gladly keep it quiet for now.'

With that, Chris ended the call. He felt like he had quite possibly thrown a grenade into an already explosive situation, but he trusted Holly to keep it to herself.

As one phone call ended, another one came through on Chris' mobile. 'Please tell me you and Greg have some good news.'

'Quite possibly, boss,' Trudie answered. 'Mr Parks handed us some receipts for payment received from Dana's mystery benefactor.'

'That's progress.'

'I wanted to ring and see what you wanted us to do next. Do you want us to bring him in?'

'Hold fire on that one. If you and Greg head back here, we can get the documents analysed. He's bound to have slipped up somewhere.'

'Think they could be fake, boss?'

'I've not heard back from Julie about "Notts Gal", but it wouldn't completely surprise me if they were.'

'We'll head back now.'

'See you in a bit.'

Chris placed his phone back on his desk. Part of him wanted to phone Holly back up and tell her that everything was sorted and the landlord had found the proof they needed, but there was no point trying to go back and undo something he had already set in motion. With his coffee now on the cold side and his thoughts turning to his next shot of caffeine, he got up from his desk and headed towards the incident room to see if anyone wanted a top up.

Chapter Twenty-Two

Jen Garner

Jen and Hannah climbed out of the pool car at St Pancras, thanked the driver and headed towards King's Cross. At night, King's Cross was a very different place to how it appeared in the day.

Jen reached inside the document folder she was carrying. 'Sam managed to get Dana's photo from her asylum application. She's blown it up for us.'

'Great.' Hannah looked around at the street girls as they started to gather in small groups, with their pimps keeping a close eye. The drug dealers weren't far away either, eyeing up their next target. 'I think it might be best if we just go round and tell people we're looking for your friend and see what happens from there.'

'Sounds good.'

'If we try to approach a range of people, we might get lucky – so we're not seen as just targeting the working girls.'

Jen turned around to see a car pulling up, and the girls moved over in their tight skirts and the heels she could only wish she'd be able to balance in. 'Max said he'd get someone to keep watch on us in case we get ourselves into trouble,' Jen said as her attention returned to Hannah.

'Would it be better if we split up?'

'I guess so, but we should keep an eye on each other – just in case there's any trouble.'

Hannah momentarily studied Dana's photo and walked towards a group of girls who were chatting to each other in front of the train station. There were no trains running at this time of night, so there was only one reason they were there – and it wasn't for the last train home.

Jen noted Hannah's position and made her move. 'Excuse me, love,' she said in her best Cockney accent.

'Sorry, I don't do girls,' came the response.

'Oh no, it's just I'm looking for my friend. I wondered if you'd seen her?' Jen attempted to flash the photo at the lady she'd approached. She must have been well into her forties and layered in make-up.

'Nah, not seen her,' the woman responded dismissively without even looking at the photo.

'Will you just have a look, please?' Jen asked meekly. 'We haven't seen her for over a month and we're worried sick.'

'What, you and that pretty blonde over there?' the women asked, pointing towards Hannah who seemed to be happily chatting away.

'Yeah, that's my other friend. She's helping me look for Dana.'

'I've got no idea, love. I've not seen her.'

'Okay, thank you,' Jen said as she moved away from the older woman and surveyed where Hannah was now standing. Hannah looked like she was a natural at this. She had the girls eating out of the palm of her hand. Jen guessed she was out of touch in talking to the younger generation. If they'd been kids of Alex and Melanie's ages, she'd have been fine, though.

As she stood there, working out who to approach next, a big, burly man came and grabbed her by her arm. She felt herself tense up. She was definitely out of practice – she should have seen him coming. Now all she could do was attempt to strike up a conversation with him.

'Aw, you're hurting me,' Jen said as she attempted to get her arm free.

'What are you doing here, and why are you talking

to my girls?' he asked as he put his face within inches of Jen's, while still holding her arm.

Jen contemplated what to do next, wondering whether to knee him in the groin or try one of those other moves she'd learned years ago, in the hope she still remembered them.

'I'm just looking for my friend,' Jen answered. She didn't have to fake being scared because part of her was very scared that she was being clung onto by a six-foot man.

'And what makes you think they'll know where she is?'

'Can you let go of me please, and I'll tell you?' Jen tried to use the situation to her advantage. She had already seen Hannah clock what was going on and begin to edge closer in case she needed assistance. Time for the waterworks, which came easier than she expected because he really was hurting her.

'She ... she ... used to be a working girl before she disappeared. We just hoped that someone round here might have seen her,' Jen sobbed. At least she'd have a bruise to show for her efforts. The man released his grip so Jen could move slightly. He was still in her face, but he had softened slightly.

'Well, I can tell you for free, she ain't round here. I know all my girls,' he grunted.

'Will you just look at the picture, please?' Jen pleaded as she tried to wave it at him for his attention.

The man snatched the photo from Jen's hand.

'Nope, never seen her. She's not from round here.'

'Thank you for your time.'

'Stop harassing my girls,' he growled as he began to rip up the photo. 'Or you'll have more than a sore arm to worry about next time.'

'Okay, okay, I'm sorry. I'll just get my friend and we'll move on. We can see she isn't here.'

Hannah rushed over and played the concerned friend, and they both retreated towards where they'd been dropped off.

'Prick,' Jen said, rubbing her arm. 'When this is all over, I'm going to come back and floor him.'

'You sure you'll remember how to?' Hannah laughed.

'I'm sure I can learn again pretty fast.'

'Look, let's grab a milkshake. We can move on to somewhere else in a bit when he's gone.'

'Sounds good. You can tell me all about the dishy detective. And make sure you act like my friend. I've just told that prick we are.'

Jen and Hannah found the nearest takeaway that had seating, grabbed a couple of milkshakes and sat down.

'So ... Detective Jackson?' Jen probed

'If I'm honest, it's a bit of a crazy situation.' Hannah sighed. 'After they let me out of the hospital last year, I travelled down to Derby and turned up at his flat – but it was all lust then.'

'And now?'

'It's kinda carried on that way.'

'But you want more?'

'You know when you've finished a case, or something has worked out so you've made a difference, and you get such a high that nothing else can reach that feeling?'

'Only too well. That's why Chloe and I started going out, getting drunk and taking random strangers to hotels.'

'Well, I go to Derby and see Chris, we have amazing sex and everything is great, and then I return to London. But the more time I spend with him, the more I get this feeling that I want more than just sex.'

'You spoken to him about it?'

'Hell no, he'd probably run a mile. He's probably enjoying these no-strings sexual encounters. Plus, there's my job. Who would want to be in a relationship with an undercover officer, never mind one who could quite possibly make DCI when Max retires?'

'Hmm, but I bet he's married to his job just as much. You two would make a right pair.'

'That's why it works at the moment. I don't ask for anything from him, and he doesn't ask anything of me. We don't spend our lives waiting for a text message and arriving home to cold dinner left on the table.'

'Yeah, he just arrives home to find you on the table.'

'You could say that. What about you and James? You two must have come out the other side okay?' Hannah looked curious.

'To be honest, Han, it depends where the other side is. Plus, I've got Melanie and Alex to think about.'

'Well, you're here, aren't you?'

'Oh yeah, he told me to come, but we had Max in the house. He and James had been talking about the good old days.'

'You think Max being there swayed him?'

'Who knows? James and I seem to be getting along fine and back to how we used to be. Then something goes wrong or one of us says the wrong thing, and we're back to lying on opposite sides of the bed.'

'See, this is what I don't want to happen with Chris. He's a great bloke, there's no question of that, but what if the service gets in the way of all that?'

'But isn't his job just as likely to?'

'We can't have emotional ties in this job, Jen. It's too dangerous. You yourself know that.'

'Now you're making excuses,' Jen said. 'The bad guys could already know about your relationship and use it to their advantage. That's why Chloe and I used to have one-night stands.'

'And that worked out well.'

'Yeah, I suppose it did before James came along. Maybe you just need to talk to him, Han. Find out how he's feeling. I quit the service because I was scared that I'd lose James if he knew the truth, and I almost did anyway.'

'Hmmm.' Hannah didn't seem to have anything else to say on the subject and returned to slurping her milkshake.

'Did you get anywhere with the girls you spoke to, before we were rudely interrupted?' Jen asked, noticing the change in Hannah's body language.

'No, not really. I didn't get enough time to speak to them properly. I showed them her photo and told them I was looking for our friend.'

'Then that idiot stepped in. He's made me so cross, Han. I just want to go out there and punch him, but what use would it do? The girls would still go back to him.'

'One of the girls did mention a local charity that it might be worth contacting. We could see if they recognise her.'

'Fancy trying our luck at the Bird Cage? It's just outside the station.'

'And if all else fails, we can play on the swing.' Hannah laughed, finishing her remaining milkshake and brushing herself down.

Jen and Hannah walked together to Battle Bridge Place and the famous Bird Cage, which was lit up with its bright neon lights.

'Hopefully we won't bump into the same pimp round here,' Jen said as they both came to a stop. 'Same plan as last time?'

'Try not to get manhandled this time, though,' Hannah responded as she took her share of the photos and moved towards her targets. 'Hi, I wonder if you could help me? I'm looking for my friend.'

Most of the girls that Jen spoke to gave her a non-committal response but, after a while, just when she was thinking about calling it a night, she found someone who seemed more willing to help.

Jen approached an older looking woman, who appeared to be closer to Dana's age, and finally she got the response she'd been waiting for.

'I wondered where she'd disappeared to. I used to see her, you know, at the parties? But she kinda disappeared.'

'When was the last time you saw her? What was she like? Was she okay? Do you know where she went?' Jen started moving from one foot to another, throwing questions at the poor girl like any worried best friend would.

'Woah! Slow down, hun.'

'I'm sorry. I've just been so worried about her.'

'Look, time is money. Meet me tomorrow and I'll talk – but it's gonna cost you.'

'Anything,' Jen said, summoning as much enthusiasm as she could muster.

'Meet me here, 11 a.m. You can buy me breakfast.'

'Yeah, of course. Thank you so much. I'll go and tell my friend now.'

'Try not to make a scene, hun. No one likes a snitch.' And with that, the woman walked towards the nearest waiting car and hung herself through the window, touting her business.

Jen signalled over to Hannah, who had had another group of girls eating out of her hand like before.

'I think we've got something. Girl over there, standing talking to the Merc driver. She said she used to see Dana at parties. She's going to meet with us tomorrow.'

'Did she say much more?'

'Not much, other than it's going to cost us breakfast … and no doubt more.'

'Shall we make our getaway, seeing as it's getting late and at least one of us needs our beauty sleep? You wanna stay over?' Hannah asked as she waved at the group of girls she'd been talking to and linked arms with Jen.

'If you don't mind. I hate turning up late at Max's. I feel like I'm a teenager trying to sneak in after a night out.' Jen pulled out her phone and put a call in for a car to meet them. Once she was back at Hannah's, she could work out her strategy for tomorrow.

Chapter Twenty-Three

Dana

As the years passed and Mikel got older, I found it harder and harder to keep him out of the way when the money for the landlord was due. I began to trust Holly and confided in her how I had been trafficked over and admitted I was in the UK illegally. She didn't judge me and suggested that I apply for asylum status. She made me believe I could be free. I never told my other visitors about my plans, because I was too scared that they wouldn't work out.

My mystery friend started to comment on how much happier I was and said that she hoped one day we would both be free. She never said anything, but I suspected she was suffering the same fate as me. She was always so positive and kind. Us working girls knew how to hide the bruises and the scars left on us by others, and I knew just because I couldn't see her scars, it didn't mean they weren't there.

I was so nervous when I had my interview, but I explained everything to the man who was conducting it. Then Holly met me afterwards and took me for tea and cake. I was starting to believe ... that was until things went wrong again, as they always did for me when I thought I could finally see a way out of this mess. The same man who had abducted me arrived at my flat one night with his mate, Clive, who I recognised as somebody who used to visit me regularly at the brothel – I was never usually told the punters' names, but this guy was a regular who seemed to know the house madam. They warned me they were going to take me and Mikel back to London soon. They didn't seem to know about my application status, so

149

at least I was able to keep that from them. They warned me that my time in Nottingham was running out, and I knew far too well what would happen if I tried to run. Shortly afterwards, my asylum was declined and I was ordered to return to Iraq. I could feel everything around me crumbling into tiny pieces. There was no escape.

Chapter Twenty-Four

Jen Garner

'Morning all.' Max walked through into the meeting room from his office. 'Do we have DI Jackson on the line?' he asked he sat at the head of the table.

'Just dialling through now,' Sam responded as she reached across to the phone.

'Did you two have a successful night?' Max asked, turning towards where Jen and Hannah were sitting.

It had been close to 3 a.m. by the time they had arrived back at Hannah's from central London. As soon as Jen's head had hit the pillow, she was out like a light. She dreamt of happier times spent with the kids, who she hadn't spoken to since she'd left for London. Though she hadn't spoken properly to James, he had texted several times to check she was still okay, and she'd replied, telling him everything was fine. She knew she had to promise herself that this would be it; this would be the end of her time as an undercover detective – but what if something else came along? Though she could see herself in the police force, she worried that she'd end up wanting more and resenting the kids and James for holding her back, but then she'd think back to her conversation with Hannah about her relationship with Chris and how *she* found herself wanting more than just sex. It was just that the coming-down-from-a-case high was so unique that no one else could ever begin to imagine what it was like.

Jen had momentarily zoned out when she was brought back into the room with everyone looking at her, waiting for an answer to a question she'd not heard.

'Max wanted to know about the girl you spoke to last

night?' Hannah reminded her, just as the DI answered his phone.

'Morning all. Julie is with me again today.' Chris' voice came through the speakers.

'Morning Julie, Chris,' Max responded. 'Just so you know to start with, Angela is happy for us to continue working the case at our end but has asked to be kept in the loop.'

'I spent some time talking to Angela yesterday. She still isn't sure why Dana wasn't on the system after her arrest, but she said she's looking into it,' Sam offered.

'Chris, any more news from your end?' Max prompted.

'Starting with Mikel, I spoke to DI Holman and received a very defensive answer from her. No missing person's report has been added to the system for the boy, as they believe he left with his father.'

'What the hell?' Jen couldn't believe what she was hearing. 'What the fuck is she playing at? Other forces could be keeping a look out for him but, without his missing person's report on the system, no one else will know about him!'

'The fire is being treated as arson, but again DI Holman doesn't necessarily think that Mikel's disappearance and that are connected. Paula, Mikel's emergency foster parent, has housed hundreds of children placed into emergency care over the years. It seems that in DI Holman's mind, there are any number of people who could have done it.'

'What are your thoughts on this, Chris?' Max asked.

'Personally, I don't buy it. Although, her excuses about why witness statements weren't available on the system are believable, when you look at how under-resourced some teams now are in Nottingham.'

'Do you need me to look into it at all?' Max asked. Jen knew that his powers extended far beyond London.

'I want to say no, but I'm worried that they're missing something.'

'I will see what strings I can pull this end, Detective.'

'Before I hand over, we did have a breakthrough regarding Dana and where she was tenanted after the birth of Mikel. I will let Julie explain this.'

'We are all ears.'

'To bring everyone up to speed,' Julie began, 'the landlord who owned the property where Dana was staying has an interesting history. One of the team was doing a general internet search when they hit upon a message board where a Nottingham student had posted about what a creep this particular landlord was. The student implied he had told her she could pay in sexual favours if she was short for rent.'

'And did they?' Max questioned.

'I'm guessing not. We spent yesterday trying to trace the message poster, "Notts Gal", and we're expecting a call back from the university this morning. We also continued to do a background check on Gordon Parks, the landlord, and discovered he has been pulled over on more than one occasion for kerb crawling,' Chris continued on from where Julie left off.

'So, do you think Dana was paying for rent in sexual favours?' Jen asked.

'Mr Parks claimed that the money was paid a year in advance but was unable to show us any proof until two of my colleagues went to visit him yesterday, when the receipts magically turned up,' Julie explained.

'Do you think they're faked?'

'Most certainly. I've emailed a copy over to Hannah, so you can have a look for yourselves,' Chris responded.

'Sounds good,' Max said as Hannah searched her email. 'What are your team telling you down there, Chris?'

'They're pretty much in agreement with me and Julie. We're just waiting for the confirmation from this "Notts Gal" before we bring him in.'

'Keep us up to date on that one. Now, over to us. Jen, how was your night on the streets of King's Cross?'

'Eventful,' Hannah responded as she nudged Jen.

'Other than being threatened by a pimp, who I *will* be returning to visit once this is over, it went pretty well.'

Everyone laughed as the tension was lifted slightly.

'She wants to go and show him who's boss,' Hannah added before Max cleared his throat to silence the room.

'We came across a girl who Hannah and I are meeting later on this morning. She claimed to have seen Dana at some parties or something.'

'Parties?' Chris asked.

'I'm guessing she meant sex parties, but I'll get that confirmed when I speak to her later.'

'How reliable is her intel?' Max didn't look completely convinced.

'I'm not sure. We know these parties exist. She did mention the information was going to cost me breakfast.'

'Sounds a classy bird,' came a voice over the speaker.

'Any further questions from your end, Chris?' Max asked, clearly eager to bring the conference call to an end.

'No, I think we're good. I'd be grateful if you can see what information you can get from DI Holman, and we'll continue working the landlord angle.'

'Great. Jen, Hannah, go and meet this girl and see what you can find out from her. I'd be interested to know where Mikel was during all of this,' Max commented as he ended the call. 'What do we all think?'

'Do you think DI Holman is trying to hide something?' Sam asked.

'Quite possibly. It seems she's keen to put a nice, neat bow on things rather than investigating what's right in front of her.'

'I'll be interested to find out what the landlord knows as well. If Dana was paying for rent via sexual favours, whose idea was it? And was that the reason she left Nottingham again in the first place?' Jen mused.

'Whatever happened, the sex trade seems to be playing rather heavily in all of this. Might be worth getting the DI up here if things dry out in Nottingham,' Hannah said absentmindedly. 'I mean to help with the investigation into the case,' she added, but was too late as the laughter began again.

DI Chris Jackson

At the exact same time as Max ended the call, there was a knock on Chris' door.

'Sorry to disturb you, boss,' Trudie said, peering round the corner and surveying who was there.

'Come in. Julie and I have just finished. What can I do for you?'

Trudie entered and stood, leaning back on the office wall. 'We've managed to trace this "Notts Gal" and have arranged to meet her once she's finished university for the day. At around lunch time.'

Chris studied his watch, checking how long they had before the meeting. 'Did she mention anything about the landlord?'

'Only what she had written on the message board, so I asked her if she'd be happy to meet us and have a chat about possibly taking a statement,' Trudie replied. 'She didn't contact us when it happened because she didn't think anything would be done.'

'Okay, that gives us a couple of hours to play with. Julie, what did you make of the conference call?'

'Do you need me to leave, boss?' Trudie asked, looking slightly uncomfortable.

'You can stay. We've just had our daily briefing with our friends in London.'

'Friends?' Trudie looked interested. 'Is this all connected to why Jennifer Garner was here, boss?'

'I'm afraid so. Grab a seat, Trudie, and we'll fill you in,' Chris said as he directed Trudie towards the free chair. 'So …' Chris began giving Trudie the edited highlights of the case.

'So, that's what she and the random bloke were doing here then?'

'The bloke was her boss, DCI Max Carver. I'd had dealings with him last year.'

'We had royalty in and no one said anything?' Trudie gasped.

'It puts a whole new spin on this case, if I'm honest with you.' Just then Chris' email pinged and his attention was drawn back to the computer screen in front of him.

'Looks like our luck's in, ladies. DI Holman has just forwarded over all the witness statements and fire report,' Chris announced as he flicked through the various files which had just arrived. 'Max has obviously waved a magic wand or something.' Chris typed out a quick thank you email before standing up. 'I think we need to rally the troops,' he said. 'I'll go and put the kettle on and meet you back in the incident room.' *Time for some more pain relief for this headache*, he thought grimly.

Julie and Trudie got up and followed Chris out of his office, talking amongst themselves about the new revelations.

'We now have everything DI Holman had on the

investigation into the house fire and subsequent disappearance of Mikel Antwar,' Chris announced to his team as he strolled into the incident room. 'Julie, can you look over the missing person's report for Mikel, please, now we can access it?'

'Do you want me to alert the media too, boss?'

'Let's see if we can keep it quiet for now. We don't want to scare whoever has Mikel. If you could get the artist's impression and Mikel's photo out to all forces too, that would be great. Can you get back on the petrol, Greg? You can liaise with Julie and her contact at Notts fire and rescue about what caused the fire and start checking CCTV. Colin, can you look over the witness statements and see if there is anything of interest? I'm also keen to know why Jill didn't push for the missing person's report, and I'd like to hear more from Paula too.'

'Do you want me to contact Holly Lord as well, boss?' Colin asked

'No, I'm pretty confident she's in the clear on this one.'

The incident room was buzzing again, and everyone was happy to be on task. As Chris sloped back to his office, he wondered how Hannah and Jen were getting on speaking to their mystery street girl. He also wondered what Max had done to make all the files suddenly appear.

Chapter Twenty-Five

Jen Garner

Hannah and Jen were dropped off in the same place as the night before and made their way to Battle Bridge Place. It was all change in the daytime, and the streets that were once lined with women in tight skirts and high heels were now lined with tourists waiting for their connection or a friend, or perhaps just sitting and watching the world go by in the summer sunshine.

'Do you think she'll show?' Hannah asked.

'I'm really not sure.'

'So, just to clarify, you're my friend and we're looking for your friend Dana?'

'Yep,' Jen agreed. She was a little distracted as she noticed how different the Bird Cage looked during the day. Long gone were the neon lights, and all that was left was the rivalry between the younger generation to have a go on the swing. 'There she is.' Jen regained focus and signalled towards their lead as they made their way over. 'Hi, thanks for meeting me again,' Jen said as she approached her.

'Not a problem, doll.'

'My name's Lizzy, and this is my friend, Monica.' Jen introduced them and held out her hand.

'Candy,' the woman said.

'Where's the best place to get a decent breakfast around here?' Jen was keen to move the conversation away from the crowded square.

'There's a greasy spoon this way,' Candy said as she began to walk off, clearly expecting Jen and Hannah to follow. Hannah gave Jen a look of concern as they were led past the train station and up a little side street.

'You can always get a good meal here,' Candy said, opening the door. 'No matter who you are.'

Surveying the small café, Jen followed Candy in with Hannah following behind.

'Morning, ladies,' the owner said to them as they entered.

'Morning, Ken. Full English over here when you've got a moment,' Candy called back.

'Friendly with the owner?' Jen asked.

'Yeah, he's one of the good guys.' Candy took a seat and waited for Jen and Hannah to join her.

'Can I get you two lovely ladies anything?' Ken came over and looked at her.

'Just a tea, please,' Jen said quickly.

'You sure, Lizzy? You already skipped breakfast earlier.' Hannah feigned concern.

'I'm too worried about Dana to eat,' Jen responded, playing along. 'You said something about seeing my friend?' Jen continued, once she was sure Ken was out of earshot.

'Can I look at the photo again?'

'Certainly.' Jen dug around in her bag. 'It's in here somewhere.'

Candy laughed in amusement. 'Spend a night on the streets, doll, you'll soon learn to carry less.'

Jen pulled out the photo and handed it over to Candy, who studied it for a while before responding.

'Yeah. I think I remember seeing her at a couple of the parties recently ...'

'Someone's birthday?' Jen asked with added enthusiasm.

'Ha ... no. How best to put it?' Candy smirked. 'Orgies.'

Jen took a huge breath in. 'What was she doing at a sex party?' Jen asked, looking towards Hannah for comfort.

Hannah moved her hand onto Jen's arm. 'Wait till we find out more,' Hannah responded perfectly.

'They happen more or less every month, depending on who's running them. Someone books a group of us girls and we all go along and provide the entertainment. Of course there are plenty of drugs around, but that just adds to the fun of it.'

'And that's the last place you saw my friend?'

At that point, their breakfasts arrived. As Candy and Hannah tucked in, Jen fiddled with the sugar pot.

'So, who books these parties? And who are they for?' Jen eventually asked, fed up of waiting for Candy to say more.

'I don't know. I just get a message on my phone and then I just turn up. They're worth it. Really well paid.'

'So, Dana was at these parties too. Did she look okay?'

'She looked fine, doll. Enjoying herself along with everyone else.'

'Where do they take place?'

'It depends who's organising them, though it's hard to tell who it is at the best of times.'

'What do you mean?' Hannah put her hand on Jen's arm again. 'Oh okay ...' Jen said, pretending to finally get the point. 'So, can you get me into one of these parties so I can find my friend?'

'I'd love to, doll. Monica would make a killing,' Candy said, looking over towards Hannah.

'She'll go,' Jen said quickly.

'Will I?' Hannah raised her eyebrows.

'If it means we can find Dana.'

'Lizzy, I'm not prepared to go to one of these sex parties to be hit on and plied with drugs just to find Dana.'

'But Mon ...'

'Listen, hun. Like I said, I just get a text message and then I turn up. I have no clue who runs them or how you get invited. Plus Dana wasn't at the last one, so there's no guarantee she'll be at the next one.'

'Why wasn't she there?' Jen asked, feigning panic.

'I told you, doll. I just get a text.'

'So, who else goes to them? Somebody must know where Dana is.'

Candy laughed. 'Ha! Good luck getting the richest people in London to talk.'

'So, you're saying someone could have done something to her?'

'Lizzy.' Hannah stepped in again and turned to Candy. 'Where have these parties taken place in the past?'

'All over. Sometimes in Camden or Soho, or some random mansion in the countryside.'

'Is there anything you can tell us to help us find Dana?' Hannah asked as she kept her hand on Jen's arm.

'Like I said, I didn't see her at the last party.'

'But she was at the one before. When was it?' Jen started up again.

'Oh, erm ...' Candy stalled.

'Look, I'll pay you,' Jen said, searching in her bag and bringing out her purse.

'Oh, but you already have, doll. This was on you, remember? Look, there is one thing that might help. There used to be a regular ... you know ... "queen bee" at these parties. But last year she seemed to vanish.'

'Do you have a name?'

'I don't, although there was this rumour going round that she'd been arrested or something. But you know what it's like once the queen bee is dead? Someone is always quick to take her place. I think I heard that a bloke was hosting them now. I can't remember his name but all the girls want a piece of him – a tall, dark stranger with money.'

'So, do you think this "queen bee" will know where my friend is?'

'Possibly, as they both disappeared at the same time. Maybe they ran off into the sunset together.' Candy gave a throaty laugh and then started to cough. 'You're so cute.'

'So, you've actually got no idea where my friend is?'

'Nope, like I said to you, I used to see her at the parties. That's all.'

Jen stood up. 'Come on, Monica. We're leaving.'

'Good luck finding her.' Candy laughed

'Thanks for your help,' Hannah said curtly, getting up from the table and throwing some money down.

Jen was now in full hysterics, playing the concerned friend as she fled the café with Hannah not far behind. Hannah chased Jen up the road and back towards the train station, where they would both get lost in the crowds and return to the office safely.

Feeling emotionally drained, Jen sat in the back of the car heading to the office, with Hannah following somewhere behind. She was getting too old for this shit. As she leaned back on the headrest, she hardly dared to close her eyes for a second, afraid that sleep would take her away for those moments of alone time and silence as they travelled between King's Cross and her destination.

Hannah returned to find Jen sat on one of the more comfy chairs in Max's office.

'Successful breakfast meeting?' Max asked as he came in.

'Possibly. What did you make of it, Jen?'

'Bloody exhausting,' Jen said as she propped herself up and reached over to where her cup of tea was sat. 'I don't think it was a wasted journey, though. Even though Candy might think she's messed us around, she did tell us more about the parties.'

'And you tried to get me on the guest list. As a hooker.' Hannah laughed, seeing the funny side to it to Jen's relief.

'You're in better shape than me. I'm just a washed-up detective.'

'She did also mention that the "queen bee", as she called it, had changed. The previous one stopped showing up at these parties. Which got me thinking—'

'Jessica,' Jen concluded before Hannah could take a breath.

'It fits the timeline. Unless there have been any other drug busts we aren't aware of,' Hannah mused.

'Right.' Max got up from his chair. 'Let's move this into the meeting room and call Sam over to join us.'

Jen sighed. She had just found a comfy position on the chair she was occupying, but she managed to hoist herself up again.

'I'll go and get some drinks and let Sam know,' she said as she left Max's office and headed towards Sam and the kitchen. As she did, she stole a look at Chloe's old desk, which had now been tidied and left almost as a permanent memorial to her – well, at least until someone else came along and needed a desk space. Plus, it was tidy – so not much of a memorial to the chaos of her former life.

'Sam, you're wanted in the meeting room.'

Sam looked up, confused. 'Are they wanting coffees?' she asked, clearly wondering why she had been called.

'Nope, I'm off to get those sorted.'

'Paper?'

'I think Max wants you in on this case.' Jen smiled encouragingly at her.

'Oh, okay then.' Sam stood up hurriedly and grabbed her array of different coloured pens.

'Everyone settled?' Max put his paperwork on the table as Jen walked in with a round of drinks for them all. 'Just so everyone is up to speed, this morning Jen and Hannah met with Candy, the girl who they spoke to near King's Cross last night. Though it wasn't the most useful of trips, we've managed to get some key information. Hannah, the floor is yours.'

'Okay, Candy was basically looking for a free breakfast, *but* she did manage to give us some interesting information that I think we need to take forward. First off, Candy gets invited to what are essentially orgies, or sex parties. They are well paid and she and other girls are expected to keep the clients happy. It sounds like it's usually high-end clientele.'

'So, I'm thinking, basically, the rich and famous, politicians, footballers ... those who wouldn't like this "hobby" exposed,' Jen added as Hannah wrote on the main screen.

'Candy informed us that she had seen Dana at several of these parties, but she had not been in attendance at the last one. She only finds out about the parties via a text message inviting her to attend,' Hannah continued.

'Do we think someone has a database with a list of all the working girls available for parties?' Sam asked.

'Quite possibly, but I wouldn't know where to start looking for it,' Hannah responded.

'One thing that did come out of the meeting was a mention of a "queen bee", who had recently stopped attending the parties, although somebody has apparently already taken over the spot,' Jen added.

'Jen and I wondered if this could be Jessica,' Hannah

added. With that, a photo of Jessica filled the screen. There was silence in the room as they all reflected on last year's case.

'Jessica is currently residing in prison on drug possession and intent to supply charges, along with murder and assault charges. She is more famously linked to her dad, George Crawford but, prior to her arrest, there hadn't been any contact between the two of them,' Hannah continued.

'Did we ever discover how Jessica ended up in the drug trade? More specifically, dealing Crawford-branded drugs?' Jen asked.

'Jessica claimed to have fallen into the role after a family friend contacted her to tell her she could continue her dad's legacy,' Hannah explained. 'This is also the same friend who recognised Chloe,' she added grimly.

'Can we assume that this family friend has taken over the sex parties?' Sam asked as she flicked through something on the screen in front of her. 'We know the drugs are slowly disappearing now we've cut the source off, but we didn't know about the sex parties till today. They're still carrying on, even with Jessica locked up.'

'I don't think we can ignore the connection between George, Jessica and Dana.' Jen folded her arms.

'But was Dana brought over here by Jessica or George?' Sam queried.

'We know from the police reports that Dana was hooking prior to Mikel's birth. She only arrived in Nottingham to give birth to Mikel, as far as we're aware,' Hannah said, tapping away on the computer in front of her.

'Have the team back in Nottingham made any progress in locating Mikel?' Jen asked.

'They now have access to all the reports and witness

statements from the fire, so hopefully they will start making some in-roads,' Max responded. 'Though I did get a copy of the artist's impression of the man who took Mikel.'

'Do you want me to run it through the facial recognition, boss?' Sam asked.

'Might be a good idea.'

'Oh, and is it worth setting up a tail on Candy?' Sam started to gather up the coloured pens and highlighters that she had randomly brought into the meeting.

'We don't know when the next party is due, so we could end up following her for twenty-nine days and achieving nothing. Would you have a look and see if we have any assets close to Candy and find out if they've picked up any chatter about the events?' Max instructed.

'On it, boss,' Sam said as she stood up.

'I don't know what you think, Max, but there is one person we could go and see who might be able to tell us what happened to Dana in those three years …'

Chapter Twenty-Six

DI Chris Jackson

Trudie and Chris arrived at the campus and saw a girl sat alone at one of the picnic benches in front of the university.

'Hi.' The girl stood up, holding out her hand to greet them. 'I'm Kathryn.'

'Detective Constable Trudie Clarke. We spoke on the phone,' Trudie said, showing her identification, 'and this is my colleague, Detective Inspector Chris Jackson.'

'Thank you for agreeing to meet up with us.' Chris acknowledged the girl stood in front of him.

'Kathryn, we were hoping you'd be able to tell us in your own words what happened with Mr Parks, the landlord at Regatta house,' Trudie began.

Kathryn picked up the fizzy drink can she'd been sipping from and began to study it.

'He was kinda sleazy, if I'm honest with you.'

'Let's start at the beginning. How did you end up renting at Regatta House?' Trudie continued, clearly trying to steer the conversation.

'I was planning to spend six months abroad, so I needed a short let. And the flat seemed ideal for what I was looking for.'

'Okay, so when did you start having problems with Mr Parks?'

'If I'd known what was going to happen, I wouldn't have rented there.'

'When did you start to feel uncomfortable around him?'

Kathryn shifted on the bench. 'I never really had anything to do with him as my rent was paid in advance via direct debt. But, towards the end of my let, I started to have problems financially. So, I contacted Mr Parks to explain my rent would be late.'

'And how did he react?'

'When I spoke to him, he seemed very understanding and told me it wasn't a problem.'

'What happened next?'

'Well, he started coming round my flat. At first I thought he was checking up on me.'

'Was anyone with you when he visited?'

'This is it. He always managed to come round late in the evening, like really late, and he would insist on coming in, even when I told him I was about to go to bed, or off out.' Kathryn picked up her drink again and stared at it. 'At first I thought he was joking when he turned round to me and said if I was struggling with the rent, I could pay him in sexual favours. He must have seen I was shocked, because he just laughed it off and went.'

'Did he ever try to make a move on you?' Trudie asked calmly.

'He started coming round every night at various times, asking for my rent. I told him I was sorry but, as explained on the phone, I was struggling financially. He started to get more and more suggestive about what I could do to pay.'

'I know this is difficult, Kathryn, but did Mr Parks ever mention anything about anyone else in the flat block paying in sexual favours?'

'I don't know.' A tear ran down Kathryn's cheek. 'I ended up phoning my mum and asking if she could pay that month's rent for me. My independence went straight out the window.' Kathryn started to sob. Trudie moved from her seat and went to put her arm around the distressed student.

'Take some deep breaths,' Trudie said soothingly. 'Chris, can you grab some tissues?'

'It's ... it's my mum. She'll just throw it in my face now.' Kathryn continued to choke back the tears. 'But I didn't feel safe, and asking her for money was the only way I knew I could pay my rent and be out of there.'

'Have you spoken to her since?' Trudie asked sympathetically. 'And explained why you needed the money?'

'I've not had a chance since moving out of the flat and all this getting ready to go abroad.'

'I'm sure if you explained the circumstances to her, she'd understand.'

Kathryn went quiet for a while as she caught her breath.

'So, what happened after you paid him the rent?' Chris asked, steering the conversation back.

'I don't know. I paid the money and moved in with my friend the very same day.'

'So, you never heard from Mr Parks again?'

'I had a phone call from him about a flat inspection, but I didn't want to be left alone with him, so I just ignored him and tried to forget about it.'

'Okay, thank you, Kathryn. You've been very helpful.' Trudie smiled encouragingly at her.

Kathryn nodded and rubbed her face.

'Would you be willing to make a statement about your dealings with Mr Parks?' Chris asked.

'I didn't think there was anything you could do, which is why I never reported it originally.'

'What you experienced was sexual harassment, Kathryn. We can and will do something about it.'

'Okay, yeah, I'll make a statement then. Will I need to go to court?'

'Let's just take things a step at a time,' Chris reassured her.

'Can I suggest you speak to your mum as well, honey? It will make you feel better,' Trudie added kindly.

'I will. Thank you, Detectives.'

'What did you make of all that?' Trudie turned to Chris as he climbed into the car next to her.

'It sounds to me like our Mr Parks saw a vulnerable female student who had run into trouble and decided to try to take advantage of her.'

'I couldn't agree more. It makes me so cross. Instead of being supportive of her, he's gone out of his way to be a pervert.'

Chris stared into space as Trudie drove back to the station. As the world passed by, he tried to work through what felt like cotton wool inside his head, squeezing everything down into smaller blocks so the information about the case could take priority.

'Right, team, who's got some good news for me?' Chris asked as he took his place at the front of the incident room.

'I have something about the fire.'

'The floor is yours, Julie.' Chris relaxed into his seat.

'I've spoken to Watch Manager Kevin Teddington, and he gave me the name of someone at the fire investigations unit who was in charge of writing the report, although Kevin kindly offered to give me the edited highlights to save me ringing around. He informed me that it was as suspected: arson. As we all know, an accelerant was posted through Ms Seamoor's letter box. The fire investigations unit have reiterated that if there hadn't been an automatic fire alarm fitted, it could have been much worse. Whoever caused it was going for maximum effect.'

'Where does that fit with the idea that the fire was started to get Mikel out of the house?' Chris asked.

'I think it is very likely.'

'Looking back over the statements from the fire, is there any report of anyone seeing a suspicious person in the area at the time?' Chris questioned.

'No, boss. There weren't really any witnesses to the fire starting – quiet area, everyone asleep, only woken up by the fire service asking them to leave their houses,' Colin jumped in.

'Did DI Holman and her team conduct a further house to house?'

'Looking over what was sent through, it doesn't look like it.'

'Do you think it would be worth setting one up now, boss?' Trudie asked.

'Yes and no. It's now a couple of days since the incident. All street residents were asked to vacate their homes at the time of the fire, so I'm pretty sure the officer on the scene spoke to everyone, either outside their homes or later on. Julie?'

'Agreed, boss. There were a number of officers talking to residents.'

'I'm torn. If everyone was asleep, which we are assuming they were, it isn't likely they're going to remember anything now.'

'I agree with you, boss,' Colin said, poring over the statements in front of him on the desk.

'That reminds me. Colin, did you get anywhere with speaking to either Paula or Jill?'

'I spoke to Paula briefly on the phone. She still seems to be pretty shaken up by what happened. She's been an emergency foster carer for years, but she's never been involved in an incident like this.'

'There has to have been a leak somewhere within social services for the information about Mikel's whereabouts to get out.' Chris sighed. 'Aren't these emergency foster homes supposed to be anonymous, safe places?'

'Boss, are you sure this mystery Lisa Carter doesn't have anything to do with it?' Greg asked suddenly.

'Again, I can categorically say that Lisa Carter has no involvement in Mikel's disappearance,' Chris informed his team. With only Julie and himself knowing Lisa's real identity, maybe it was best to keep it between them. 'Where are we with Jill?' he asked, trying to change the subject.

'I've tried to get in touch with her with little success. Paula commented that she hadn't spoken to her since the fire and had been waiting to hear from her, but understood she was probably busy since Mikel vanished.'

'Thanks, Colin. Can you try again with Jill tomorrow? Even if you have to phone the social services directly.'

'Boss.'

'If you're still having issues, let me know, and I'll speak to my contact. Okay … Greg?'

'Not much success this end; the fire investigation team confirmed that the petrol used was supermarket brand due to its low quality. So, I went back to those supermarkets I had already approached for CCTV and asked if they had any recent transactions recorded for anyone buying petrol in a canister.'

'They manage to find any transactions?'

'Nope. I could expand our search area, but it's like we're looking for a needle in a haystack, to be honest.'

'If you wouldn't mind continuing your search, that would be helpful.'

'Okay, boss.' Greg appeared to suppress a sigh.

'Well, the good news from our end is Trudie and I went up to the university and spoke to our "Notts Gal", who is actually called Kathryn. Two uniformed officers are going to see her tomorrow to get a full statement, all being well. From talking to us, there is definitely a case for sexual harassment on the landlord's part. It looks as though our Mr Parks tried to take advantage of a young, vulnerable girl living in his premises.' Chris looked around at the team for a response. 'Julie, do you mind contacting the university and informing them what we have found out about Mr Parks?'

Julie nodded. 'Of course.'

'Hopefully we can get Mr Parks and Regatta House removed from the university-approved renting list, at least,' Colin piped up.

'But do we have enough to bring Mr Parks in?' Trudie asked.

'I think we have a cause for concern. If he harassed a young student, I wouldn't put it past him to try it on with another vulnerable person.'

'Do we think that's why Dana ended up in the Trent? I mean, could Mr Parks be behind it?'

'I'm not sure, Colin. Remember, there were three years between Dana leaving Regatta House and appearing in the Trent.' Chris paused for a moment. 'Trudie, get a team together and let's bring Mr Parks in and see what he has to say for himself.'

'Hell yeah, some action at last,' Colin cheered, clearly bored with everything else that was going on.

'I'll go and see if I can grab a couple of uniforms. Julie, you okay organising a search warrant?' Trudie asked.

'Hold fire on that for now,' Chris told them. 'Let's see what he has to say for himself first.'

Having been sat in the silence of his office for some time, trying to ease his headache, Chris knew that his team had arrived back from bringing in Gordon Parks, as the sounds emanating from the incident room got louder and more frenzied. He got up to join in the conversation.

'What did Mr Parks have to say for himself when you brought him in?' Chris asked as he walked into the incident room.

'Pretty much as we expected. Apparently he doesn't know anything about any sexual harassment, and the documents that he provided us were certainly not forged.' Trudie raised her eyebrows.

'He tried to be all buddy-buddy with me, boss. Made some comments about a girl on the way in, that sort of stuff. Trudie did nearly slam the brakes on a couple of times,' Greg said.

'Would you say that he seems different now to when you first met him?' Chris asked Trudie.

'Hard to tell, boss. When we first met him, he was all nicey-nice to me, but there's definitely something creepy about him too. I wonder if my thoughts are clouded with what we know, though.'

'Would you be happy to lead the interview, Trudie?'

'Certainly, boss. I thought you would want to lead, though?'

'You've already built up a relationship with him. Take Colin in with you. He's your typical young lad trying to get laid, after all.'

'Hey!' Colin gave Chris a look of sheer shock but then laughed.

'I'll let you both decide how you want to play this, but our primary goal is to find out how Dana was paying her rent. If we can score one for Kathryn, then that's even better.' Chris got up from where he sat, wobbled a bit and headed back to his office, leaving Trudie and Colin to discuss tactics.

'Boss!' Julie shouted after him as he opened his office door.

Sitting down at his desk, he wiggled the mouse, waiting for the computer to come back to life. 'How did you get on with the universities?' he asked as Julie walked in.

'Yeah, good. I spoke to their letting agents, who is, unsurprisingly, the same person for both universities. I spoke to him for a while about what checks they did before adding a building to the site. They're pretty thorough: inspections, background checks, all that.'

'I wonder how Mr Parks made the list …'

'I mentioned how he had been arrested a couple of times for kerb crawling, and there was an ongoing investigation for sexual harassment,' Julie replied.

'So, does that mean Regatta House is being removed from the letting site?'

'Yes and no, boss. The university wants to carry out its own investigations and asked me to keep them informed of our progress.'

'Great. I just hope there isn't a student living there who is dealing with sexual harassment as we speak.' Chris wondered if there was a way that he could get the word out about Mr Parks and his reputation. 'You thought of going higher up the food chain?' he mused.

'Not as such, boss. Do we know who was sent to take Kathryn's statement?'

'I'm not sure, but I suspect it was Officers Haywood and Curtis.'

'I'll go and have a look for them while you're with the landlord.'

'Sorry, boss,' Trudie interrupted, poking her head around the door. 'Mr Parks is ready for the interview, if you wanted to observe.'

'Let me grab a coffee. I'll sit and watch on the screens.'

Chris sat with his notebook and a cup of coffee, with Mr Parks' interview playing out in front of him. Despite the allegations, he seemed pretty relaxed and unaffected by the interrogation. Taking a sip of coffee, Chris placed the headset on so he could listen in.

'Mr Parks, we'd like to discuss one of your previous tenants, with you,' Julie began.

'Which one? I've had hundreds pass through my door.'

'We have briefly spoken about her before – Dana Antwar. We want to know more about her letting agreement. We also believe that the rent statements and receipts you provided to us before were forged.'

'What makes you say that?' the man asked.

'Well, Mr Parks, it took you three days to provide them.'

'You've seen my office, love. It's a mess.'

'I know what it's like; you do one favour for one tenant, then they tell someone else, and suddenly everyone is behind in their rent, taking advantage of your generosity,' Colin commented, playing the "good cop" role.

'Was Dana like that? Did she never pay on time? So you thought of other ways she could pay …?'

'Absolutely not.'

'So, why did you tell Kathryn Lewis she could pay using sexual favours?'

'I was joking around.' He chuckled and sank further into the chair. 'I didn't mean any harm by it.' Chris could see that Mr Parks was now so relaxed, he was almost horizontal.

'That isn't how she tells it. You tried to take advantage of a vulnerable girl. You made her feel unsafe and scared in her home.'

Mr Parks remained silent.

'Was Dana paying her rent in sexual favours?'

'No, never.'

176

'So why fake the rent statements?'

'I swear, someone used to pay the money directly into my account once a year for her rent.'

'And did you ever meet this mystery person?'

'No.'

'Not even when the arrangement was made?'

'No ... I mean, yes! Look, Dana and I ... we were in love.'

Chris hadn't been expecting that response, and he quickly scribbled it into his notebook.

'Ah, so you and Dana were in love. Anyone else know about this relationship of yours?'

'No, she wanted to keep it a secret. She was afraid she'd lose her son. I let her stay in the flat rent free. We were lovers.'

'Is Mikel your son, Mr Parks?'

'Absolutely not,' he said, seeming to suddenly become very aware of his surroundings.

'So, explain something to me: Dana moved into the flat at Regatta House straight after the birth of her son. When did this relationship start up? There is no mention of you in the social services reports. Dana stated she was single.'

'Like I said, we fell in love.'

'So, where is the first month's rent statement from before you fell head over heels in love?' Trudie changed her stance. 'I think you're talking rubbish, Mr Parks. I don't believe anyone paid the rent; I certainly don't believe you were head over heels in love.'

'Where's Mikel?' Colin prompted, leaning forward in his seat

'I have no idea where that brat is.'

'Mr Parks, Dana lived in Regatta House for three years, which you claim was because you were in a relationship. You also stated that she did a moonlight flit, and you didn't notice she was gone until her social worker came looking,' Trudie concluded.

'We decided to end the relationship. It wasn't working ... she had too much baggage.'

'You mean a young son, Mr Parks? Or the "brat" as you described him?' Colin pressed.

'You know what I think, Mr Parks? I think you took advantage of a new mother and made her perform sexual favours.' Trudie sat forward. 'Did you get off having sex with a woman who'd just given birth?'

The man seemed to be lost for words as Trudie and Colin continued to fire questions.

'That could be classed as rape, Mr Parks. Maybe we need to speak to the CPS about you.'

'You seem very quiet, Mr Parks.'

'Look, I can give you information.' The landlord stiffened, and there was a tremor in his voice. 'But you need to guarantee me protection.' As he spoke his eyes darted around the room, like he was checking that no one else was in there with them.

'What do you need protection from?' Trudie pressed.

'I'm not saying anything until you can guarantee my safety.' He put his elbows on the interview table and rested his chin on his hands.

'From what? We can't go and make deals without any information.'

'I have information about where Dana came from,' he replied as his body seemed to slump.

'Right ...'

'Look, someone found out about my history and my relationships with my tenants.'

'You mean there are more tenants paying rent in sexual favours? You're not showing yourself in a very positive light, Mr Parks.'

'I was approached by someone and asked to give Dana a flat.' Mr Parks suddenly became very interested in a speck of dust on the interview room table. Chris could see him moving it around with his finger.

'Okay. Who?'

'I told you, I'm not saying anything until you can guarantee me I'll be protected.' He appeared to push the speck of dust off the table with his index finger.

'Let me sum things up, and you can tell me whether I'm right. You were approached by someone who blackmailed you into giving Dana a flat. You then went on to take payment from her on a monthly basis in sexual favours.' Trudie folded her arms.

Mr Parks didn't say anything. He didn't need to. Chris knew exactly what had happened to Dana all those years she was at Regatta House. *Why hadn't she reached out to her social worker?* Chris was sure that Holly would have done all she could to help.

'Boss,' Trudie said, making him jump. He hadn't realised the interview had been paused. 'What do you reckon?'

'That he's a bigger creep than we first thought?'

'Is it worth speaking to the CPS to see if we can get him a deal?'

'I'd personally throw him to the wolves.' Chris got up from his seat and wobbled a bit as he lost his balance again.

'Would the CPS agree to cut a deal?'

'I doubt it,' Chris replied, deflated. He headed out of the small office space and towards the interview room where Mr Parks was sitting.

'For the benefit of the recording, Detective Inspector Jackson and Detective Constable Trudie Clarke have entered the room,' Colin said to the tape as Chris took a seat opposite the landlord, leaving Trudie to stand somewhere behind them.

'Mr Parks,' Chris began. 'Let me get this straight. You are refusing to tell us who asked you to house Dana Antwar?'

'Yes. Unless you guarantee my safety.'

'According to our records, you were housing Dana for several years. You claimed to be in a relationship with her during this period.'

'That is correct.'

'So, you want us to protect you from someone who was blackmailing you six years ago, when you raped Dana on a monthly basis so she didn't have to pay you rent?'

'It wasn't like that. I swear we were in love.'

'You were so much in love that you didn't know where she was until we found her in the Trent?'

'No—I don't know.'

'Well, you aren't housing Dana now, are you? She's in the city morgue and her son is under the care of social services.' Chris stopped to take a breath. 'Mr Parks, we will not be offering you any form of protection and, if you manage to wangle your way out of this, I will make it my mission that your name is out there as a police informant. I will paint a red target on your back and make sure they come after you for what you've done to Dana and no doubt countless other vulnerable women.' Chris stood up suddenly and instantly regretted it. He grabbed the table in an attempt to steady himself. 'Take him back to his cell, Detective. I think Mr Parks needs to have a long think about things.'

Colin stood up and moved around the table to the landlord.

'Interview suspended at sixteen hundred hours,' Chris spoke into the tape as he moved over to stop the recording.

'Hang on, I'll talk,' the man shouted as Colin took a step back. 'Someone called Jess first contacted me and told me she knew all about what I was getting up to with my tenants. I ignored her at first, thinking that there was no way anyone would know ... but then I started to get photos.'

'What sort of photos, Mr Parks?'

'You know, long-range camera sort of stuff. Photos of me in compromising positions with sex workers, photos of me with ...' Mr Parks paused '... with my tenants. This Jess said to me that she wanted me to house someone for her while she recovered. If I did what she asked, she wouldn't make the photos public to the universities.'

'Recovered from what? A broken leg?'

'Well, that's what I thought until, one day, this lad turned up at my office with a woman and a newborn baby. He told me Jess had sent him.'

'I'm guessing it was Dana and Mikel?'

'Yeah. When I tried to contact this Jess and ask her what I was supposed to do with her and, you know, who would be paying the rent, she told me that she was sure I'd think of ways of getting the rent from her.'

'So, you decided, out of the goodness of your heart, you'd make her pay with sexual favours?'

'Yes.'

Chris could tell Mr Parks had finally told the truth as a look of guilt passed over his face.

'So, who was this Jess then?'

'I don't know. She just signed the emails "Jess".'

'And the email came from?'

'I can't remember, but I can go back to the office and look?'

'I'll send some of my team over. And the bloke who brought Dana and Mikel?' Chris knew exactly what

Mr Parks was going to say before he said it. He had this sinking feeling in the pit of his stomach.

'I don't know who he was, except he was short and had carrot-ginger hair. You don't see that colour much, so it stuck in my mind.'

'And he never gave a name or anything?'

'No. I'm telling the truth! I never saw him again either.'

'Thank you, Mr Parks, for finally being honest with us. It's just a shame I had to be dragged away from finding out what happened to Dana to force the information out of you.' Chris stood up again, but more slowly this time, and managed to keep his balance. 'Trudie, Colin, he's all yours,' he said as he headed out of the interview room and back towards his office. He needed to phone London.

Jen Garner

'Can we have a meeting in five? I've just had the DI on the phone,' Max shouted out of his office door.

'What's gone down?' Hannah turned and asked Jen.

'I have no idea, but it must be something serious if he wants us in five.'

They had both been busy trying to trace the last three years of Dana's life before she returned to Nottingham, with little success.

'There seems to be a lot of chatter around this brothel in Camden and a possible sighting of a young boy. No description though, so it could be anyone.'

'What are they saying? Any hints of abuse?' Jen asked, concerned for Mikel's safety.

'Not that I'm picking up.'

Relief washed over Jen. The last thing she wanted was for something bad to be happening to that little boy.

'I'm struggling to find anything about these sex parties

Candy mentioned. There's nothing on the usual internet forums. I've contacted our sources on the ground and other communication channels. If we could just find out when the next one is and wangle an invite …'

'Isn't there someone in the government we can squeeze, or some film exec?' Jen joked.

'I'm not getting anything from the face recognition software either,' Sam commented, joining the conversation.

'So, unless our DI can pull something out of the bag, we're no closer to finding Mikel or what happened to Dana.' Jen sighed. *Why were things so hard?* Dana, or whoever was controlling her, managed to keep her off the map in life and in death. Jen stood up, pushing her desk chair in. 'I've got to visit the ladies'. Meet you all in the meeting room.' Jen didn't wait for a response as she wandered off; if nothing else, she needed to splash some cold water on her face. It was at times like these that she used to sneak off with Chloe for a quick fag outside the fire exit.

When she got back, she stretched out in her seat and prayed that there'd been some break-through somewhere; there was only so much chatter she could listen to, hoping for news of Mikel or sex parties. She logged on to the integrated tablet and waited.

'So, we've had some developments from the team down in Nottingham,' Max announced to the room. The fact that Max was now talking about Chris and his officers as "the Nottingham team" meant something had happened and he needed them on board more than ever. 'We've had a turn of events with Dana's old landlord, Gordon Parks,' Max explained. 'As you will be aware, DI Jackson and his team were investigating Dana's time at Regatta House, and it has now come to light that somebody called Jess was blackmailing Gordon because of his rent collection techniques. She instructed Mr Parks to give Dana and her new son a home.'

'Free of charge?' Jen asked.

'This is where things get a bit clouded. Gordon is saying that he was instructed to give Dana a flat. There was no agreement regarding rent or how it was to be paid.'

'So, he decided to revert to his usual collection methods?'

'It is looking that way, yes, although there is something else ... which brings a lot of last year into question.'

Jen knew, deep down, what was coming.

'This is where you tell us Harry was somehow involved, isn't it?' she asked.

'Afraid so. Again, according to Gordon, six years ago someone who very much fits the description of Harry brought Dana and her new baby to the flat.'

Jen put her head down on the table as a sign of defeat.

'The DI is showing Gordon Parks some photo-fits. As much as we don't want it to be true, it sounds like Jessica was operating some six years before we caught up with her.'

'So, that means pretty much everything we knew about Chloe's investigation and last year could be wrong?' Sam asked slowly.

'I don't think we got everything wrong.' Hannah joined in the debate, having sat silently taking it all in. 'Jessica was no doubt the reason the Crawford drugs were back on the market. Look what we found at the Silverdale Gateway – and Harry's house, for that matter.'

'There was something she said to us at the Gateway that never made sense at the time, and I never managed to put my finger on what she meant,' Jen mused.

'What, about us being there on the wrong day?' Hannah questioned.

'Yeah. What if she was expecting a shipment of something else … like people?'

'We got her for the drugs, and she admitted as much, but what if we missed the bigger picture?'

'But Max, didn't you say at the time you thought Chloe had only been investigating Jessica for a couple of years?' Jen looked over towards her old boss. She needed his reassurance that Chloe hadn't been on her doorstep for longer than Jen had even imagined.

Sam suddenly began to tap away on the screen in front of her. 'Hang on! If I remember rightly, Jessica was recorded saying that one of her dad's old friends had told her she could start off where George had left off. What if we got the timeline wrong?'

'Why? Because the items that were delivered to Jen came several years after Jessica had learned about taking over the drug manufacturing side of her father's business?' Hannah asked.

'That would be the only way to explain why Jess wasn't clocked sooner; she was involved in other criminal activities before she restarted the Crawford brand … maybe these parties?'

'Could there be a second Crawford daughter out there somewhere?' Sam asked. 'Because the age range doesn't fit. Tilly, who used to visit George with her mother, is listed as a child. So, how old must she have been? Ten? What ten-year-old goes on to blackmail pervy landlords at fourteen?'

'So where is Tilly now?' Jen questioned. 'And is she even related to all this?'

'We now have a possible second Crawford sister,' Hannah said, getting up and noting things on the board at the front of the room. 'Jen, you left the service when you were how old?'

'Twenty-five.'

'Right, so you'd been out of the force for, what, ten years up until last year, making you thirty-five now. Correct?'

'Yes.'

'Would you say Jessica was the same age as you and James?'

'Yeah. Early thirties?'

'So, if we look at this mathematically, there is no way Tilly and Jessica are the same people,' Hannah finished, as the numbers began to add up.

'I think we were so blindsided by Harry Greenidge's involvement that we didn't even think to check the ages matched up.' Sam sighed.

'Max, when are you expecting to hear back from Nottingham on the photo-fits?' Hannah asked.

'Shortly, I'd expect,' he responded as he scrolled through something on his tablet.

'I think we need to go and have a chat with Harry,' Jen suddenly said. 'I have a bad feeling that he's more caught up in this than we even realised. Especially if he delivered Dana to Regatta House.'

'Do we know what Harry's status is, Max?' Hannah asked.

'Still pretty much protesting his innocence.'

'James went every day to the trial. Harry was so convinced that some hot-shot lawyer was going to turn up and save him, or someone would tamper with the jury so he wouldn't get sent down. When the guilty verdict was read, he was a broken man. James even said he felt sorry for him. It was like he'd suddenly woken up in the big boys' world.'

'If I remember rightly, Jessica pretty much sold him down the river as well,' Hannah added. Jen hadn't gone to Jess's trial but had been told the edited highlights from Max each night.

'Okay.' Max had seemingly organised his thoughts. 'Hannah, get yourself up to Nottingham and HMP Shelham, speak to Harry and see what he has to say about Dana and Regatta House. Take someone along with you from the Nottingham team – I'm sure you'll have plenty of willing volunteers. Jen, Sam, let's arrange a raid at this brothel in Camden where the chatter is coming from. Hopefully we'll get lucky and find Mikel there. We can discuss the Crawford family another time; I think our priority needs to be finding this little boy.'

'Is it worth popping in on Jessica too?' Jen asked.

'She isn't going anywhere any time soon, and neither is that father of hers. If Harry is as innocent as he makes out, maybe he'll want to help and give us something.' Max stood up. 'I'm going to phone Angela and let her know how things are working out here.'

'I should have looked into this more than I did.' Sam looked upset. 'Then I would have noticed the age difference and not just assumed that Tilly and Jessica were one and the same.'

'Don't be silly, Sam. I put too much on you in the heat of the moment.' Jen tried to reassure her. 'Plus, I know it sounds harsh, but you were the fricking PA, not some highly trained officer. That'll change, though.'

'Jen's right,' Hannah said, joining in the conversation. 'And look at it another way, you get to kick some doors down tomorrow with the big boys.'

'While you're cosying up to Detective Inspector Jackson?' Jen teased.

'Oh, you never know, Detective Ryan might decide she wants to join me instead, or that Sally what's-her-name? She seriously hated me.'

'I suppose that's one way to keep the DI safe from a femme fatale.'

Chapter Twenty-Seven

Dana

As I expected, the day came when Mikel and I were bundled into a van in the middle of the night and taken back to London. I had to leave everything behind; all my clothes and the few belongings I had. We were taken to a different house this time, and I wondered what the catch was going to be. We were set up in a room, and I was introduced to the other girls and told it was time to start paying back the money again. I'd had three years of freedom, but now it was time to repay the debt. It was different this time, though. I was now a high-end call girl. The girls quickly took me under their wings. I was still expected to perform various acts, but these were now at classy hotels. I was arm candy at events. I supplied various clients all the drugs they wanted to shove up their noses. I was now miles away from my days in a grubby house, serving whoever walked through the door. I often thought back to my days in Nottingham, my asylum request, Holly, my pervy landlord and watching Mikel grow into the little person he was becoming. Every night I spent away from Mikel, I worried about him and what they were planning for him. There was no way they would let a toddler run around freely and grow into a young boy. What worried me the most was that Clive, who'd been involved in bringing me back to London, was starting to take a particular interest in him and his development. I tried hard to keep Mikel protected from the world he was growing up in, I knew soon he would start asking more questions. But the girls where great with him. We celebrated every birthday and Christmas with him, trying to make him believe the world he was living in was normal.

Chapter Twenty-Eight

DI Chris Jackson

Mr Parks had positively identified both Jessica and Harry as the people responsible for bringing Dana to Regatta House. Once the identification was made, Chris had been in no mood to sit around and listen to his excuses and requests for protection. As far as he was concerned, Jessica was safely tucked up in one prison and Harry in another. In his mind, Mr Parks deserved everything that was about to happen to him, and Chris himself would make sure Kathryn got justice for the way he had treated her.

When Max had thanked him for his work so far and put a request in for one of his team to meet Hannah at HPS Shelham, he had half expected Hannah to be waiting at home for him that evening. The headaches, balance issues and blurred vision seemed to be getting worse and, as much as he loved coming home to find Hannah there, he was sort of relieved to return to an empty flat and the cat, who wasn't exactly fond of Hannah's random appearances and loss of Chris' full attention – as well as her spot on the bed.

He hadn't been stood near the main entrance of Shelham Prison long when he noticed Hannah walking towards him. As she moved closer, the sun turned her to a silhouette – but he'd have known her slim figure anywhere. Shielding his eyes from the light, he greeted her. 'Hi.'

'Hey,' she replied, leaning in to kiss him.

Having her this close made his body tingle – he wanted to touch her. Unsure how he'd react if their lips met, he turned his head and kissed her on the cheek. 'I was half expecting you to be at mine when I got in from work last night,' he said as he pulled away.

'We didn't finish till late organising the raid in London, so I came up first thing.'

'Everything okay with the case?'

'I think so. I'm not sure how useful the information about Harry and Jessica is going to prove, but we'll see. Hopefully he'll be able to help with timelines.'

'I can't say I was totally surprised when Max phoned and said I needed to send one of my team to meet you.'

'No one else fancy the morning out?'

'Nope, sadly just me. Everyone else is tied up with this fire investigation.'

'DI Holman playing ball now?'

'For the most part, but I think Julie may have managed to charm the watch manager, so she's been going direct.'

'Shall we?' Hannah turned to walk towards the entrance. When Chris had left home that morning, he'd been unsure what to wear: should he go for exhausted DI or smartly dressed and meaning business? Last time he'd seen Harry had been at the trial and full police uniform had been called for, but this was different. As he watched Hannah stride away, he noticed her long legs and knee-high pencil skirt, clearly worn for effect – but for him or Harry?

'Detective Littlefair and DI Jackson. We have an interview with Harry Greenidge,' she told the reception as Chris flashed his credentials.

'If you'd like to take a seat, I'll inform the governor you're here.'

Chris led Hannah to what looked like the most uncomfortable green plastic seats in the world.

'Have you had any thought on how you want to play this?' he asked as she sat down. 'He certainly doesn't like me very much and the last time he saw you ...' Chris let his mind wander for a moment back to that night in the club where their bodies first met.

'If it's okay with you, I'd like to lead. If he doesn't respond well to either of us, then we'll revert to good cop, bad cop,' Hannah instructed.

The air inside the reception was so stuffy and close, Chris was almost grateful when one of the doors was unlocked and an officer, with keys jangling from his belt, let in a gust of air.

'Detectives Littlefair and Jackson?' he called out to the small waiting room.

Chris and Hannah stood up.

'If you'd like to follow me. The guv is a bit tied up at the moment so has instructed me to take you through security and onto your meeting.'

'Thank you, Officer,' Hannah said as she pushed a strand of hair from her face and handed over her items.

'Phone, Detective?' The officer motioned to the open collection hatch.

Chris checked his phone and turned it off – not that he had any signal in the prison, anyway. Once they were cleared, they were led through more corridors to an empty interview room.

'As you can see, all interview rooms are fitted with CCTV surveillance,' said the officer as he pointed out the camera in the corner.

'Can I ask if sound is also captured?' Hannah asked.

'It is.'

'There might be some concerns regarding national security. Is there any way the microphone can be turned off?'

191

'Inspector, I can assure you that whatever is said between you and the inmate remains on a secure server.'

'Is there any way that we can have a confidential conversation with the inmate?' Chris asked, stepping forward momentarily and confusing the guard. 'You know, client lawyer confidentiality and all that?' Chris continued. 'As my colleague explained, this could be a matter of national security.'

The guard turned to speak to Hannah again. 'I'll speak to the governor and see what we can do.'

'Thank you, Officer,' Chris said as he and Hannah moved towards the seats, hoping they might be more comfy than those out in reception.

'I'll be back shortly.' The guard left the room.

'There's someone else who clearly doesn't like you either,' Hannah said with a wicked smile on her face. 'Any plans for this afternoon?' She placed her hand on his thigh.

'Well, piles of paperwork. I need to book an eye test. Oh yeah, and there is this case I'm investigating ...'

'You're no fun,' she teased as she moved her hand further up.

'Next you'll be asking me if I'm nervous yet?'

Hannah looked at him, clearly confused as to what he was talking about.

'Never mind. It was a game they used to play at school,' Chris explained.

Just then the door was opened again, and Harry was escorted into the room flanked by two other officers. Unsure whether he should stand up or not, Chris decided he'd better put on a good show in an attempt to get on Harry's good side.

'Mr Greenidge. I'm Detective Inspector Jackson, and this is my colleague, Detective Littlefair.'

'I remember you from the trial,' Harry said, sitting down and ignoring the offer of a handshake. 'You, I'm not so sure of.' He looked at Hannah with interest. 'I was told Nottingham's finest wanted to come and talk to me,' he carried on, as he continued to stare at Hannah, almost like he recognised her but couldn't place her.

Chris watched Hannah as her body language changed to sheer disgust at being stared at like a piece of meat. 'Harry, we've come to speak to you about when you and Jessica dated,' she started, clearly trying to distract Harry from his inspection of her.

'What, before or after she hung me out to dry?'

'The DI and I wondered if you'd mind looking at a photo and telling us whether you recognise the person.'

Chris unfolded the photo from his jacket pocket and slid it over towards Harry.

'Erm.' Harry looked at the photo for a couple of moments before he responded. 'Oh yeah, that's Jess's friend, Dana – but I've not seen her in a while. Why, has something happened?'

'We pulled her out of the Trent a few days ago.'

'Oh God. What happened to her?' Harry asked, seemingly full of concern.

'We aren't sure at the moment. That's why we've come to speak to you.'

'Ah, well, that's something Jess can't blame on me then, because, as the DI will know, I've been stuck in here for six months now.'

'How did you and Jessica come to know Dana?' Hannah continued.

'I got a call from Jess while she was in London. She told me one of her friends had gone into labour. She'd promised to pick her up from the hospital but, as the baby had come early, she was stuck in London. She asked whether I'd mind picking her up and taking her to her flat in Nottingham city centre.'

'Which you did.'

'Yes, of course. We used to go and visit Dana and her son – I think he was called Mikel – and Jess would get all broody.'

'Dana and Jess were good friends, were they?'

'They seemed to be. We went to visit her quite a lot, actually.'

'Do you know where Dana moved to after she left Regatta House, Harry?' Chris asked.

'Haven't the foggiest. You'll have to ask Jess that one.'

'This might seem like a strange question. Did you ever sleep with Dana – with or without Jess?'

'No!' Harry laughed. 'I liked the girl but not that much.'

'And what about the drugs you were caught selling?'

'*Now* I know who you are.' Something seemed to spark in Harry's memory. 'You were that girl who set me up in the club.' Hannah didn't respond. 'As for the drugs, like I said, Jess made me sell them. They were her drugs.'

'So you keep saying Harry, but do you not think it's time to wake up and smell the coffee and start telling the truth?' Hannah asked.

Harry seemed riled up now. 'Look, I don't have to speak to either of you. I did not have any sexual contact with Dana, did not sell her drugs or make her sell drugs for me. God knows if Jess did, you'd have to ask her.'

'We will, Mr Greenidge.'

'Well, while you're at it, see if you can find out why she set me up.'

Hannah clearly didn't see any point in rising to that one. Harry had already admitted taking Dana to Regatta House and visiting regularly with Jess. They had the confirmation they needed.

'You say Dana is dead, but what happened to her little boy?' Harry asked out of the blue. 'He was a good little dude. Rather clever if I remember rightly.'

'He's currently in the care of social services,' Hannah lied. 'You're not his biological father, Harry?'

'*Ha*!' Harry spat. 'Which part of "I never slept with her" are you struggling with? When I took her to the flat, it was the first time I met the woman.'

'Okay, one more thing before we leave you – did you and Jess ever attend any sex parties together?'

'Sex parties? Now they sound like fun. How do I go about getting a ticket to one of those?'

'I take that as a no.'

'You can take that however you want.' Then he looked over towards Chris. 'Does she still dress up like that for you on your days off?'

It took a few seconds for Chris to work out what Harry was referring to. 'I should be so lucky, mate,' he replied, gritting his teeth as he was friendly with a guy who made his skin crawl. Now he knew that Harry had played a part in keeping Dana captive.

'What about your sex life, Harry, I mean before you ended up in here?' Hannah asked as she drew Harry's attention back to herself.

'Jess and I had great sex. She was very adventurous. We did it with various people in various places and positions.'

'But she never took you to a sex party? Seems a little strange to me.'

'You'll have to speak to her on that one. I might not have always known who we were shagging, but I certainly know I wasn't at a party doing it.'

'So other people were involved in your … sessions?' Chris questioned.

'Like I told you, she was adventurous.'

195

'Don't suppose you were ever introduced to any of Jess' other, let's say, friends?' Hannah looked at Harry intently.

'There was this one guy who would turn up all the time with bunches of flowers. Think she said it was her godfather or something – one of her dad's friends from way back when.'

'Don't suppose he had a name, Harry?'

'Clive or Clyde, or something. Can't remember. I always thought he was very creepy – would pat Jess on the bum and tell her she was a good girl. Always got the impression he was into some weird shit.'

'Weird as in …?'

'I made a throw away comment once about Jess sleeping with him, and she just laughed and said she wasn't his type and not to worry because I wasn't either.'

'Well I think that's everything then Harry.' Hannah suddenly began to stand up.

'The pleasure was all mine,' Harry said, holding his hand out for Hannah to shake. 'If you ever feel like a repeat performance of that night, without grumpy here, you know where I am.' He kept hold of Hannah's hand for a little longer than was necessary.

'I'll keep you in mind next time I'm out,' Hannah muttered, pulling away. 'If you remember anything else about Dana and Mikel, feel free to give DI Jackson's office a call.'

Chris reached into his pocket for one of his cards. 'Guard!' he shouted as he handed over his card. Moments later, the same officers returned to escort Harry back to his cell.

Once he was out of sight, Hannah visibly shuddered. 'Nice guy.' She grimaced.

'Oh, isn't he just? But he has answered a lot of

unanswered questions about Dana. Who on earth is this Clive bloke, though?'

'Yeah, I need to tell the team in London about him. I don't think a Clive has popped up in anything so far. I still find Harry creepy, though.' Hannah shuddered, but then Chris saw her smile. 'Do *you* want a repeat performance of that night, Detective?' she teased as she followed him from the interview room.

Chapter Twenty-Nine

Jen Garner

'Go, go, go!'

'Entrance to the property has been achieved,'

'Stay where you are.'

All of this came through Jen's earpiece followed by the words she had been waiting for: "clear".

'The property has been secured.' Jen looked over to where Sam had been sat next to her for the past hour while strategy had been discussed around them. Detective Angela Currant had been quite animated in the mission planning. Her main concern was for the girls and their welfare.

'You ready?' Jen asked as she turned towards Sam.

'I guess so, but it sounds like we've missed all the action.'

'Oh, you'll still get a hit of adrenaline as you rush towards the house to look for Mikel. But we'll know the house has been secured.'

'I'll head in with the welfare team,' Angela told them as they began to leave the van.

Jen jumped out, followed by Sam and several other officers from the local team. She really hoped they would find Mikel inside, though part of her doubted it. It would be far too easy if Mikel was just there waiting for her. But if he was, it would mean she might get to go home as early as tomorrow and see her family.

'All clear, Officer?' Jen asked.

'Yes ma'am.'

'Any signs of the boy?'

'Not that I'm aware of.'

'Thank you, Officer,' she said as she stepped through the

door. She wasn't sure what she was expecting when she walked in. From outside, it looked like any normal house.

'Will you and Sam check upstairs and see if there are any signs of the boy,' Jen instructed one of the eagerly waiting officers as she saw the women coming down the stairs, scantily clad and clearly strung out on something.

'Ma'am.'

Jen moved into the main living area, and the smell of cigarettes immediately hit her as she walked through the door.

'Ma'am, this is Josephine Bale. She's the madam here,' a young officer told her enthusiastically.

'Thank you, Officer. Have her sit over there away from the girls. I don't want them talking to each other.'

Several girls filed into the room and sat on the various sofas and chairs.

'Where is the boy?' Jen asked them to no avail. She turned towards Josephine. 'Where is the boy who's been seen here?'

'I don't know what you're talking about,' came the answer back, full of spite.

'Officer, will you keep an eye on this lot while I check the rest of the building?'

'Ma'am.'

Jen left the living area and entered a second room along the hallway. This looked to be one of the girls' rooms. It was dark with fairy lights hung on the walls.

'Ma'am,' Officer Hopkins shouted as he stood in the doorway of one of the other rooms.

'What is it?'

Jen walked through into what appeared to be a lounge area where the punters were all sat, looking dishevelled and in shock. Jen was surprised to see that there was an older woman among them who looked just as surprised.

'Are we sure these are all the punters?' Jen asked, not wanting to ask whether the older woman was a working girl.

'One hundred per cent, ma'am,' came the response she was hoping for.

'Okay, whoever answers this question correctly will win a prize,' Jen said, looking at the assembled people. 'Where is the boy?'

A blank look fell across all their faces, and she could tell they didn't know what she was talking about. It looked like they had either missed Mikel or someone had hidden him somewhere.

'You okay to stay with these till we can get someone to pick them up, Officer Hopkins?'

'Yes, ma'am.'

Jen left the room and found the tactical command officer.

'Thank you for your assistance. You can stand down your men.'

'Will do, ma'am.' This was followed by the orders to stand down in her ear.

Jen took the radio that had been clipped on her stab vest. 'Site clear, send in the welfare team.' The girls could wait to be interviewed. She wanted to get them somewhere they would be safe, and Angela Currant would be able to arrange that. 'But leave the madam here. She can be taken in with the rest of them,' she ordered.

God, she'd forgotten how good this felt; issuing orders and being in command.

'Sam,' she shouted up the stairs as she took them two at a time.

'Up here in the loft,' came Sam's muffled response as Jen noticed a step ladder hanging down from a hole in the ceiling. Jen ignored the rooms either side of her. They all had their doors wide open so had obviously been cleared by the entrance team.

'Sam?' Jen poked her head through the loft hatch.

'Looks like whoever runs this place keeps a close eye on all their girls.'

Jen looked over at the bank of television screens and heard the whirring of DVD recorders.

'Good find, Sam. No sign of Mikel, though?'

'Sorry, Jen. I know how important he is to you.'

'Just leave everything how you found it. I'll get the tech team up here and try to salvage what we can. Who knows? We might find something interesting on the DVDs.'

'Ma'am,' came the shout from below.

Jen made her way down the steps and into the room where the voice had come from.

'I've just found something behind the mirror.'

'Let me guess, a CCTV camera?'

'How did you guess?'

'Sam has just found the recording equipment in the loft.'

'Want me to check all rooms for the same?'

'No, leave as is. We'll get the crime scene techs in here.' Jen exhaled as she headed downstairs to see the working girls receiving care from the welfare team and Angela. The madam had been removed from the room so she couldn't intimidate the girls.

'Seven in the morning,' she said to herself as she looked at her watch and pulled out her mobile phone to let Max know the outcome of the raid. But first, there were two little people whose voices she really needed to hear.

'Well, someone is positively glowing,' Sam said as Jen climbed into the pool car.

Was she really making it so obvious that she was enjoying this?

'Can I tell you something, Sam?'

'Of course.'

'I kind of miss it. I know last year was a whole different ball game, and I wasn't exactly front line. But since all this Mikel stuff started happening, I've found myself wanting to go back.'

'You mean back undercover?' Sam looked shocked.

'I know I could never go back undercover as I've got the family to think about, but just the rush of today and the stuff I did back home with the DI ... I kinda want in again.'

Sam appeared unsure how to respond. 'I know Max is looking to retire,' she said, more to fill the silence, it seemed.

'To spend more time with my kids.' Jen laughed. 'That would work out well. He retires to spend more time with my family, and I take up his job as the head of the unit.'

'Hmm, maybe that wouldn't work out ...'

'I think Hannah has her eyes set on that role now anyway. Max seems to be pushing her forward and letting her coordinate.'

'I just hope it works out better than Chloe did.' Sam clearly regretted the words as soon as they were out of her mouth. 'I'm sorry, I didn't mean it like that.'

'Don't be silly. I knew what you meant,' Jen reassured her. The silence fell in the car again as Sam returned to looking out of the window and Jen sat pondering what she'd just said. *Did this mean she really wanted it, now she had spoken it out loud to someone?*

The kids had been so happy to hear from her when she'd talked to them on the phone at their grandparents' house, and she'd also phoned James who sounded stressed out about something going on at work. She promised them all she was getting close to cracking the case and coming back but, in all honesty, she had no clue when she would be home.

The car pulled up outside the police station, and Jen and Sam climbed out. They were greeted by the station's DI.

'Carolyn Hallam. I hear you had a successful morning,' she said as she held out her hand to them both.

'We didn't find the boy, but at least the girls we pulled out of there will have the chance to get clean,' Jen said as she shook the DI's hand.

'I understand they're being looked after by the Met's exploitation team, so they'll be in safe hands.' The DI nodded.

'This is my colleague, Samantha Jones,' Jen said as Sam also shook hands with Carolyn. 'Thank you for lending us your staff at such short notice.'

'Not a problem. Would you like to follow me to my office? We can chat more there.' Carolyn held open the door for Jen and Sam to enter the station. 'We've had that particular location on our radar for a while. I'm just glad we've managed to close them down.'

'Glad to have been of assistance,' Jen said as she followed Carolyn up several flights of stairs and into her comfortable office.

'Tea, Detectives?' she asked as they all sat down.

Jen declined the offer whilst Sam requested water.

'I must say, I was pleasantly surprised when I received the call from Max asking if you could borrow some staff for an early morning raid,' Carolyn said as she handed a glass over to Sam.

'We had picked up a lot of chatter about a child being seen at the residence, so we wanted to get in there and get him out if we could.'

'Yes, Max said that last night on the phone. Did you find any sign of him?'

'I'm afraid not. We called the forensics team in as soon as we cleared the house. We also found some CCTV cameras, so who knows? We might strike lucky there.'

'Well, if there's anything further that my team can help with, just let me know.'

'We will.' Jen nodded

Just then, there was a knock.

'Sorry, ma'am, Detectives. The madam from this morning's raid, Josephine Bale, says she has information on the child.'

Jen whipped round to look at the officer stood in the doorway. 'Did she give any indication as to what she knows?'

'No, just that she wanted to speak to "that woman who was asking after the boy".'

'Do you mind if we speak to her?' Jen turned to Carolyn, keen not to step on anyone's toes.

'Be my guest. Do you want one of my team to sit in with you?'

Jen turned and looked at Sam, unsure how she would handle an interview scenario and whether she'd had enough training. In all honesty, Jen knew she was a little rusty herself, but that didn't matter. She just wanted to know where Mikel was and how to get him back.

'If I could borrow one of your officers, that would be great. I'm a little out of practice myself, so it would be good to have someone show me the ropes again.' As Jen spoke, she watched the relief spread across Sam's face.

'Tell you what, it will be interesting to see what she has to say for herself and, as I'm free at the moment, I'll join you ... if that's okay?'

'Sure. It will be good to have someone in there with knowledge of the brothel.'

Chapter Thirty

DI Chris Jackson

Chris was glad to be out of the prison and back into civilisation. The air felt cleaner outside for some unknown reason. As he and Hannah turned their phones back on, they were met with a barrage of message. Chris noticed a voicemail message too. If only he could escape the real world, just that bit longer. Hannah had walked a little way off to return some calls, and he headed to the safety of his car to search out some pain relief for his headache. He was searching his glove box when he heard Hannah shout for him and rush up towards where he was parked.

'Look, Hannah, I'm sorry. I'm really tired and I just need to get to work and make a start on the paperwork and joining the dots of what Harry has told us and how it affects the Nottingham investigation.'

'You've not read your messages, have you?'

'Nope. Was planning to avoid them till I got back to the office. Why?'

'There's been a development. There's a car coming to pick us both up and take us somewhere in the Derbyshire Dales.'

'Right ... okay,' Chris climbed out of his car and began scrolling through his messages just as a black Jaguar appeared from round the corner and pulled up in front of them.

'Afternoon, Detectives,' the driver said as he got out of the car.

'What's going on, Officer?' Chris asked, assuming that he was speaking to a fellow officer.

'I have no idea, sir. My instructions are to drive you both to Waterland Cottage in Bakewell.'

'Han?'

'I'm just trying to get Max now,' came her response, her phone glued to her ear.

Chris wandered around to the passenger side door and peered into the car.

'A bit posh for driving two officers to a cottage in Bakewell, isn't it?'

'I know, sir. I couldn't believe my luck when I was asked if I wanted the job. I expected one of the battered pool cars.'

Chris nodded as he waited for Hannah to finish on the phone to whoever she was speaking animatedly to.

'Just spoken to Max. He said there's been a development since the raid this morning, and we need to get to Bakewell. He said something about a video conference once we get there so we're up to speed on the developments.'

'Do my team know?'

'I'm not sure, Chris, but I suggest we get on the road. You can give them a call from the car to check in.' Hannah moved around to the other side of the Jaguar. 'Front or back?'

'Whichever is easiest for you.'

'Front it is, then.' Hannah said as she got into the car next to the driver.

'Barry Flint,' the man introduced himself.

Hannah smiled her dazzling smile at him and then turned and glanced at Chris. He noticed but was too busy on his phone to fully return her gaze.

'Julie, it's Chris.'

'I wondered when you'd be free from Shelham. How did it go?'

'Looks like our landlord was right about Harry and Jessica. It also sounds like Harry and Jess visited Dana regularly,' Chris said as he looked out of the window at the passing traffic.

'Do you think they were keeping an eye on her then?'

'I'm beginning to think that.'

'You on your way back in, boss?'

'Afraid not. Something has happened this morning at a raid in London. I'm guessing it has to do with Dana and Mikel. Right now, I'm sat in the back of a car being taken to Bakewell with Hannah and Barry Flint.'

'Oh … okay. We've not heard anything from anyone here. Do you want me to look into it and see what I can find out?'

'If you could just keep on with the fire investigation stuff for now, that would be great. I've been promised an update once we get to this cottage in Bakewell.'

'Well, at least make sure you bring me back some tart, boss.'

'I'll ask Hannah to pop back with me.'

Julie laughed at the other end of the phone as Hannah turned towards Chris with a confused expression on her face.

'If you need me, give me a call. I'll try and let you know in advance if I'm going to be unavailable.'

'Okay, boss. See you soon, hopefully.'

Chris ended the call and went back to checking his emails on his phone while Hannah made conversation with Barry. His headache was back, and he'd not found any pills in his glove box. Why he couldn't have driven himself to this place, he'd never know. He closed his eyes and massaged his temples, hoping for some form of release.

*

'Well, this is where I was instructed to bring you,' Barry said, turning around to look at Chris slumped in the back seat. 'So, I hope you both know more than I know.'

'Thanks, Barry,' Hannah said as she got out of the car. 'I'm pretty sure we'll figure it out.'

'I'd invite you in for a cuppa, but I don't even know if we'll have tea or coffee to start with,' Chris said as he got out of the car. He hoped they had coffee in there because his head was killing him. If there was no pain relief, then caffeine would have to do. As Barry turned and drove off, Hannah and Chris walked towards the front of the cottage. Hannah gave a customary knock and gently pushed the front door to see if it would open.

'Hello?' Hannah called out as she entered the house.

'Come through. I'm just setting up the video conference,' came the response from one of the other rooms. Hannah and Chris started to walk towards the voice, pushing open one of the doors which led to an expansive living room.

'Wow!' Hannah said as she walked in. 'This place is massive.' Chris looked around, taking it all in. The living room was a large circular room which was located in the centre of the house. From where he was standing, he could see into the dining room and kitchen area. There was also a spiral staircase that led to the upstairs.

'Next time your boss needs video conferencing setting up, ask him to send me somewhere that at least has an internet connection,' the man groaned as he stood up. 'You must be Detectives Littlefair and Jackson.' He held out his hand. 'I'm Daniel.'

'Hi, Daniel,' Hannah replied, leaving Chris to continue taking in his surroundings. 'So what's happened? Why have we been brought here and not back to London?'

'Your guess is as good as mine. I'm just a tech wizard

– but the way things are going right now, I might end up being just a tech guy.'

Hannah laughed and pushed that strand of hair behind her ear once again.

'Is there anything to drink?' Chris asked, keen to survey the downstairs of the cottage further.

'When I arrived, I had a quick look through the cupboards. There seems to be a range of refreshments, yes.'

'Can I get you anything?' Chris offered as he silently longed for another coffee.

'Whisky. But I didn't see any in the cupboards, so it'll have to be a coffee.'

'Hannah?'

'Tea. Two sugars, please.'

Chris wandered into the kitchen, leaving Hannah and Daniel talking away. Locating the kettle, he turned it on and began a forensic fingertip search of the cupboard to see what he could find. There seemed to be fresh milk, and tea and coffee making facilities, along with plates and all the necessary crockery, but no sign of any food. He doubted there were any takeaways nearby so, unless they weren't staying, he wasn't sure what they were going to do about sustenance – or headache relief, for that matter.

'I think we're cooking,' came the shout from the living room as Chris began to pour the hot water into the mugs he had found. *Proper drinking mugs.* He'd chuckled to himself when he'd found them sitting in the back of a cupboard.

Carrying all three of the cups back into the living room, he could see the Met logo on the laptop screen Daniel and Hannah were looking intently at.

'I'm not sure how good the network connection is going to be.'

'I'm sure it will be fine. Thank you for getting it set up for us. I don't think either of us would have known where to start,' Hannah said, taking a drink from Chris and passing it over to Daniel.

'No biscuits, I'm afraid ... or any other food, for that matter.'

'Typical. Government cutting your funding so much, you can't even afford to offer your guests biscuits.' Daniel tutted.

Just then the familiar ringing of Skype began, and Max's face filled the screen.

'Think this might be my cue to leave,' Daniel said as Hannah leant over to accept the call.

'Afternoon, Hannah, Inspector Jackson.'

'Afternoon, Max.'

'I see Daniel got you all set up.'

'Make sure you send them somewhere with a better internet connection next time,' Daniel shouted from where he was beginning to pack his things up.

'And he wants biscuits, too,' Chris cut in.

'Bloody government cutting your funding,' Daniel began to mumble to himself again for effect.

'Thank you, Daniel. I will keep your requests in mind for the next time we need somewhere setting up fast,' Max said dryly.

'Well, thank you for your hospitality – all twenty minutes of it,' Daniel said, picking his bags up. 'Send my love to the missus, Max,' he shouted towards the screen, and then he left the room and the cottage fell silent again.

'I didn't think you had a missus?' Hannah said in surprise.

'He means my cat ... it's best not to ask.'

'Yeah, Chris has one of those. *She* doesn't like me much

either. So, what happened, boss? Why have Chris and I been shipped to the middle of nowhere?'

'There was a breakthrough at the brothel raid this morning. I'm going to need you to go undercover again.'

'Okay, boss. How long for? Where am I going?'

Chris watched Hannah as she seamlessly fell into mission mode. She had been called on to serve her country, and she was ready to go without even a thought for herself.

'I don't know how much you have explained to the DI, but we believe Dana was involved in sex parties before she ended up in Nottingham.'

'We spoke about said parties briefly before we interviewed Harry.'

'The house madam Jen and Sam arrested this morning was very keen to cut a deal in return for telling us about a party she was sending some girls to tonight.'

'That fits in with what Candy told me and Jen, boss.'

'That's right. So, we need you to go undercover at one of these parties and see if you can sniff out Mikel.'

'Can this madam be trusted though, boss?'

'Well, this is one of my concerns too.'

Chris began to get the feeling he knew what was coming.

'I can't send Jen in for obvious reasons, in case she gets clocked. Sam isn't ready, and I wouldn't feel comfortable sending Hannah in on her own.'

'So, I'm guessing the reason I'm still here is you want me to go along too?' Chris asked, glancing at Hannah and back to the screen again.

'If it's okay with you, Inspector? You and Hannah are let's say ... acquainted ... with each other in more ways than one. Plus, I would be happier sending Hannah into this situation with someone she knows and not just a random detective who's never seen her naked.'

Hannah almost spat out her drink as Max finished his sentence. 'I can't believe I just heard that!'

'It is the safest way I can think of to send you in, Hannah. I don't want you going in as a sex worker for obvious reasons and, come on, I've heard all the details about you and the Inspector from overhearing you and Sam. At least it isn't going to look unnatural.'

'Excuse me …' Hannah seemed to stop herself finishing the sentence.

'So, if the Inspector is happy to escort you to this party tonight, it would make me feel a whole lot better about sending you in.'

Hannah looked over at Chris, clearly curious to what his answer would be.

'How do you know you can get us in without us being clocked? They must know exactly who's coming to these parties?'

'Now we know where the party is and when it is, I've got the tech team on it. They're hacking into the systems and getting you both on the guest list.'

'Is it not best just to send me in as a sex worker, boss?'

'What, so you'll be forced to perform sex acts on people you don't even know?'

'Okay, I get your point.'

'I don't like putting you girls at risk as it is, and this is the best way I can think of to make sure you're safe.'

'So where is this party then?' Chris asked.

'Yorkshire Dales. Some farmhouse, apparently.'

'Yorkshire! Why are we in Bakewell then?'

'Because we're going to fly you in.'

Hannah looked at Chris. 'You ever jumped out of a plane?' she asked teasingly.

'Hannah, you and the Inspector are going to go on a little helicopter ride. You're going in as a wealthy, newly married couple.'

'How is sending us to Yorkshire going to find Mikel?' Chris wasn't sure he liked any of this.

'We're hoping he's going to be there.'

'Then what? You're going to swoop in and get him out?'

'Most probably not, as I suspect there are going to be lots of very rich and influential people there. The last thing the government want is to go upsetting these people. If Mikel is there, we can work out a plan to get him out later.'

'My team in Nottingham ... where do they think I am?'

'I've got them looking at the fire at the foster mother's home,' Max assured him. 'So, what will it be, Inspector?'

'In all honesty, I don't know. Aren't there safeguarding issues to be considered, if we know Mikel is going to be there? Are you sure there's no other way we can get him out?'

'Chris, can I call you Chris? Let's be serious. We are a team that operate outside the rules of what you bobbies on the front line follow. We get stuff done. We may go about it an unorthodox fashion sometimes, but we get results. For that reason, the powers that be usually turn a blind eye to what we do. But, I can tell you for sure, I will never put one of my team in harm's way unless I trust them and know how to get them out if something goes wrong.'

Chris didn't really know how to respond. He didn't want to bring Chloe up. They clearly hadn't got her out in time, and it was Chris who'd been left to pick up the pieces. 'I need some air,' he said as he stood up and headed towards the door they had come in through. He needed

213

time to think about what he was possibly about to do or not do. He realised that if he didn't go, Hannah might be forced to go alone or with some other detective. He walked out of the front door and into the warm summer air. He needed to work shit out. He had his failing health to consider and his relationship with Hannah, that had all been a bit of fun up until the moment they left Shelham Prison in the black Jag.

He hadn't been out in the country air for long when he heard Hannah coming up behind him.

She was so beautiful. The thought of her being leered at and made to perform sexual favours for other random men made his skin crawl. He did question how much he'd been looking through rose-tinted glasses, though. How many people had she slept with in her line of work? He remembered the day he'd first met her – what if he'd followed her into the shower that night? Would he have just become a name in a little black book somewhere?

He felt her wrap her arms around him, and she rested her chin on his shoulder.

'Go on. Ask me,' she said after a while. 'Ask me how many people I've slept with for the benefit of my country.'

'Han ...'

'I don't mind, I'm used to it. I can't have relationships in the real world because of it.'

'Because of what you do as a day job?'

Hannah moved to stand in front of him. 'Chris, people don't trust me. How many times have you sat at your desk and thought "I wonder what Hannah is up to?"'

Chris was quiet for a moment.

'After today's chat with Max, it's going to change to "I wonder who Hannah is doing".'

Chris didn't know how to respond.

'Everything I do, the ends justify the means. I didn't

have to come and see you when we closed the case last year. They wanted me to stay in hospital, but I felt something for you, Chris. There was something there between us, and I wanted to touch it and see if it was real.' Hannah started to move away from him, and Chris began to get the sense that he was about to lose her.

'Believe it or not, you're the first mark I've ever gone back to. That's probably why I keep coming back to you and why you come home to find me in your bed. I'm drunk on you, Chris. I can't get enough of you.'

'So, is this the breaking up speech? "Come undercover with me or we're over?"' Chris could see in Hannah's eyes that he had crossed a line.

'Would you seriously ever be able to look at me the same way if I went off on this mission tonight and you went back to your comfy lifestyle chasing down minor criminals?'

Chris knew what his answer was. He'd been ridiculous to think that no one else had ever touched her the way he did.

'I don't want to lose you, Chris, but this is my job; my bit in saving the world, my way of chasing down the bad guys and putting things right.'

'I need time to think. I need to process everything.'

'Well, don't be too long. I can disappear as fast as I appeared, Detective.' Hannah started to march back towards the cottage.

He noticed how he wasn't Chris to her any more. He was just plain old detective.

'Oh – and, Detective,' she shouted as she turned around one last time, 'the answer is none, because I've always found some other way to do the right thing.'

Chris stood there and watched Hannah walking away and, for a moment, he really did feel like this was the end of the road. He started along the pathway towards the unknown, towards what he thought might be a village pub or somewhere he could mourn having just lost the most amazingly beautiful girl he had ever known – and, for once, it wasn't because of what *he* did for a living. It was her job that had got in the way.

As he continued to walk, looking for any signs of life, he began to think about Jen and why she had never told James about her life before; why she had given it all up for love. Were Chris' feelings for Hannah deeper than he had ever dared to acknowledge? Did he really want more from her than what they already had and, if he did, would he be able to accept what she did for a living? He thought back to his parents' relationship, and how he'd always hoped he would find someone to love as much as his parents loved each other. He wanted to share that same love with someone – but every relationship he had, the job always got in the way. That was, until he'd met Hannah … but they weren't in a relationship. If this case had never come along, would Hannah and him have just fizzled out? Would she have just stopped appearing, or would he have found someone else?

He felt like he was at a crossroads and, though his phone felt heavy in his pocket, he knew he needed to make a decision that there would be no going back from. If he went back to the cottage and Hannah, at least if she had to do anything at the party it would be with him and not some random stranger. At least he would be by her side as her new husband. If he kept walking, could he let go of Hannah and what he felt for her? It felt like that time he'd been left heartbroken in the playground at school, when his year six girlfriend broke up with him because she liked his best mate more.

He needed to make a decision, and as he stood there

he felt his phone vibrate in his pocket. The name coming up on the screen almost made him laugh to himself, given who he'd just been thinking about.

'Mum?' he answered, almost unsure whether it would be her on the other end of the phone. He was greeted by the sound of someone coughing.

'Sorry ... Christopher?'

'Is everything okay, Mum? You sound awful.'

'Ah, just this cold thing that's going round. It's the middle of bloody summer and here I am hacking up a lung.'

'Have you been to see the doctor or anything?'

'Oh no, don't be silly. Your dad is looking after me like he always does. If I'm honest with you, he's being a bit of a pain.'

'Look, Mum, I'm really sorry but I'm busy. Can I call you back later?'

'As long as you do. We haven't heard from you in such a long time.'

'I promise I'll phone back over the next couple of days.'

'Okay. Goodbye, Christopher. Keep safe.'

He had made his decision. His dad looked after his mum no matter what. What if he'd already found that someone to love in the kind of way his parents loved each other? And he was about to let her go off to who knows where, to fuck who knows who? It was his duty to keep her safe.

Detective Hannah Littlefair

Hannah walked back into the cottage, slammed the front door and sank towards the floor. At least she hadn't let him see her cry. She had held out till she had got back to the cottage before breaking down. She didn't even know

217

why she was crying. Why had her weekend fuck had such an impact on her that she was now sat on the floor in tears, having basically just been dumped?

She hated to admit it, but Jen was the perfect example of why you couldn't have this job and love someone. She now understood why Jen had left the service when she met James. She even understood why Chloe had kept her relationship quiet and ended up dating one of the druggies she was investigating. Whereas, here she was, sat sobbing her heart out over a guy she wasn't meant to feel anything for. He was meant to be her weekend plaything, but then why did she always leave his flat wanting more? As she sat there, she heard footsteps on the other side of the door and car doors slamming. The door vibrated against her back as they knocked. It would be the crack team Max had told her would be on their way to get the evening's events rolling – and Chris' replacement, who she wouldn't fall for but would fuck like the world depended on it if she had to.

'One moment,' she shouted as she picked herself up off the floor and tried to mop away any sign of tears. Then, she plastered a smile on her face like battle paint and reached to open the door ...

Chapter Thirty-One

Jen Garner

'We got back here as soon as we could, Max,' Jen said, knocking and walking into his office. 'How did Hannah and Chris get on with Harry?'

'I've not had a chance to debrief her. I decided it best to get them to a location where we can prepare for tonight's op.'

'You mean you're sending them in together?'

'Well, the thought had crossed my mind, but I was on a conference call with our detective a moment ago and he freaked out and left.'

'Hannah been caught mixing business and pleasure?' Jen asked, concerned for her friend.

'Possibly ...'

'And there you have it: the reason I *left* the service for love.'

'I think you did the right thing. As much as I was disappointed in you, looking back now ... and the life I've lived.' Max sighed. 'Anyway, enough about my officers' relationships. How did our new recruit get on at the raid?'

'Like a pro, boss.'

'Maybe I should send her out instead of Hannah tonight.'

'I don't think she's quite ready for seduction 101,' Jen said as she changed her position in her chair. 'She was a bit disappointed about not being first through the door, but when she did get in the house, she followed instructions and couldn't stop talking about it on the way back.'

'Where is she now?'

'Not sure. She said something about wanting to get changed?'

'Ah, that sounds more like my PA.' Max smiled.

'I'm guessing with Hannah out in the field, you got something from Josephine's intel?' Jen asked.

'We did, and the tech team are working double time to ensure we get Hannah and her partner in there tonight without any hitches.'

'What do we know?'

'Highgrove Farm is a disused farm up in the Yorkshire Dales. There hasn't been any intel on anything suspicious going on up there. The owner of the manor checks out; no criminal record, nothing.'

'So, why holding sex parties? And, more importantly, why has he got Mikel?'

'I phoned the poor guy, asking questions about tonight's party and he told me I'd need to contact the organisers because he only hires that place out. From what I can see, he has absolutely no link to George Crawford.'

'So whoever is running these parties hires the venues.' The cogs continued to turn in Jen's brain. 'Do you think this is the contact Jessica mentioned – the old friend of her father's?'

'It could be, but I can't find any links between the three of them.'

'I'm just still trying to work out why they snatched Mikel.'

'From what I remember you saying after meeting Mikel, he was scared of the men that used to do horrible things to his mum. He can more or less identify them, so isn't it better to keep him close?'

'I hope to God they aren't abusing him. If he's going to be there tonight, it doesn't bear thinking about.' Jen felt a shiver run down her spine and began to think of her little people at home, safe in their little bubbles.

'I'm sure if Hannah can find a way of getting him out of there, she will. At least if we know where he is, we stand more of a chance of getting him back than if we didn't.'

'True.' Jen sighed. Silence fell between them as they both tried to think of a strategy to get Mikel out and away from the horrors he could quite possibly be facing.

'When we do get him out, he's going to be one messed up kid. He'll probably be in witness protection for the rest of his life.'

'Maybe that's what we should have done with him the first time we found him?'

'Afternoon, boss.' Sam entered the office, balancing coffee and biscuits. Her timing was spot on as it broke the gloominess of Jen and Max's conversation.

'So, I hear you're leaving me for a life of kicking doors down?' Max smiled wryly as she passed out the drinks.

'Well, once you go, boss. I don't think I could be the PA to the next unit boss.'

'Yeah, I'd make Hannah write all her own stuff too.' Jen laughed.

'Ah, but what if she doesn't get the job, or decides she wants to stay out in the field?' Sam wondered out loud.

'Compared to a nice office job, I know which one I'd pick,' Jen joked.

'You know, Jen, the job was always meant to be yours.'

'Let's not have this conversation,' Jen said before she really did start regretting some of her choices. 'Any luck locating Candy?' She quickly changed the subject.

'Have you checked in my bottom drawer?' Sam immediately said, leaving Max and Jen to exchange glances as they wondered if she was being serious or just trying to be funny.

'At this moment in time, no,' Max answered.

'I think we should, because she's the only other person who could really blow Hannah's cover.'

'I've got my best team on the ground looking for her now.'

'Any luck with phone records?'

'Tech are working on it as we speak. They're triangulating her location, and I've got a team on standby.'

'Great. We need to make sure she's out of the way before Hannah even sets foot in that place.'

'Max, how far away are back-up going to be from Highgrove Farm? Just in case Hannah gets in trouble?' Sam asked, looking anxious.

'I've got special forces setting up as close as they can get without being spotted, though I suspect they won't be able to get too close if all the rich and the famous are in attendance tonight.'

'Is Ant Middleton on the payroll for special forces?'

'Sorry. Who, Sam?'

'It's best not to ask, Max. Sam, I doubt it. Isn't he busy with some survival show?'

'It was worth asking.' Sam sighed as Max looked confused as to what they were going on about.

'I need to brief the special forces guys before we send Hannah in. You're more than welcome to come and listen in. They might know if Ant Middleton is on the team.' Max got up and walked towards the meeting room door.

'Trust me, he won't be.' Jen tried to make sure Sam wasn't getting her hopes up.

'Maybe he'll be there as a bodyguard?'

'No, Sam,' Jen said, shaking her head.

'Who's the other bodyguard to the stars, on the same programme as Ant Middleton ... same name as a famous author?'

'Enid Blyton?' Max smiled as he pushed open the door.

DI Chris Jackson

Chris had walked back to the cottage in hope of having a conversation with Hannah about what had just happened, but was instead greeted by a group of people who had been sent to get them ready for the evening's event.

'Chris Jackson?' somebody said as he walked in and looked around.

'Yeah, do you know where Hannah is?'

'Probably busy getting ready for tonight. Speaking of which, we need to get you ready too – unless you've come to say your goodbyes? In which case, I'm sure she'll phone you when she gets back.'

'Can I have a minute to speak to Hannah privately?'

'Not at the moment, I'm afraid. So, what's it going to be? Are you in?'

'I'm in. But can I at least get some pain relief for this—?' At that point, he was dragged away to be made over, fitted into an expensive suit, his hair styled and sprayed with something that smelt expensive but he certainly didn't like.

The next time he saw Hannah, she was sat next to him ready for their briefing. There was so much he wanted to say to her before they were both sucked into something that possibly neither of them were prepared for.

'Right, you two. I see you're both dressed up and ready to go. This is your brief: you are a young, just married couple, and this is the first stop on your honeymoon. You decided you would bring your new wife to one of these parties as a wedding present.' A uniformed officer started to instruct them.

'Good to see I've married a classy man,' Hannah muttered.

'I need to warn you both: there will be drugs on offer at this party, seeing as we have intel that these parties were happening when Jessica Adams was running the show. You may find yourself in the situation where you have no choice but to take something. You need to be sensible. I suggest you work in partnership – one of you takes the drug while the other one stays clean. You need to watch out for each other, because we're not going to be in there with you. There is no way we can attach earpieces or other obvious communication devices to you. We will be around but not at the party itself.'

'Thank God for that. Don't fancy making out with one of you lot,' Hannah joked, clearly trying to ease the tension in the room.

'If you do run into trouble and need us to get you out, you have one of two choices. Each of those pins in your hair, Hannah? Well, if you snap one we'll know you're in trouble. With the watch you'll be wearing Chris – though it looks like a designer brand, all you need to do is pull the pin out and we'll be there. Just be careful, please. We don't want to crash the party unless we have to.'

'I can't think of anything we'd be doing to cause it to happen accidentally.' Hannah looked over, giving her flirtatious smile to the Gold Command.

'Once the helicopter drops you at the venue, we'll have no further communication with you, unless, like I said, you snap a hair pin or the watch pin gets pulled out.'

'Won't we be checked?'

'Hannah's dress leaves little to the imagination, so there'll be no way she's hiding anything, although they might opt for a feel to get them off for the night. You will be subjected to a search, Chris.'

'For the same reason,' Hannah teased.

'Let's make this a clean investigation. Go and have fun, do what you need to do, and the helicopter will pick you up first thing and bring you both back here for a medical check over. Then we'll get you back to London for debrief. Understand?'

'Yes, boss,' Hannah responded.

'You shouldn't face any checks on your identity while you're there – but, just to confirm, you've made your millions on stocks and shares, Chris. And remember, it's the day after your wedding, and this is part of your wife's wedding present because you like to see her enjoying herself.'

Chris glanced over towards where Hannah was now stood, looking stunning in a gold dress which hugged her curves.

'We haven't had a chance to clear the venue, so I suggest that you both stay in your roles from the moment you step out of the helicopter.'

'Has there been any news on Candy?' Hannah asked.

'Not that I've heard, but I will contact control and make sure we get the information to you while you're in the air.'

'Right, I'm going to leave you to come up with your cover story and let the guys know we're good to go,' Gold Command informed them.

'Thank you, Officer.'

Hannah turned and looked over at Chris. 'It's not too late. You can change your mind. I'm sure they'll take you back to Nottingham.'

'I want to be here, Han. If you need to do this, I'd rather you were doing it with me instead of someone else.'

Hannah moved over towards Chris and kissed him.

'Look, when this is all over, let's start again, me and you,' she whispered.

'I'd like that.'

There was a knock on the door as one of the female officers walked into the room.

'Miss, it's been suggested you take this in advance. I'll make sure there's one waiting for you back here in the morning.' Chris watched Hannah take the small pill, wondering what it was and why she would need one in the morning.

'Birds and the bees,' the officer said to him as she noticed him watching Hannah.

In the distance, they could hear the sounds of a helicopter coming in over the hills of Derbyshire.

'And a little thing called love,' Hannah added.

'Sounds like your ride is here. Stay safe,' the officer said as she saluted them both and left the room.

The cottage shook slightly and the wind picked up as the helicopter landed. There was a knock on the door. 'We're good to go when you are,' came a voice.

'Chris?' Hannah looked at him meaningfully. 'What I said still stands. You don't have to do this.'

Chris twisted the wedding band that had been placed on his left hand. He didn't know what to think or how to feel. He was okay going into scenarios and playing his part, but going to an all-out orgy? He wasn't sure about that.

Then there was the constant reminder of what else was going on in his head: the balance issues, the blurred vision. What if he took something and it aggravated matters more? What if his sex drive was about to fail him at the moment he most needed it? He needed to remember the reason he was going into this, and that was to get Mikel out of there and keep Hannah safe.

'Chris?' Hannah asked again, bringing him back to reality.

'After you,' he replied as he stretched out his left hand to take in the wedding ring and an expensive looking watch. This hadn't been how he'd expected to spend his evening when driving to the prison that morning.

He stopped and turned as he reached the front door, casting a last look behind him at all the people who had arrived to make this mission possible; all the people tasked with keeping them safe. He took a deep breath as he stepped outside, leaving behind a safety net for the unknown.

Chapter Thirty-Two

Jen Garner

Jen, Sam and Max stood peering at the map of the area where Hannah and Chris were due to land.

'Special forces will be situated in these fields.' Max pointed out. 'This is the closest they can get to the house without being spotted. There'll also be a drone in the air, watching the situation from above – so, though we'll lose communication with the guys below, we'll be able to see what's going on.'

'Do you think they'll be okay?' Sam asked, looking anxious again.

'Hannah is an experienced officer. She'll be fine.'

'And the detective?'

'I honestly don't know. Hannah assured me that she didn't need a replacement and that Chris would be fine, after his initial wobbles.' Max moved over to the main screen, turning it on and handing out the headsets.

'This is Gold Command. Our officers are in the air. Over.'

'Thanks, control. Over,' Max responded. 'We have Detective Garner and Sam also on the frequency.'

'Hannah asked before take-off if there'd been any news on Candy?' came the response.

'I'm awaiting news.'

'Officers, T-minus ten minutes to location,' came a different voice.

'Excuse me, incoming call,' Max said, taking off his headset and leaving the meeting room.

'Drone is airborne. Over.'

Suddenly the screen was filled with the landscape below and the night sky as the drone took off.

Jen remained silent, watching the ground fall further away as she stared at the screen in wonderment. She could just make out images of the building below.

'Drone at 14,000 feet. Over.'

'Moving towards the target.'

Just then, Max re-entered from his office, replacing his headset.

'Gold Command, Candy has been neutralised.'

'Message received and relayed.'

'Have you managed to find Candy?' Jen asked as she instinctively pressed the mute button on the side of her headset.

'Tim's got to her. Slipped her some Rohypnol and, other than having to spend the night in her grotty flat, he has her immobilised.'

'Tim?'

'Detective Brown. I know you two had your differences last year, but he is a good officer.'

The news surprised Jen more than anything. After Tim's behaviour towards her last year, she hadn't expected him to be so willing to help in any way.

'We all look after each other, no matter our differences,' came Max's warning.

'Good to know.' Jen was conscious of conversations going on in her ear.

'Hotel One to Gold Command, permission to land has been granted. Over.'

'Okay to proceed,' came the response back.

'Will lose communication in sixty seconds and counting. Fifty-nine, fifty-eight …'

'Right you two. It's show time,' came the voice through their headsets as Chris felt the helicopter begin to descend. He'd been quiet during the short flight over, looking at the night sky, pondering everything about life and beyond the stars.

'Just to let you both know, Candy has been immobilised and holds no threat.'

'That's one less thing to worry about,' came Hannah's response as she also stared out at the night. Chris felt the squeeze of her hand as the helicopter touched down on the ground. *Show time*. One final twist of his fake wedding band and a deep breath.

'God, you make me horny,' Hannah whispered into his ear with the flirtatious laughter that made his head spin.

Chris opened the doors and jumped out, turning to lift his new wife out. As he slowly lowered her to the ground, their lips brushed past each other. He could feel the temptation and lust dripping from Hannah as she turned and grabbed his hand.

'So, why have you brought me all the way out here?' came the question he'd been waiting for.

'Call it an early wedding present,' he said as he led her towards the house.

Truth be known, he'd have had her there and then, but this wasn't about them. Chris led her up to the imposing manor door and knocked. Seconds later, a well-dressed man appeared.

'Sir, madam.' He gave them both the once-over and stood aside as they walked through the door into the entrance hall. 'We were all a bit excited when we saw the helicopter land,' he told them as he closed the door behind them.

'I'm sorry. My wife was taking forever to get out of that wedding dress and, I must say, I was a little preoccupied myself, so asked my pilot to run us over.'

'Understandable, sir. I would be distracted by your wife, too.'

'Come and find us when you clock off. I like to watch her having fun.' Chris couldn't believe the words that were coming out of his mouth. God help him if his mother ever found out about this.

The guy just laughed and muttered something about not being able to fraternise with the guests. Chris ran his hand down Hannah's back, and she gave him those lustful eyes.

'I just need you both to pass through these security scanners, tick your names off the guest list and I'll show you to your suite.'

Ever the gentleman, though right now he felt like a dirty old man, Chris let Hannah walk through without an issue.

'Do you need me to take my jacket off and put my watch through separately?' he asked, like he was talking to check-in staff at the airport.

'No, sir, we just screen for guns and the like.'

Chris wandered through after Hannah, again without a hitch.

'Now, your names please?'

'Joe and Katie Kendal.' For a heartbeat, Chris panicked that they wouldn't be on the list, but they were found without an issue. Then they walked through a second set of doors that opened up in front of them into a vast circular room. There were a couple of steps down into what looked like a fish bowl with a bar in the middle. There were sofas around the edge, where couples sat in various formations and positions.

'So this is our main area, where we encourage our guests to mingle and get to know each other. At the bar we have a range of champagne, wines and spirits.' They were led towards an expansive marble staircase and began to climb several flights of stairs. 'So, here is your suite. It can be locked from the inside only – although, we'll encourage you to keep your door open because, like yourself, sir, some people just like to watch.'

In the room, they found a vast double bed and a stack of various sex toys, some of which Chris had never seen before; without closer inspection, he wondered how the hell they all worked.

'We have staff here at your service. As long as they aren't busy with another couple, they are yours to do with as you wish.'

As Chris looked round, he noticed several white lines of powder on a silver tray that had been placed on a shelf in front of a mirror.

'Those, sir, are your welcome present from our hosts, who will be down to mix with you later. You'll find the coke at almost one hundred per cent purity for the most incredible buzz you've ever had.'

'Thank you for your assistance,' Chris said, reaching into his pocket and giving the guy a fifty pound note he'd stored in there earlier. Then they were left alone in the room.

Hannah moved over towards the shelf and sniffed back the coke before Chris had even realised what she was doing. He watched her eyes roll back as it hit.

'I want you.' He crept up behind her, put his arms around her and began to lift up her tightly fitted dress. As she let it happen, he began to doubt himself and what he was about to do. 'God forgive me,' he whispered to himself as he looked up at the ceiling and

232

noticed the red flashing light of a camera. *No backing out now ...*

Though feeling unsteady on his feet and hyper aware of his surroundings, Chris had fallen into the playboy role a bit too comfortably. He was shocked at how easy it had been to embody the sort of pricks he arrested, and Hannah was all too happy to play along as the sexy seductress who was pulling him further into temptation. He'd had a drink of the champagne but left the coke for Hannah to consume; from the look in her eyes as the initial buzz hit, he knew he needed to stay alert and keep her safe. Chris found himself keen to explore this strange world of sex and seduction he had been pulled into – and there was plenty of it going around. The air was charged and, though he noticed many of the staff were stunning as they made eye contact with him, enticing him to touch them, he had made a promise to himself that he wouldn't do anything without Hannah by his side. He hoped she felt the same way. As he walked the long corridors and began to descend the stairs, staring around at his surroundings, he knew he needed to act naturally. He stopped midway on the stairs to watch another couple, before he continued on down and moved into the fish bowl. Chris tried not to study the faces for too long – maybe one of the people at this party could be their mystery man, Clive, who Harry had mentioned in the interview. Or maybe whoever ran these events was tucked away, watching everything on the cameras. The thought made him shudder, but then something caught his eye and brought him crashing down back to the mission.

In amongst all the adults doing things no six-year-old should be aware of, sat on one of the leather sofas, was Mikel. He appeared terrified and unsure where to look, as he sat there drinking some bright-coloured juice. As he tried to get closer to the boy, he fingered the pin on his watch. All he needed to do was pull the pin out and the shit would come down on everyone's heads – he'd seen enough A-listers and politicians to know that having the secret service crashing their party wouldn't end well. He knew he couldn't get too close – if Mikel recognised him, any trust he had built up with the boy would either vanish and he'd lose him forever, or he would blow his cover. So, his circle to get close to the child began to widen again. *Stay safe little one*, he whispered to himself. *The good guys are coming to get you out of this misery.*

As he circled back to find something – or someone – to take back to Hannah, like she was a lioness waiting for her kill, he felt a tap on his shoulder.

'I see you looking at the boy,' a male voice broke into his thoughts. 'Does he interest you, sir?' The question was out there and, at that point, Chris realised why Mikel was there. He'd been silly to think that just because the place was streaming with all types of people getting off with each other, child abuse was a taboo that was off the cards. He knew he couldn't take him back to Hannah; the flashing red light in their room was a constant reminder that they were being watched and monitored, and someone, somewhere, was no doubt getting off on their sexual adventures fuelled by drugs and lust.

'Who is he?' Chris turned and asked, keen to play along.

'He belongs to the organiser, but I'm sure he won't mind you borrowing him.'

Chris felt his skin begin to crawl. 'I don't think my new wife would approve,' he replied, giving the man a knowing look.

'I understand, sir. I really do,' came the reply.

'Do you think the organiser would let me borrow him at some other point in the near future?'

'I can ask.'

'Tell him I want to test the goods. I'm sure he'll get the gist.' Chris felt himself sinking to a new low that he wasn't prepared for.

'I'll get you an answer before you leave tomorrow.'

'Just between us, mind you. Let's leave the missus out of it. She might need time to come round to the idea.'

The man disappeared into the sea of bodies. Chris felt himself wanting to retch, but he needed to stay focused – even more so as his vision blurred. *God, he didn't need this now of all times*. As he moved over towards one of the sofas, a girl appeared next to him. She placed a hand on his thigh and started to lick his ear. This was turning him on far more than it should. He needed to take control of the situation as he turned towards her and kissed her softly at first, and then more aggressively. As she stood in front of him, with a knowing sparkle in her eyes, she held out her hand.

'I've got someone I'd like you to meet,' he said as he stood up. He had found his prey, and he was taking her back to his lair and his mistress.

Chapter Thirty-Three

Dana

Things came to a head one evening when we were all told to get dressed up because we were going to a party. We were supplied with various drugs that we were expected to give to those in attendance. We were to perform whichever sexual acts they requested. This was the first time all the girls had been invited, so who was going to sit in and look after Mikel? I had no choice but to leave him with one of the men, but it scared me what they might do to him. I had witnessed and been subjected to so much violence in my life, but this ...

It turned out that Jess was now running things with that ginger bloke, and these parties were for her best clients to use and abuse us while filling themselves with coke. There were literal bags of coke lying around for them to help themselves to. I had been clean since before the birth of Mikel, so I did my best to decline the stuff. I noticed my friend, who had visited me in Nottingham, was in attendance too. She was there with Jess, making out and performing sex acts with strangers. I noticed Clive watching them from a distance, and I found myself shuddering at his leering expression.

But then everything suddenly stopped. My friend was thrown into the centre of the room and an announcement was made. They said that this person was an undercover officer by the name of Chloe Seaward and that she was there to spy on us.

Then things got scary. We were made to watch as she was raped and beaten. We were told if one of us was ever caught reporting back to the police that this would happen to us too. I met Chloe's eye on several occasions during the beating; she was no longer that kind girl who'd come to visit me on a monthly basis. Her body was crumpled on the floor, broken. Another announcement came that the party was to carry on and no one was to approach Chloe. It was like she was nothing, and we had to avoid her like the plague. As the evening continued, I was sure the person lying on the floor was still breathing as I tried to carry on with my duties for that evening.

They were about to drag her out when I couldn't take it any more and rushed over to help her. I knew right away I shouldn't have and, trust me, I paid for it, but I felt that she should leave with some of her dignity. I didn't want to think where they were taking her to, but I went over and tried to re-dress her the best I could. That's when she told me to find Lisa Carter. I wasn't sure what she was saying at first; she sounded so frail. She asked me to promise her that I'd find her, and I gave her my word as they dragged her away. Later, they asked me what she'd said to me. I lied and told them I didn't know, that I couldn't make anything out. The party still carried on as if nothing had happened, but with the announcement ringing in our ears that if anyone else thought about spying, they would share the same fate.

Chapter Thirty-Four

DI Chris Jackson

Chris woke up in a tangle of limbs and silk bed sheets and, from the moment he opened his eyes, he felt like hell. His mouth felt like it was full of cotton wool, and he reached over for some form of liquid to restore the moisture. Aware that he was on camera, he played the dutiful husband role and Hannah played along once she woke up. If she felt as rough as he did, she didn't show it. As they left their suite, Chris noticed the various bodies crashed out across the floor and evidence of the coke that had been consumed at the party. As they crossed the main area, his mind returned to Mikel, alone and no doubt scared about what was going on around him.

'Sir.' The man from the night before approached Chris. 'I've been asked to make sure you have this before you leave.' He passed over a business card. 'The organiser said to contact him. He has something that will interest you very much.'

Chris turned the business card over in his hand. *Ablaze Events*. 'Thank them and tell them I'll be in touch.'

'What is it, honey?' Hannah asked as she tried to study the card in his hand.

'Nothing for you to worry about, sweetie. Why don't you go and jump into the helicopter?' And with that, Hannah kissed him and disappeared towards the awaiting chopper.

'Is the boy here now?' Chris turned back to ask.

'I'm not sure. I haven't seen him since late last night.'

'Not to worry, maybe another time.' Chris smiled and

went to follow his wife, only turning back to hand the guy another crisp note from his pocket.

'It's been my pleasure, sir. Safe trip home.'

And with that, Chris headed towards the helicopter, climbed in and kissed his wife, as the rotor blades began to turn.

'Package picked up. Over,' came the call signal he had been dying to hear.

'Hotel One, in the air and returning to base. Over.'

As Chris watched the clouds come closer and the ground fall away, he took Hannah's hand. There was so much he wanted to say to her, so much he needed to tell her. Did he need to apologise? She was no longer glowing like she had done the previous night as her mask finally dropped, but he relaxed as she squeezed his hand back. That was the other signal he had been waiting for and, though he felt like shit, everything was okay ... *wasn't it?*

The helicopter set them back down where it had all begun, at the cottage in Bakewell. As Chris opened the door, a team of people hurried towards them. Blankets were wrapped around Hannah as she was escorted into the cottage. Chris turned and thanked the pilot for their lift home and followed Hannah in. He was soon greeted by his own team of concerned officers.

He finally got to sit down and, though he was part of the buzz of communication that was going on around him, he was glad to have time with his own thoughts as he replayed the events of that night in his mind, mentally checking himself over.

After he'd pissed in a pot and they'd taken blood from him, he was allowed to strip off and get in the shower. As the hot water ran over him, he was finally able to properly relax and, as he expected, felt the beginnings of a headache. He wondered if dehydration was causing this particular pulsing headache or the stress of the night. There was so much he needed to tell Hannah, and no doubt she'd be the same. Hopefully they would get a chance to talk on the car journey back to the office. Climbing out of the shower, he found someone had left him a clean set of clothes on the back of the door.

Feeling almost human again, he went to join the others.

A woman in her early forties greeted him as he walked into the living room. He didn't recognise her from the previous night, but then he'd seen so many people before he and Hannah had been flown out to the party.

'Inspector Jackson. You're looking much better than when you arrived earlier,' she said to him as he sat down on one of the sofas.

'It's amazing what a shower can do.'

'Successful night?'

'I would say so,' Chris said, remembering the card. 'I need to get something out of one of the pockets of the suit before you take it away.'

'Not a problem.'

'And is Hannah okay? I've not seen her since we landed.'

'She's with medical. I'm sure you two will be reunited in no time.'

'Chance of a coffee?' Chris asked. 'And maybe several painkillers to get rid of this headache?'

'I'll see what I can do.'

Chris was sat on the same sofa that they'd sat on at the beginning of the operation. The woman Chris had been speaking to disappeared, hopefully in search of caffeine and pain relief. As Chris rested his head back, his eyes became heavy and he felt something drag him downwards into the cold earth below.

'Detective.'

'Hannah?' Chris started awake, opening his eyes to find Hannah looking over him.

'Wakey, wakey.'

Chris looked around the room, noticing the cup of coffee he had asked for next to a small pile of pills.

'Our chauffeur back to London awaits. You've been fast asleep for ages.'

Chris stretched. Admittedly, he did feel better after having a proper sleep, even if it had been on a sofa. 'I saw Mikel,' he said, suddenly remembering.

'When?' Hannah's eyes widened. 'Why didn't you tell me?'

'I didn't get the chance. We were being filmed, so I didn't want to blow cover.'

'Did you get to speak to him?'

'No. I was spotted, but I think I know how we can get him back.'

'Have you told this lot?'

'Not had the chance.'

'I spoke to Gold Command while you were asleep. They seem happy with the mission.'

'Shouldn't we tell them, so they can get things moving?'

'No point,' Hannah reassured him. 'Let's get back to HQ and work out our next move.'

'I just need the card out of that suit before we leave.'

'Yeah, and I think they'll want their watch back too.'

Chris stood up and wobbled slightly as he removed the watch. 'Do you think if I pulled the pin now, special services would burst in?'

'They're already here …'

Chris went round and thanked everyone who had been part of the mission the night before. As he and Hannah departed with Barry, he realised they were leaving a house full of people who had probably had less sleep than he'd had, because they'd been up all night keeping him and Hannah safe. They had assured him that a copy of the business card would be sent to the team in London and they'd make a start with the investigation while they journeyed back.

As they left the cottage, he noticed Hannah on her phone. He realised he really needed to get his turned back on and check in with the investigation at home.

'Ready?' she asked as she ended the call.

Chris moved around to the back of the car and climbed in. 'Thanks for coming to get us,' Chris said to Barry.

'Not a problem. Did you both have a good night?'

'You could say that ...'

To Chris' surprise, Hannah got into the back of the car with him. 'Not sitting up front?' he asked her.

'Will you hold me?' she whispered.

'You okay?'

'I think so, but I just need to lay in your arms and feel safe again.'

Chapter Thirty-Five

DI Chris Jackson

Hannah had slept peacefully in his arms during the journey back to London. He had never seen her so vulnerable. The outgoing, friendly, flirtatious girl he knew had vanished now it was just the two of them in the back of the car. He couldn't take his eyes off her. Though he had watched her sleep before, this was different somehow. He almost wanted to bottle this precious moment so it could last forever. Was this the *real* Hannah he had in his arms?

Once the car had arrived back at the office, Hannah woke up, and the moment was lost as she returned to her normal outgoing self, almost like a light switch had been turned back on.

She had whizzed him through security and then into the office and the meeting room, where he was now sat waiting to debrief. He wondered about his team back home, making another mental note that he needed to check in with them in case something important had come up.

As Chris surveyed the room, he noticed a map on the wall of where he had spent the night with Hannah, and several blurry mug shots that had been taken from a distance. He didn't recognise anyone in the photos but was more than one hundred per cent sure there were people there who shouldn't have been.

As he pondered, the screen in front of him flickered to life at the same time as a young woman carrying glasses and jugs of water came in.

'Good night, Detective?'

'Long,' Chris replied as the girl giggled. *Had Hannah said something?*

'I'm Sam, by the way. PA-cum- trainee detective,' she introduced herself.

Jen and Hannah followed a few minutes later, all smiles and knowing looks.

'Right, let's get started,' Max said, strolling in from his office through the connecting door with another man. 'This is Captain Tucker. He spent last night with his team keeping Hannah and our detective safe,' Max introduced the thick-set man in military uniform.

'Good afternoon, all.'

'Chris, let's start with you. I hear you saw Mikel?'

'Yes, but only briefly. I toyed with the idea of calling the good guys in but decided against it as there were too many powerful people there. I was approached by an unknown male, who had noticed me looking and struck up a conversation with me about Mikel. There was a camera in the room Hannah and I were in, and no doubt further cameras behind the mirror, so I wasn't prepared to bring Mikel into the room with us.'

'Wise decision.' Max nodded in approval.

'How did he look? Was he okay?' Jen sounded anxious.

'Like I said, I didn't want to get to close, but he seemed spaced out and not aware of what was going on around him.'

'Do you think they had drugged him?' Jen pushed.

'I'm not sure. He was drinking some brightly coloured liquid. I thought it was juice.'

'Did you see anyone take or do anything to Mikel?' Jen asked, and he noticed her shudder.

'I wasn't able to keep an eye on him without causing further suspicion, so I made the decision to return to our room.'

'I think you made the right call, Chris.' Max spoke up. He knew Max was trying to make him feel better, but it didn't stop Chris feeling racked with guilt. He may have made the right decision at the time, but where was Mikel now? And what had happened to him last night?

'When Hannah and I came to leave I asked after Mikel again, but I was informed he was no longer on the premises. However, I was given a business card which I was told had been copied to you guys while we were on our way back.'

'Yes, it's been loaded up onto the system. We've been searching for records of Ablaze Events and their phone number,' Sam confirmed.

'Captain Tucker, did your team witness the boy leaving at all?' Jen queried.

'No, we would have intercepted them once they were clear.'

'So, does that mean he's still there now?' Jen questioned. 'Couldn't you just raid the manor?'

'I don't think it's wise,' the captain said carefully.

'I agree,' Max said as Jen tutted. 'If we send a team in there now, that's Hannah and Chris' cover blown, and we still have an in with this business card.'

'I will keep a team on site until we know the building is clear.' Captain Tucker spoke. 'If the boy leaves, we will intercept him once it's safe to do so.'

'Before we move onto this business card and its meaning, do you have anything for us, Hannah?'

'I wasn't in the position to investigate much. Upon our arrival, they seemed to be very excited about the helicopter so were pretty much tripping over themselves to buddy up with Chris. Seeing as he had made the initial connection, I didn't want to be seen as taking over and potentially blowing our cover.'

'Did you find out anything from the other people in attendance?'

'The girls weren't that talkative. I did try to engage in conversation, but the ones I tried to talk to were very … robotic? They were there to do a job, and they didn't want to talk about life outside of the manor,' Hannah explained.

'Thank you for keeping my guys safe last night, Captain Tucker.' Max turned to the other man.

'No a problem. Like I said, I will keep my guys on the ground till the scene is either clear or we are asked to pull back.' Captain Tucker stood up and Max mirrored him.

'Let me show you out.'

Jen Garner

'Do you think we've stumbled upon a paedophile ring?' Jen couldn't believe she was even thinking about this. She felt sick to the pit of her stomach. She couldn't begin to imagine the things that Mikel must have witnessed, maybe even made to take part in. There was silence in the room as everyone reflected on what could possibly be going on.

'So, this business card …' Max re-entered the room. 'Sam, did you find anything?'

'No, boss. The number isn't on our system and, as for the company name on the card, there's no record I can find.'

'Chris, can you tell us more?'

'I was given it as we were leaving, after I had made enquiries about Mikel and discussed … wanting to test out the merchandise.' There was an awkward silence in the room as they all realised what Chris was implying.

'And did they say anything else?' Max pressed.

'Just to contact the organiser. The thing that concerns

246

me is that if child abuse was going on at this party last night, which we can probably assume it was, who else asked after Mikel and got given the same details?'

'There is something else we need to discuss,' Hannah said as she watched the colour in Jen's face start to change. 'Harry mentioned someone called Clive – apparently he was on old friend, possibly even Jessica's godfather.'

'Her *godfather*? Sorry, I need to get some air ... I can't breathe,' Jen said as she scraped her chair back and rushed for the door. She'd thought she was tougher than this, she'd thought she'd seen and heard the worst humanity could do. Hannah hurried to her side and helped her from the room. 'I think I'm going to be sick.' Jen choked out.

'It's okay, hun. Let's get you to the fire exit. I'll find you some water.'

Jen needed to get out of there, she needed to get out of the building, she needed to go home, she needed to be free from this.

Everything was becoming a bit too close for comfort. *How the hell could a paedophile ring be linked to her?* She knew that George Crawford had links to people trafficking, but that had been about young people who had wanted to escape their war-torn countries. Even he wouldn't have stooped to that, and now there was this mystery Clive person ...

'Are you feeling any better?' Hannah asked, once Jen was sat on the step outside.

'In need of a double vodka, I think.'

'I'm afraid I could only find water,' Hannah said, handing her the plastic cup. 'Wanna talk? We worked together enough last year that I know when something is wrong.'

'It's the case. I'm just feeling like I came speeding back to London thinking this was all about me again, and it's not. You and Chris seem to have this all pretty much sewn up, and you're on the verge of cracking a possible paedophile ring. I might as well just go home and back to domestic life.' Jen sighed. 'I'm beginning to feel like there's no way to leave this all behind while I keep looking for reasons to come back.'

'Jen, you're forgetting Mikel. He was asking for you when he was found, wasn't he? So of course you rushed back here. There was no way Max was sending his prize asset in last night for a night of sex, drugs and rock'n' roll when she has a family back home, plus you might have been spotted and we'd have lost Mikel forever.'

'Are *you* okay? Sounds like Chris did most of the work last night,' Jen said, desperate to change the subject. At least she was starting to feel a bit better now.

'I'm fine.' Hannah laughed. 'It was easier to let him get on with it. I was just the new wife.'

'And everything else?'

'Honestly, Jen, there's nothing else to report.'

'And you've taken a tablet?'

'Yes, boss. No babies happening here any time soon.' Hannah patted her tummy. 'Chris kept me safe anyway.' She looked serious again. 'When did you last speak to James and the kids?'

'A couple of days ago? I'm not sure, to be honest. Obviously I've let them know I'm safe.'

'Here, take my phone.' Hannah passed it to her. 'Ring and check in with your little people.'

Chapter Thirty-Six

DI Chris Jackson

While Jen had left to get some air, they'd decided between them to contact the number on the card – but first Chris needed his second identity brought to life. He soon found himself the owner of new Facebook, Twitter and LinkedIn pages, populated with work colleagues he'd never meet. Then there was also the latest smartphone and watch combo, a laptop and a new wife. It was just a shame all this had to be returned when it was all over. Well, maybe not the wife. He was amazed by how someone's social media presence for the past year could be created in an hour.

'So are we clear, Chris?' Max asked him as if he was a new team member on his first day. When Chris had originally joined the force, this is where he'd dreamed of ending up. Running undercover missions and kicking down doors. Sat in the meeting room of the team who already did, he realised he missed the mean streets of Nottingham. Plus, he was becoming increasingly concerned about his health. That would need to wait until they'd brought Mikel home, though.

'Do we need to run through things?' Hannah asked as Jen re-entered the room.

'Isn't it like ordering pizza?' He attempted a joke. 'Yeah, I'm good. Let's roll.'

The team donned their headsets, ready to listen in to the call he was about to make. Chris hadn't dared think about what he was about to insinuate as he dialled the number and counted the rings. The more times it rung, the more butterflies danced around in his stomach. The bile rose at the back of his throat as he thought more about what he was about to do.

'Hello?' came the answer he'd been waiting for.

'Hi, I was given this number at the party last night.' There was a silence on the line and murmurs in the background.

'Mr Devonshire, wasn't it?' Chris knew that this could be a test – either that, or he'd been right, and the number had been given to more people than just him. He didn't dare look over at the others who he knew would be signalling at him.

'No.' Now the ball was in their court.

'Erm, let me check something,' came the response. 'Ah, Mr Kendal – the man with the stunning wife.'

Chris stole a look at Hannah. *Did he recognise the voice from the previous night?* Maybe he was mistaken in thinking he'd heard it somewhere before ...

'We were checking through the CCTV footage from last night, and I must say—'

Chris' mind ran back through the events of the previous evening, and he knew he had to change the subject quickly. 'Don't they say what happens at Highgrove Farm stays at Highgrove Farm?' He laughed.

'Indeed, Mr Kendal, indeed.'

'Please call me Joe.'

'Joe, how can I be of help?'

'I was told by one of your associates that you'd be the one to talk to about the boy at the party.'

'Ah yes, Jake.'

Chris was confused for a second, but then realised they must be using a fake name for Mikel. 'I'd like to see him.'

'Are you interested in little boys?'

Chris' skin started to crawl. 'I like their company.'

'I can introduce you to lots of young boys, Joe.'

'Is ... Jake ... not available?'

'He is, but I thought you might want to check what else I have on offer.'

'You have others? I only saw Jake at the party.'

'I can provide you with whatever you desire.'

Chris felt sick. 'So, where do we go from here?' he asked through gritted teeth.

'Well, that is totally up to you, Joe.'

'Is there any way I can see these boys?'

'Maybe it's best I send you some photos. Can I send them to the number you've called on now?'

'It might be best if you email me. I don't want my wife checking my phone and finding out my little secret just yet,' explained Chris, before giving the man the email address that had just been set up for him.

The man on the phone laughed. 'I understand. Trust me, I do. I'll send you something shortly, Joe.'

'Thank you for all of your help.'

At that point, Max ended the call. 'I think we need to get the tech guys down here and get Angela back,' he said, immediately springing into action.

'Think that might be a good idea, boss. We need their knowledge before this gets any more complicated,' Hannah agreed.

'Take five. I'll get everyone together.'

'I'll get everything sent up, boss,' Sam said as she clicked back into PA mode.

'Take a break, Sam,' Max instructed. 'You're going to need it later.'

'Afternoon, all. Thank you for coming down so swiftly to join us, Angela, Sean. I wanted someone to have a look at that email before we opened it on our system,' Max explained.

'I decided it might be best not to open the email sent to Chris' on Joe's laptop until I had completed some further checks on it first,' Sean added.

'Did you find anything suspicious?' Max asked.

'Afraid so. Also hidden within the image file was some malware and spy software.'

'Okay, so where do we go from here?'

'As this laptop was requested as part of an undercover operation, it has been set up to look like Joe's personal computer, so I also made sure that it isn't connected to our mainframe.'

'So, when the spyware gets onto Joe's system, it will just look like his own personal laptop connected to a normal internet provider?' Jen asked.

'Correct. I've also managed to isolate it so we can transfer anything onto the main screen here without too much of an issue.'

'So, there is no harm in opening the email then?'

'Not that I can see.' Sean looked rather pleased with himself.

'Well, let's rock and roll and see what we've been sent,' Jen instructed as Sean clicked to open the PDF and transferred it to the main screen. The team were presented with what could only be described as a catalogue full of naked children.

'What ... the?' Sean asked as the silence stretched on whilst everyone took in what was in front of them.

'Angela?' Max said through gritted teeth, breaking the deadlock.

'I'm afraid this isn't uncommon. We seem to be seeing it more and more as criminals get more technical-minded,' Angela responded.

'I don't know what I expected when he said he was going to send me something, but this ...' Chris glanced at the screen briefly, but then had to look away again.

'I'm afraid my colleague will back me up that this is already happening on the dark web,' Angela said as she looked over towards Sean.

'Do you recognise any of the faces here, Angela?' Jen asked.

'We look at so many images a week, I'm not sure. If you could remove all the nasty stuff from the email, Sean, I'll get the document through the facial recognition software.'

'I can do that, no problem.'

'So, where do we go from here? Is Mikel featured in this brochure?' Jen pressed.

Sean started to flick through the pages of what looked scarily like a glossy magazine.

'I don't see him,' Hannah responded. 'Anyone else?'

They sat and studied the screen as Sean continued to flick through. Chris knew that the graphic images would be burned onto his brain for a long time to come. 'Nope. Max?'

'I think this is where we can start from then. We can get Chris to email back and question where Mikel – or Jake as they're calling him – is and why he isn't featured,' Max suggested.

There was a resounding hum of agreement from the room.

'Angela, if you can run this through your facial software, hopefully we might be able to identify at least one of these children and where they come from.'

'Do I need to do anything before I reply, Sean?' Chris asked.

'No, you can pretty much treat this as your own personal laptop.'

'And it's all secure from the service mainframe?'

'Yep. Though you are using the same server as the rest of us, anyone from the outside trying to look in won't know,' Sean explained. 'I will access the email from our systems and get a clean copy over to Angela for her analysis, so just carry on as normal.'

'Sorry, Sean. Can we not send the same spyware back when Chris replies?' Jen asked.

'We could, but if they know about adding stuff to Joe's email I worry that they'll notice if we try the same trick.'

'Okay, just a thought.'

'I'll be in touch as soon as I've run the software, Max,' Angela promised him.

'Thank you both,' Jen said as Sean and Angela got up to leave the room, followed by Max as he saw them out of the office.

'Well, I guess our first plan of action is for me to write an email back to this guy asking where Mikel is?' Chris said as he looked at his watch. It was getting late and it was looking unlikely he would be getting back to Nottingham tonight, which meant he would either be staying with Hannah or at some hotel. At least if he was staying with Hannah, he would finally be able to speak to her about the previous night.

Chapter Thirty-Seven

Dana

I was never able to forget what happened to the girl I once knew. She was always so kind and caring towards me and Mikel. It took me a few months, but I knew I needed to do something, I knew I had to find Lisa Carter, and I began to plan our escape. The more I thought about it, the more I knew it wouldn't be easy. I had been located once before. How had I ever thought I could be free? I knew that in Nottingham there were people who could protect Mikel, who was becoming more and more withdrawn. I dreaded to think what Clive and his friends were doing to him when I was having to work. So I did what I did best and managed to steal some money, and Mikel and I started the journey back; if nothing else, at least when he was found wandering the streets he would be taken into a home where he would be safe. I knew this would be the last time I would ever spend with Mikel, so I kept him close and made sure he knew how much I loved him and always would.

Once we arrived in Nottingham, I posted the letter I needed to send. Then I took Mikel to the market square. I told him I'd made a promise to find somebody called Lisa Carter. I explained he wasn't allowed to speak to anyone other than Lisa Carter. He promised me he would find her, and I said I'd see him again once he had. I walked away and left Mikel wandering the streets of Nottingham alone, asking for Lisa. I wasn't sure whether Lisa even lived in Nottingham but, right now, I needed to protect Mikel and keep him safe.

Then I made my way to the River Trent along the scenic route I used to always walk when I lived here. I knew, in my heart of hearts, that I had no choice …

Chapter Thirty-Eight

DI Chris Jackson

Chris had woken up with Hannah still laying in his arms. All he knew was that as soon as his head had hit the pillow, he'd been asleep. No doubt Hannah had been the same as they were in the same position as when they'd got into bed. He wasn't sure what time it was, but it was light outside – although that didn't mean much in the summer months. He decided he'd let Hannah sleep. Things had changed between them since the party, and he was beginning to see a different side to her from the highly sexualised persona she liked to portray. He had wanted to talk to her last night about the party, but they were both too tired for anything when they'd finally arrived back from the office. As he lay in the silence of Hannah's flat, he began to wonder whether Angela had found anything using the facial recognition software to at least put a name to these poor kids. He had left his new work laptop in the office so had no idea if his mystery man had replied either. He was distracted from his thoughts by Hannah beginning to stir. 'Good morning, beautiful,' he said.

'Hey.'

'You sleep okay?'

'Yeah, I was so tired when we got back. I've not even bothered to take my make-up off. I bet I look like a panda.'

'Han … we need to talk about the other night.'

'The mass orgy?' she questioned.

'If you want to put it like that … it's just, you've not said anything about it since.'

'I didn't think there was anything to say?'

'So, we just carry on like we are?'

'It was a mission. I was just lucky enough to get to go on it with the man I love.'

The L word took Chris aback for a second.

'We went there, we did what we had to do and then, when it was all over, we were brought back to London and reality. I didn't think there was any more that needed saying.'

'So you're okay?'

'Yes, aren't you?'

'I guess normal police life isn't as intense as the other night and the things we did, and I'm just a bit ...' Chris didn't have the right words to explain how he was feeling. He couldn't question Hannah's change in personality; he liked her better this way ... and she'd basically admitted that she loved him.

'I guess that's why the department exists, so you don't have to do the stuff we did. We do it all for you.' Hannah climbed out of bed. 'I'm gonna shower, then we'll head in. Help yourself to anything you find in the kitchen,' she added as she disappeared from the bedroom. No offers for him to join her in there, then? Had he really woken up next to the same girl?

'Unless you want to join me?' she asked as she popped her head back into the room.

Ah ... there she was.

Jen Garner

Jen had been sat alone in the meeting room, waiting for others to arrive. Max had gone back into his office to get updated from Angela on the facial recognition search, and she was left alone to think.

Jen had spent a lot of that night on the phone to James.

She couldn't understand why she was finding the distance between them so challenging with this case. What had happened to her? She had seen cases similar to this before and they'd not affected her, but this one really was hitting a bit too close to home. Maybe it was because she knew Mikel and had met him before he disappeared ...

'Morning.' Sam breezed into the meeting room, jugs of water in hand as always. 'Did you have a good night?'

'Didn't sleep too well again. What about you?'

'I guess so. I couldn't get those images out of my mind, though.'

'Tell me about it.'

'How do you think Inspector Jackson is coping with it all? This is a bit of a step up from Nottingham major crimes, surely?' Sam commented as she practically danced around the room, setting the place up.

'I've not really spoken to him to be fair, plus we don't really know what went on at that party, seeing as we couldn't get anywhere near it.' Jen slouched back in her chair.

'Maybe we could ask Hannah for the gossip later.'

'Hmm, I get the feeling Hannah will give us information on his performance ... but it will have nothing to do about undercover policing.' Both the girls laughed, then Sam continued to set up the room while Jen stared into space. After a moment's silence, Sam began to talk again. Jen had noticed that Sam didn't seem to like the silence, seemingly always feeling she had to fill it in some way.

'I'm sorry I had to split the other night. I just couldn't keep my eyes open,' she apologised.

'Like I said, you didn't miss much ... lots of cloud, the odd star, a tree maybe.'

'I noticed you climbing the walls a bit before I left, though.'

'Was I that obvious?' Jen straightened herself up in her chair.

'At points, I thought you were about to get up and drive to the farm yourself.'

'I was just missing the buzz and the thrill of the mission. It becomes like a drug. It just felt like I was sat watching a screen of nothingness.'

'Was that when you and Chloe used to party hard?'

'Yeah, it was just so we could continue feeling that high a bit longer.' Jen sighed as Hannah and Chris entered the room.

'Morning, you two. Have a good night?' Sam asked them both.

'I was asleep before my head hit the pillow.' Hannah smiled coyly.

'Do we know if Joe got any response to his email?' Chris asked quickly, before Hannah clicked fully back into sex kitten mode.

'Not sure. Max went straight into his office when he got in, so you might want to hold fire just in case something has happened,' Jen suggested before she turned her attention back to chatting to Hannah and Sam.

'Right, are we all ready?' Max asked, marching out of his office. 'We've had a response back from Angela, and I'm afraid it isn't all good news.' They all stopped talking and looked at Max. 'Okay, the good news is that Angela managed to name every single person in the document that our mystery person sent over. The bad news is, well, all these kids were reported as missing from care.'

'*What?*' asked Jen in complete disbelief.

'All the kids we're looking at were reported as missing from care homes,' Max repeated.

'Why were these kids never looked for?' Jen couldn't believe what she was hearing.

'From what Angela said, so many kids go missing from care for various reasons. Not all of them are located.'

'Fuck.'

'So, where do we go from here?' Hannah asked. 'Do we think Mikel is with all these other kids?'

'I'd say it's a distinct possibility. This case has just got a whole lot bigger, and more complicated, than we originally thought.'

'Our mystery person, whoever he is, is taking kids out of care, bringing them to orgies and selling them on to the highest bidder,' Jen concluded.

'There's also something else Angela said that I think we need to discuss,' Max added as the room fell silent. It felt like one of those moments in a movie when you know the big reveal is coming, and the tension ramps up as everyone holds their breath. 'All the kids have been reported missing from the East Midlands area.'

'Hang on. You're telling me that all those kids are missing from my patch?' Chris looked appalled.

'From what Angela has said, yes. I made her double and triple check, but she still came back with the same result.'

Jen noticed that Chris was turning very pale.

'Okay, team. We need to be productive on this,' Hannah interrupted, trying to rally the troops again. 'Firstly, have we had a response from our mystery man?' she asked as Chris pulled the laptop closer to him.

'I'll check now,' Chris said as he logged on to the laptop and clicked through to his emails. The team gathered round to look over his shoulder. Sure enough, there was a reply.

Joe,
I'm beginning to wonder why you are so interested in Jake?

I have plans for him, and I'm very keen on keeping him close.

Let me know if any of the other children spark your interest and we can arrange for you to meet them.

Regards.

'Right,' Hannah began as she looked over towards Max, perhaps to make sure she wasn't stepping on his toes. 'Chris, you've said before you have a contact with social services back in Nottingham?'

'Yeah, Holly Lord. I know Mikel was only one of them, but Jill Stokes said she was responsible for all the kids who went into care because they had no parents,' Chris said, standing up.

'I can ask Angela if she is able to trace these children's care history,' Max offered.

'But would she be able to do that, seeing as her angle is sexual exploitation?' Jen asked.

'All these kids are missing from the East Midlands ... so our mystery person must be getting the kids from someone who has an endless supply of kids no one is looking for?' Chris ran his hands over his face, clearly deep in thought.

'But who is the mystery person actually selling these kids? Has someone in the Crawford circle decided to branch out from selling drugs and sex parties?' Hannah pondered.

'I honestly don't know.' Max sighed 'We know that whoever we are communicating with now is male, though. That's one thing I'm sure of.'

'Jen, pack your bags. You're going home,' Hannah said out of nowhere.

'What? Why?'

'We need to keep Chris here for obvious reasons

and, as I'm the dashing wife, I don't think I'd better be disappearing anywhere. I need you to go back to Nottingham, find this Jill Stokes and start digging into these kids and how they got from the care system to sex slavery.'

'I'll give Julie a call and see if she'll hook up with you, Jen,' Chris offered.

'Okkkaay.'

'Julie is my right hand. Out of all the team, I think she's best placed to help you find what you need. I'll start making calls to the office.' Chris pulled out his phone.

'Sam,' Sam looked up at Hannah, clearly confused as to why she was being given a job. 'I'm afraid this isn't that exciting, but I need you to go back through all of Jen's case files, and I want to know where every single person who was connected to George Crawford is. Right down to his paper boy.'

'Okay, Hannah.'

'For these parties to be continuing, this mystery person must have a connection to Jess and maybe George too. Let's see if we can search him out with some good old-fashioned police work,' Hannah said, clearly trying to motivate her troops.

'Everybody happy?' Max asked, turning to look round the room.

They all stood up and got to work.

Detective Hannah Littlefair

After they had all dispersed to complete their various tasks, Hannah sat down and looked at the email again. While the others were trying to sneak up on their suspect from behind, she was ready to take a more direct route.

*I understand your concerns regarding Jake
and wanting to keep him close. How about we
compromise? I will pay you £30,000 for one night
with him. £15,000 up front and £15,000 on his return.*

Regards,

Joe Kendal

Hannah had been so engrossed in writing and sending the email, she jumped when Max cleared his throat behind her. 'You're getting just as reckless as Jen was.'

Chapter Thirty-Nine

Jen Garner

Julie had met Jen and directed her into a parking space. Jen had debated on her drive up to Nottingham whether to pop home but came to the conclusion that the sooner she got the job done at the office, the sooner she'd be able to see her family.

'Detective Garner,' Julie said as Jen climbed out of her car. For a moment she was taken aback. *Who was Julie speaking to?* Then it clicked.

'Please Julie, call me Jen. It's been so long since I was referred to as Detective anything. I might end up completely ignoring you or thinking that you're talking to someone else.'

'No problem.' Julie smiled her response.

Though Jen had been at the office when Mikel had gone missing, she couldn't help but feel that there was an atmosphere between them both. 'How are you guys holding up without Chris?' Jen asked, regretting the question. She wondered if it made her sound like she was checking up on the team.

'We've more or less all been assigned to something else. There's always some major crime going on in Nottingham, usually drugs or stabbings – but wherever the wind takes us.'

Anything that Jen could say at this point had the potential to be taken the wrong way. 'What are your thoughts on Hannah and your DI's relationship?' *Go for the girl talk*, she thought to herself, as they began to climb the stairs towards the team's office.

'Other than last year, I've not really seen her. I know

when she's been over at his because he usually comes in either completely exhausted on a Monday, or positively glowing if he's expecting her.'

'Admittedly, I don't know either of them that well, but they seem good together.'

Julie opened the door and led Jen into another corridor that she kind of recognised as she read the posters and notices on the walls.

'Are you wanting to set up in Chris' office?' Julie asked as she stopped outside an office that Jen also recognised.

'Oh no, no. I'm not here in that capacity.' Jen panicked. 'Plus, I don't want to go moving stuff around that he'll be cursing me for when he returns.'

'Okay, well, this is our office,' Julie said, walking through into a busy room. 'It's a bit different to when you were last here – everything we had has now been transferred to you guys in London. Like I said, we're kinda working on different stuff.'

'Where can I sit and not be in the way?' Jen asked.

'Anywhere that's empty,' Julie said, rather shortly.

The two of them were both taking part in some form of spoken dance battle, each making a step and waiting for the other to respond. Jen dropped her bag on a desk and plonked herself down on a chair. 'I guess I'll be here then,' she said softly, looking around at the other people nearby.

'Can I get you a drink?' Julie offered after a couple of tense seconds.

'Please. Tea, milk, no sugar if that's okay? I can make it if you direct me to where I need to be.'

'No, it's good. I'm about to make a round anyway.'

'Thanks, Julie. I know this is awkward and everything. I'm as surprised as you are that I've been sent back here.'

'Not a problem Jen. Make yourself at home. I'll do the teas.'

'Okay, thanks.'

'While I remember, Chris sent me an email with some interesting pictures attached. He said something about needing them for Jill's interview.' Julie turned back to speak to Jen.

'Ah yes, those will be of our victims.'

Jen surveyed the office once Julie had gone, turning to look out of the window she had sat herself next to and wondering if she could see her husband's workplace from there. She looked at the busy roundabout below and the few business professionals who were crossing at the lights. Was this what it would be like if she put her plan into action? Jen had already come to terms with the fact that, if anything did happen as far as her career was concerned, it might be a long time into the future. They had Mikel to find, and there were conversations to be had with both Chris and James before she could set the wheels in motion.

'Nice to see you back here again.' Jen was greeted by an older man who had now sat across from her at one of the other desks.

'I'm really sorry, I'm not good with faces. You'll have to remind me who you are again.'

'Greg Sanders. We met when you were here last time.'

'Ah yes. Sorry, Greg,'

'I hear you've come to join us for a couple of days?' He looked curious.

'Yes, there have been some developments on the case in London and they needed someone to come and speak to the social workers on Mikel's case. I got asked as DI Jackson is a bit ... busy ... at the moment.'

'Is that young Hannah keeping him on his toes?'

'I wouldn't want to comment.' Jen laughed.

'Good for him. He deserves to be happy and find someone nice.'

Jen bit her lip, not wanting to comment any further or say something she might later regret. It was almost like being under arrest! Anything she said could later be used against her upon Chris' return.

'I've just picked this up for you Jen,' Julie said, returning with a tray of drinks and a lanyard. 'It's the same one you had last time you were here. Save you having to going through that whole procedure business again.'

'Thanks so much.'

'Julie handed Greg his mug of something, and then proceeded to dish out the rest of the drinks on the tray.

'Where do you want to start?' Greg asked her.

'Start?' Jen was unsure what he meant.

'Sorry, I was under the impression you'd been sent back to lead the investigation.'

'Oh no, no ... I've been sent back to speak to Mikel's social workers.'

'How can we be of help then?'

Jen was speechless for a moment as Julie arrived back at her desk.

Come on, Jennifer, she thought to herself. 'Did you ever get anywhere with the CCTV from the petrol station?' she asked.

'We might have a vague image, but it isn't very clear. It looks like they knew where the cameras were and how to disguise themselves,' Julie responded as she sat on the corner of Greg's desk.

'Okay ... great.' She tried not to sound sarcastic. 'I remember there being an issue with a DI Holman getting witness reports processed. Is she in this building or situated elsewhere?'

'Afraid not, or I think we'd have all been down to her office to gee her up a bit,' Greg muttered.

'I think she's based somewhere near Radford, where the incident happened.'

'Okay, and Mikel's social worker?'

'We spoke to Holly Lord at her Nottingham office. I think she said that Jill mainly works on the road, but we have a mobile number for her.'

'Would you mind giving Jill a ring, Julie? Let's see if we can get her in'

'Not a problem.' Julie headed back to her desk.

'Greg, can you find out if Paula is back in her house? I don't think she's involved in this if she's just an emergency carer, but at least we know where she is if we need to speak to her further down the line.'

It had been so long since Jen had interviewed anyone, so she was in two minds whether to get right in there or leave the job to the pros.

'Jill says she's in the area and is going to pop in, in the next hour,' Julie said, rolling across the office on her chair.

'Thanks for that. I'll wait for Greg to finish up contacting Paula, and then I can give you both the lowdown on what we've got so far.'

'I'll get the CCTV images copied so you can have a look at those as well.'

Well, this was going down better than she'd expected. *Maybe she'd be home in time for tea after all?*

'Thank you for coming in to meet us.' Jen greeted Jill, who had sat herself down at the table opposite them. She had asked Julie to come in and assist her with the interview and be her back-up if she froze. This was Jen's moment to shine.

'That's okay. Have you got any news on Mikel?'

'Not as such, but we have a couple of interesting

developments that we're hoping you'll be able to help us with.'

'Anything I can do to help find him.'

'Our investigation has led us down a rather unexpected path.'

'Oh?'

'This might come as a shock but … we think that Mikel may have been caught up in a paedophile ring.'

'How has that happened?' Jill looked shocked. 'I thought he was taken by his dad?'

'It's all got something to do with his mum and where she came from before she was pulled out of the Trent.'

'I'm afraid you'd need to speak to Holly Lord on that one. She was his mother's social worker.'

'We've asked her to come in and speak to us later, actually.'

'I hope she'll be able to help you further.'

'Jill, I was wondering if you knew any more about the arson attack on Paula's house?' Julie asked.

'Oh my god. That was so awful. In all my time as a social worker, I've never had someone attack an emergency carer's house.'

'She was very lucky that she had an automatic fire alarm fitted. Do you know anyone who might have a grudge against Paula?' Julie continued.

'I guess there are plenty of parents whose children have been sent to live with Paula. It could have been any one of them.'

'But why wait till now?' Jen butted in.

Jill looked confused for a second. 'I honestly have no idea, but you don't think the arson had anything to do with Mikel?' Jill appeared shocked.

'I wondered if you could have a look over these

pictures for me?' Jen slipped the photo sheet Julie had received from Chris across the table and watched Jill's reaction.

'Oh my god. Are these children being ... abused?' Jill visibly swallowed.

'Maybe these are better photos for you to look at,' Julie followed up, slipping Jill another sheet.

Jill looked at the second sheet that showed the exact same children but looking healthier and happier. During the time it had taken Jen to drive up to Nottingham, Holly Lord had helped the team locate photos of the exact same children when they first went into care.

'I might recognise some of the kids in the second sheet,' came Jill's response.

'Would it surprise you if you knew that the children on the first sheet are the same as the second?' Jen asked.

'I had my suspicions, they all look so pale and ...' Jill tailed off. She put the second sheet on top of the first, as if she no longer wanted the pale and gaunt children looking up at her.

'So, you said you recognised some of them?'

'Possibly, but I'm not sure now. There's no way the children would end up there.'

'Where, Jill?' Jen asked.

'For a moment, I thought some of the kids on the second sheet were ones I had dealt with in care.' Jill fidgeted in her chair.

'Well, you're correct, Jill. All these children were in care in the East Midlands at some point.'

'No way.' *Was it Jen's imagination or had Jill responded a bit too quickly?* 'How the hell did they end up there? When I sign children off, it's because they've all been placed in suitable homes.'

'We were wondering the same thing, Jill. The other

connection is that all these kids were put into care as they had no living relatives to take them in,' Jen said.

'I'll have to go back to my office and check all this out.' Jill seemed very concerned now.

'Now, DI Jackson tells me that you are responsible for the children who are put into care in these situations,' Julie began again.

'Well ... er.' Jill began to visibly struggle. 'I can't believe I wasn't told any of this,' came her weak response.

'We managed to find out something else about these children, Jill. You were the one who signed each of them off, giving the impression they were all placed with well-respected foster families.'

'That isn't possible. There are so many kids out there who are put into care in the East Midlands. I'm not the social worker for all of them.'

'Just the ones who go missing, Jill?' Julie folded her arms and leant back slightly in her chair.

'You know what, Jill, I bet you couldn't believe your luck when Mikel appeared in Nottingham, because whoever you're working with was looking for him. Except you had to act quickly ... because he was asking for Lisa Carter.'

'I don't know what you're talking about. I'm not working with anyone, and I have no idea who this Lisa Carter is.' Jill stood up. 'I'm not under arrest here, am I?' She was starting to look panicky.

'No, you're just here to help us with our enquiries.'

'Well, in that case, I'm done. I can't really help you any further than I have, I'm afraid.'

'Let me sum all this up for you before you go,' Jen said, raising her voice slightly as Jill headed towards the door. 'I think, Jill, that the reason all these children ran away from care and ended up in a paedophile ring has something to do with you. When Mikel started talking to the police, you panicked and got someone to set fire to Paula's home so you could get him away – except there were people who cared a lot about Mikel, so you weren't able to just sweep it all under the carpet with help of an incompetent local DI.'

'I really don't know what you're talking about,' Jill muttered as she opened the interview room door.

'I'll escort you out,' Julie said, getting up from her chair.

'Don't go too far, we might need to speak to you again,' Jen shouted after her.

Jen managed to navigate herself back to the team's office, deep in thought about what they had learned from Jill. 'Can we get a tail put on Jill Stokes, the social worker?' she asked Greg as she sat down in the office chair.

'Already done. Colin is following her as we speak.'

'Perfect. Thank you, Greg.'

'I sat in and watched some of the interview. I decided pretty soon that it made sense to get someone following her.'

'Julie, she say much on the way out?' Jen asked, noticing Julie returning to the office.

'Not really, but as soon as she left she was on her phone. Do we need to be worried for the team in London?'

'I'm sure they'll be fine,' Jen replied, although she wondered if she had better phone and give them all an update on the proceedings so far.

'I'm still not sure about this house fire,' Julie said as Jen started to call London.

'What do you mean?'

'Well, do we really think it was just a ploy to get Mikel out of the house?' Jen put her phone back in her pocket and rolled her chair across the floor to Julie's desk.

'I'd say so, yes. I wonder if this mystery person found out that Mikel had been talking to the police and couldn't wait any longer, so he tried to torch the place.'

'At least Paula had that automatic fire alarm fitted then, otherwise who knows what might have happened to them both ...'

Chapter Forty

DI Chris Jackson

Nothing much had happened since Jen's departure to Nottingham, though Chris didn't know what Hannah had written in this email Max had mentioned to him. All he knew was that the ball was most definitely going to start rolling. It was just a shame that they couldn't prepare anything until they knew where they were going and who they were going after. With the help of Holly Lord, he had managed to put a photo sheet together for Jen to use in her interview with Jill, in hope it might stir a memory somewhere. He had also managed to speak to Paula, who was back in her home, trying to mask the smell and get the repairs done to her front door and hallway. He hadn't told her what was going on, just in case she was more heavily involved. He would leave that up to Jen and the team in Nottingham.

'We've had a response,' Hannah announced, and the office went into an immediate flurry of excitement.

He really hoped it would be something positive as he got up from the desk and followed Sam into the meeting room, where he found Max and Hannah in deep conversation.

'What's it say?' Sam asked before she'd even sat down.

'It says we've got four hours to mount an operation.'

'Sorry, what?' Chris couldn't tell whether he'd heard correctly.

'This mystery person has agreed to let you have Mikel for twelve hours.'

'Where do we pick him up from?' Chris asked, unsure whether his tone of voice was matching the way he felt.

'The hotel on junction 4 of the M1.'

'There's no way they're just going to let us pick him up,' Sam commented, reading Chris' thoughts.

'Well here's the thing ...' Hannah said as she began to explain to them both what she had done in order to speed things up. Chris wasn't sure what his reaction should have been to the news that Mikel was being sold to them for twelve hours for £30,000 – never mind how reckless Hannah had been. While the conversation was going on around him between Hannah and Sam, he was transported back to their argument in Bakewell. Was this another example of Hannah doing what needed to be done? The ends justifying the means? Was he really so ignorant as to how things were achieved in this murky world that she worked in? Was he living a comfortable life as a DI in Nottingham, unaware of what real police work actually involved?

'I've just got off the phone with Jen,' Max began, bringing Chris back to reality. 'She says they've interviewed the social worker, and she made a quick exit from the interview when the children were mentioned.'

'Does she think that Jill has something to do with it?' he asked.

'It looks that way. They've got a tail on her now, and requests for warrants and telephone records are being made to the courts.'

'Do we think we might have just been compromised?'

'What do you mean?' Hannah questioned.

'Well, if Jill *is* involved, she would have surely been straight on the phone to whoever-he-is, telling him the police are onto them?'

'But will she be thinking it's just the local bobbies and not the big guys?'

'I don't think it's any coincidence that we've only just received the email about Mikel,' Chris said grimly.

'That might be a risk we're going to have to take,' came the response from Hannah, which shocked him. Was she expecting him to go into this not knowing whether whoever they were going to meet knew he was being investigated and tracked down?

'Well, I'm going to put it out there then: I don't think this is necessarily a good idea.' Chris was uncertain of the reaction he was about to receive.

'I understand why you're concerned, Chris, but you can't back out now. This is our chance to get Mikel back,' came Max's response.

'Or I could just be walking into a trap and end up on a slab next to Dana?' Chris said. He sat there, letting the conversation go on around him and hoping someone would talk some sense.

'Obviously you can't be there, Hannah,' Chris heard Max say. *Was this how things had gone down with Jen last year?* They'd managed to track Jess down – but Jen and Hannah were both highly trained compared to him, and it wasn't like everyone had walked away from the incident without injury.

'Can you get a team on the ground at this hotel pretty sharp-ish?' was another snippet of information Chris heard as he was half lost in his thoughts.

'But what if this mystery guy is familiar with the staff there? Wouldn't that cause an issue?' Sam questioned.

At last someone was talking sense, he thought to himself.

'Has anyone actually thought about whether I'm expected to do something to Mikel in the presence of this person?' Chris finally spoke again, unsure whether what he was saying was in his head or out loud. He soon realised it was the latter. 'Because I'm sorry, I don't care how you guys work here. I'm not going *there*,' he finished.

'We wouldn't expect you to, Chris. There are ways around this; things these types of people do that don't involve anything sexual,' explained Hannah.

'Gee, thanks Hannah. That makes me feel tonnes better.'

'We need to prepare for all eventualities,' came Max's response.

'Hold up, how do you normally go about catching these people? Do you really abuse these kids further for your own gain?'

'Chris.'

'No, Hannah, I'm being serious. As you and Max both like to remind me, I'm just a detective inspector. I'm not some super detective who will do anything possible to save the day … I need some air.' He got up from his seat and walked out of the meeting room. He needed to be free of the stagnant air of the office and the suffocation he was feeling in that meeting.

'If the ends justify the means,' he said to himself as he sensed somebody rushing after him.

'Hannah asked me to show you to a fire exit. She didn't want you getting lost in this bloody building,' Sam said.

'Thanks, Sam.' Chris followed her in silence.

'This is where Chloe used to creep off to for a sneaky fag,' Sam said, opening the fire exit door onto a huge platform with stairs leading down to safety. 'Will you be okay getting back?' she asked Chris.

That's if I plan on actually going back, Chris thought darkly. 'Yeah, thanks Sam,' he responded as she disappeared back the way she came.

Chris sat down on the steps and looked out onto London – nothing much to see, but at least he was free for now.

Chris wasn't sure how long he'd been sat there when he

heard someone open the door. He looked up in order to apologise and saw Max standing there.

'Sorry, just getting my head together.'

'Take all the time you want. I come up here sometimes to look out over London. I tend to do it most when I'm questioning the decisions I've made.'

Chris smiled up at him and left him to ponder whatever was on his mind. He surely had more things to concern him than Chris did, who was sat there worrying about his relationship with a girl and a single difficult mission he was being asked to help with.

'She's a good girl, you know, Hannah,' Max suddenly said out of the blue. 'I know she can be ... let's say, a bit wild and impulsive ... but her heart in is the right place. She reminds me very much of how Jen used to be.'

Chris didn't really know what to say.

'I'm sorry you've been dragged into this Chris. If I'd had my way, you'd be back in your Nottingham office clueless about the world you're in now.'

'I guess Jen is to blame for all that.'

'Yes and no. You're a great guy, Chris. You were the one who tracked *us* down, remember?'

'So, it's all my fault.' Chris laughed.

'No, it's your policing DNA; your desire to get justice for whoever has been wronged, to bring Jen home to her family, to find out whatever happened to Daisy, to find Mikel. You aren't suited to local policing because you always want more than what you can achieve at the level you're currently working at.'

'I'm beginning to realise that the mean streets of Nottingham are a lot safer than here.'

'If I'd known how this was going to play out, I'd have sent someone else out with Hannah and kept you out of it.'

When he thought back to that night at the mansion, he was glad he'd been there with Hannah to do the stuff they'd done, because at least he knew she was safe with him. But would he have known this was even happening if he'd been kept out of it? There was so much he didn't know about Detective Hannah Littlefair and, though he wondered if he was just starting to see the real her now she'd dropped the sex kitten act, he knew if he hadn't been here, she would still have gone to the party ... maybe even done the same things they'd done together with another detective.

'There are lines I just can't cross,' came Chris' response as his thoughts returned to Mikel and the big event that was scheduled to happen three and a half hours from now.

'And I wouldn't ask you to, Chris. But I don't think we can do this without you. We are too far along – the end game is coming, I fear.'

Great. Now he was being guilt tripped.

'I'm going to head back and make sure Hannah hasn't made any more rash decisions. Come back when you're ready,' Max said as he made his way back through the door.

Chris realised he hadn't actually told Max one way or another whether he was going to do this. Did that mean he was going to have to do it whether he wanted to or not? Or did Max just know he would?

He sat there for a while longer and thought about Hannah and their relationship. Maybe after this was all over, he'd need to have a proper conversation with her about the future, her work and where things stood between the two of them.

Having navigated the building, Chris made it back to the meeting room and stood there for a while, unnoticed, as he watched Hannah positively glowing whilst she, Max and Sam drew up their battle plans.

Chris made his decision. If things went tits up, at least he'd have done everything in his power to bring Mikel home.

'I need someone to get me one of those matchbox cars,' Chris said as he was being fitted up in his outfit for the evening's mission.

'Why?' Hannah looked puzzled.

'Something I told Mikel when I first met him. I think it might put him at ease a bit.'

'What if he blows your cover?'

'Then you'll be there to rescue me.' *At least he hoped to God someone would.*

Chris pulled on a freshly iron shirt as Hannah demonstrated where everything was in the pair of jeans he was expected to wear.

'So your panic button is in this pocket.'

'So don't put my hands in my pockets?'

'Something like that, but once you've got them on, you can have a feel around and work out where stuff is.'

'There's more?'

'A tracking device is situated in the stitching, but you don't need to worry about that.'

'Remind me never to ask you to do my washing.'

'You've got maids who do that, remember?'

'Remind me never to introduce you.' Chris reached over towards Hannah and pushed the loose strand of hair behind her ear as the electric charge crackled between them. 'Han, if—'

'I've got your back, Chris. You've got nothing to worry about. Honest.' She smiled at him. 'You just need to remember everything from the briefing before you go.'

'Easier said than done.'

'Plus Sam will be on reception at the hotel, so you really have nothing to worry about.'

'Thanks. That makes me feel so much better.' He laughed.

'Back to your clothing,' Hannah instructed. 'The camera is located in your jacket in one of the buttons, but you won't need to worry about that, anyway. Oh, and there's also a recording device.'

'And if I take it off?'

'We'll still get everything.'

'Great.'

'You'll be fine. Once this is over, I'll let you take me away somewhere nice for the weekend.'

'Sounds lovely,' he said sarcastically, 'You got any pain relief? Headache pending.'

'I'll get you some good stuff for that.'

'Well, just make sure it doesn't completely knock me out as well.'

'We can't have you falling asleep on the job.' She finished what she was doing to his clothing. 'Right, you're kitted out. You'll need to collect a mobile phone from Max, but otherwise I think you're ready to roll,' she said, handing him the jeans. She then watched him wobbling as he put them on. 'I must say, you are looking rather hot.'

'Tell me about it. This room is far too warm.' As he finished getting dressed, Hannah moved over towards him, pulled him close and kissed him.

'Stay safe, Inspector Jackson.'

He could have easily stayed safe there with her in his arms, but he had a job to do and that involved bringing Mikel home … or die trying.

He was alone as he drove out of London, onto the M1 and up to junction 4. He'd had a briefing with Max and

Hannah. His team back in Nottingham were ready to search Jill's office and home, having already secured her mobile phone records. This was his time to shine and, though he knew back-up would be just round the corner, driving in a two-seater sports car with thirty thousand pounds sat next to him, he wondered if he could just make a run for it instead – although the mobile phone he'd been issued along with the tracking device in his jeans would make sure he didn't get too far. As he drove, he thought about his parents. He decided he'd take Hannah to meet them when this was all over because, despite the differences in their work and how they got the bad guys, the end goal was the same. He was beginning to have a strange feeling that this was the girl he wanted to spend the rest of his life with. He found himself thinking about Dana and the life she must have led – not that they knew the full extent of it, but he had a pretty good idea. He just hoped he would be able to pull this last bit of the mission off and bring her son home.

Chapter Forty-One

Detective Hannah Littlefair

'Everyone in position?' Hannah spoke through the mouthpiece. She was situated just behind the hotel in a white pick-up van with two other colleagues; not the most glamorous place to be hiding out, but the best that could be arranged at such short notice.

'In position,' came the replies from the other teams.

'Mark is showing as five minutes out; everyone hold position.'

Hannah fiddled with the screen in front of her. They had the hotel's CCTV cameras and the cameras attached to both Sam and Chris. Each of her colleagues were listening to various conversations through their headsets.

'Why haven't we got a visual on our target or the boy?' Hannah asked. 'Has anyone got a visual?' Hannah spoke again into her mouthpiece. No response came back as she scanned the hotel CCTV cameras. 'I've got something.' Hannah picked up her headset and channelled in.

'Good evening, sir. Welcome to Brokley Inn. Do you and your son have a room booked with us here today?' Sam's voice filled Hannah's earpiece.

'Target one is checking into the hotel,' Hannah repeated. 'Anyone got a visual?'

'Can I take your son's name please, sir?'

'Is that necessary?'

'No, sir. I was just going to get him a space reserved in the play area for this evening.'

'He won't be needing that, thank you. We've got an early start tomorrow. It'll be early bed for this one.'

Good try, Sam, Hannah thought to herself

'Can anyone confirm the child is Mikel?' Hannah asked again as she searched through the hotel's security cameras in hope of getting confirmation for herself.

'Your room is on the ground floor, sir. If you head towards the lifts but turn right instead, then your room is just on the left.'

'Thank you.'

'Is there anything else I can help with, sir?'

'No thanks. That will be all.'

'Have a great night.'

It was at that point Sam's camera was pointed directly at Mikel and their target.

'I want that picture circulating to everyone,' Hannah ordered as the photo filled the screen. 'We have a photo of our target. Circulating now.'

Hannah sat and looked at the photo she had in front of her. She certainly didn't recognise the guy from anywhere and didn't think she'd seen him at the party.

'Gold Command? Over.'

'Loud and clear.'

'We've got a photo of our target. I've just circulated it to our teams here. I need you to get this photo sent to the Nottingham team and Jen to see if we can get an ID.'

'Okay, Echo One. Over.'

While they were all in their positions waiting for action, Max had stayed back at the office in a similar position to the one Hannah was in, observing everything that was going on and more. He had the contacts and power to pull this whole operation if it went south.

'Mark is entering the car park,' came the notification Hannah had been waiting for.

'Everybody hold their positions,' Hannah instructed the team again as she waited for visuals of Chris arriving.

Here we go, Hannah thought to herself. *Please don't screw this up, Chris.*

DI Chris Jackson

Chris had been full of nerves as he drove into the hotel car park. He had no idea where everyone was situated; he just knew that they had his back. He could also feel a headache coming on. Hannah had given him some magic pills, but he hadn't wanted the inevitable side effects. He had enough problems with his vision and balance as it was. He knew that he should have made the team aware he was having these issues before he'd even stepped into that helicopter with Hannah. He promised himself as soon as he got back home, he'd go straight to the doctors and make sure they ran some tests at least. There was no way this was just down to stress, he realised that now.

His wristwatch pinged as he received a message on Joe's mobile.

We are in room G9.

This was it. He was committed, and there was no way he could back out now. Time to get into character.

Just parking up, will be with you shortly, Chris typed on the phone. He climbed out of the car, only just remembering to take the thirty grand with him. Hannah had reassured him that the money was trackable, so no one was going anywhere with it. He pulled his suit jacket on and headed towards the hotel where Mikel was hopefully awaiting his fate. As Chris strode towards the building, he looked around him, hoping to spot someone who would give him a tiny bit of reassurance.

His prayers were answered when the hotel reception door opened, and there was Sam at the reception desk.

'Good afternoon, sir,' she greeted him.

'Afternoon. I was wondering if you could direct me to room G9 please?'

'Certainly, sir. If you head towards the lifts but turn right, it will be on your left.'

'Thank you.'

'Is there anything else I can help you with today, sir?'

'No, thank you.'

Chris followed the directions Sam had given him. He located the room easily and knocked ...

Chapter Forty-Two

Jen Garner

'Any news on the warrants?' Jen asked as Julie put her phone down.

'There's some hold-up in court apparently, but Greg said he is trying to get them through as quickly as possible.'

'Anything from Colin?'

'The last I heard, he was sitting outside Jill's house. Officer Haywood has been sent to keep him company.'

'Saves him sitting there getting bored.'

'He said he'd radio in as soon as there was any movement.'

Jen returned to nervously fidgeting and clicking around pointless websites. There wasn't much more she could do from here until the warrants were issued, and then she didn't even know if she'd be allowed to take part in the search.

'Jen, I've just had an email through. It's addressed to you.'

'Anything interesting?' Jen asked as she moved her chair over towards Julie.

'From Max Carver.'

'Ahh, the boss. Probably checking up on me.'

Julie opened the email as Jen scooted over to see what had come through.

'Do you want me to leave you to it?' Julie asked.

'No, you're good. Don't worry.' Jen started to read that Mikel was now at the hotel and Detective Jackson was en-route.

'Open up the attachments. Let's get a look at this guy then.' Julie clicked on the image and waited for it to load up on the screen. A very pixelated image of a man appeared.

'Can we do anything to get the image cleared up?' Jen tutted.

'I can send it down to the tech guys, but it might take some time.'

'Anything is worth a try because, right now, I don't have a clue who he is,' Jen said as she screwed up her eyes, trying to spark a memory. 'Don't suppose you've got any thoughts?'

'You're asking the wrong person. A huge part of me wants to say I recognise him, but I wouldn't want to lead you to the wrong person. I might be a bit more helpful if he was a Nottingham criminal, but I've got nothing.'

'Not to worry. No doubt they'll be running it through the criminal databases in London anyway.'

It was at that point Julie's phone rang.

'It's Greg. He's got the warrants. Grab your stuff, Jen, we've got some property to search.' Julie pulled her jacket from the back of her chair. 'Trudie?' Julie shouted towards her colleague.

'Will meet you there. I'll get some uniform on the case as well.'

'Thanks, Trudie. Don't be too long or you'll miss the action.'

Jen followed Julie as she ran down the stairs and into the nearest car.

'Give Colin a call and let him know we're on our way over,' Julie said, throwing the phone over to Jen.

Jen looked at the phone, found the contact book and dialled Colin's number.

'Julie! Is there any news?'

'Er, sorry, Colin, this is Jen. We've got the warrant and we're on our way over.'

'Righto. We were starting to get bored sat here.'

'The satnav says we're five minutes out.'

'See you when you get here.'

Jen ended the call and held onto the phone as Julie raced through the streets, heading to Jill's house.

Jen really hoped that the house would give them something to go on, if only to confirm their suspicions that Jill had something to do with these kids who had found themselves part of a paedophile ring instead of a loving home. As they drove through the streets, Jen tried to think back to the original George Crawford case and all the main players. She'd been sure that they'd all been rounded up but obviously not, given what had gone on to happen to both Chloe and Dana.

'How do you think she's gonna take it?' Julie turned around and asked.

'If she's got any sense, she'll just let us do our thing and we'll be out of there.'

'Should I have organised firearms back up?' Julie suddenly sounded anxious.

'I'm sure we'll be fine. She doesn't look like the type to be in possession of a firearm.'

'Is there a type?' Julie raised her eyebrows.

'Quite possibly, yes,' Jen said, although she pondered the question herself.

They pulled up on Jill's street and parked next to Colin. 'Has there been any movement from the house?' Julie asked as her window rolled down.

'We've not seen anything, boss.'

'Have you heard anything from uniform?'

'They're waiting around the corner.'

'Ready to serve this warrant, Jen?' Julie asked as she parked the car, bringing Jen back into the moment.

'After you.' Jen opened the car door. She'd let Julie have her moment of glory.

They approached the semi-detached house, and Julie knocked on the door as well as ringing the doorbell.

'Jill Stokes, this is Nottingham major crimes unit. We have a warrant to search your premises,' Julie shouted at the top of her voice as Jill herself opened her front door.

'We have a warrant to search your home, Jill,' Jen repeated. 'If you could let us in, we'll try to make this as painless as possible.'

Jill seemed not to react as she turned and led Jen and Julie into her large living room. As they both entered the room, they started to scan the walls and surfaces, which were full of photos of her and somebody who must have been her husband.

'All clear,' Julie spoke into her radio.

'If you can tell me what you're looking for, I might be able to help you.' Jill spoke for the first time since they'd arrived.

'We have a warrant here for your home, office and car to search for anything that relates to the missing children who were previously in your care,' Julie said, handing over the warrant. Jill took it and then dropped it like it was on fire.

'Not sure if I can be any help,' Jill said as she tried to fake the bravado Jen had seen many times before.

'Good. We won't be here long, then.' Julie called for a uniformed officer to sit with Jill while she helped Jen and the team with the search.

As they turned to leave the room, Julie stopped behind Jen. 'What does your husband do?' she suddenly questioned.

'He's in the fire service.' Jill looked at her pointedly.

'Ah. Maybe that's why he looks familiar,' Julie said as she left the room. 'Found anything of interest?' she asked Jen, who had gone upstairs with Greg.

'Not at this moment in time, but there's a room with a locked door over there.' Greg pointed.

'I'll go down and ask her if she has a key,' Julie said as she headed back downstairs again. 'She says it's her husband's office,' Julie shouted up the stairs a few seconds later. 'But she doesn't have access.'

'Only one thing for it then,' Jen said as her boot made contact with the door, leaving Greg looking at her like she was crazy.

'Are you sure this is a good idea?' he questioned.

'You know what, Greg? I'm past caring,' Jen said as her boot hit the door again, and it finally gave way just as Julie came up to see what was happening.

'What the hell are you doing?' Jill shouted from the bottom of the stairs. 'I'll have you for that.'

Jen laughed as she opened the door. 'After you, boss.'

Julie walked into the room and stopped.

'What the *fuck*?' Jen gasped as she followed.

The room was covered in photos of children in A4 frames. All of them were smiling and looked happy and healthy.

'This looks like a modelling agency.'

'Yes, but I have a bad feeling it isn't,' Jen said as she opened a drawer to find office stationery.

Julie looked round at all the pictures of children. 'Do we think these are the missing kids?' she asked.

'I need this computer bagging up and rushed to the tech team,' Jen shouted out of the room as two officer came in and immediately removed the computer. Jen started to search the room when her attention was drawn to a photograph in a silver frame that was situated on the desk next to the computer. *No … it couldn't be? Could it?* Jen's attention was drawn away from the photo when she became aware that Julie had disappeared back downstairs.

'What does your husband do again?' Jen heard Julie questioning Jill.

'Like I said, he works for the fire service ... he's a watch manager.'

'What's the office upstairs all about then?'

'I have no idea. It's his personal space.' Jill's voice sounded full of concern and confusion.

'Come with me,' Julie ordered as she practically dragged Jill upstairs into the office.

Jill looked round the room, clearly trying to fake amazement. 'I've never seen any of this.'

'Come on, Jill. You must think we were born yesterday.' Jen laughed. 'We have seized the computer and are searching for other items.'

'Who are the kids?' Julie shouted as she squared up to Jill.

'I ... I have no idea.'

'They're the missing children, aren't they?' Julie shouted in her face.

It was then that something seemed to hit her. '*Shit*, Jen. I think I've figured out who's in the photo with Mikel.' Julie backed away from Jill and rushed out of the room.

'Greg, stay with her and make sure she doesn't destroy anything,' Jen shouted as she followed Julie back down the stairs and into the living room.

'I know who the guy in the photo is,' Julie said again.

'Which photo?'

'The one that's been sent down from London.' Julie pointed at one of the photos on the wall. 'The man who is with Mikel is Jill's husband. He was the watch manager at the fire at Paula's house – Kevin.'

'Oh wow ... we need to get the message back to London.' As Jen pulled out her phone to ring Max, Julie went pounding back up the stairs.

'Where is your mobile phone?' Jen heard Julie shouting.

'Downstairs! I left it downstairs,' came the response back from Jill, who now sounded scared. Though Jen knew Greg was up there already with them, she thought she'd better go and investigate. As she climbed back up the stairs, she found Jill was pinned to the wall by Julie with Greg trying to intervene.

'Have you contacted your husband since we've been here?' Julie continued to shout. 'Does he know we're here?'

'No, my phone's charging in the kitchen. Why?'

Jen watched as Julie let go of Jill, pushing past both her and Greg so she could run back down the stairs.

'Julie?' Jen shouted after her

'We need to find her phone. If she's told Kevin we're here then Chris and Mikel could be in real danger.'

Chapter Forty-Three

DI Chris Jackson

Chris could hear the sound of kids' television coming from behind the door and voices. He wasn't sure how many voices there were, or whether they were just coming from the television. He heard someone approach the door and unlock it.

'Joe Kendal?'

Chris looked directly at the man speaking to him. 'Yes. I'm here to meet the boy.'

'Ah yes, come in.'

Chris had a decision to make, and he knew that once he stepped over the threshold, there would be no turning back.

'I've brought the money,' Chris said, holding up the briefcase.

'Come and make yourself comfortable, Joe. Jake is watching TV at the moment.'

Chris walked into the hotel room and noticed Mikel perched on the end of the bed, watching some cartoon that was playing out in front of him.

'Hello,' Chris said to Mikel as he turned to acknowledge him. 'What are you watching there?'

'Have you had far to travel to meet us, Joe?' the mystery guy interrupted.

'Quite a way to meet this young man, yes. Yourself?'

'We travel quite a bit, from party to party, and meet our clients in various locations.' Now the man was in the light of the hotel room, Chris looked over at him and suddenly realised who he was talking to. Chris felt his heart rate start to increase as his vision blurred. He had spoken to this man only days before outside Paula's house. *Just breathe*, he told himself.

'It was a good party the other night,' Chris said. 'I don't think I saw you?'

'No, I stay out the way and let the staff do all the work. I must say your new wife is very attractive.'

Chris smiled. 'In truth, she's as thick as pig shit – a total bimbo who only married me for my money, and she thinks I don't realise it. She has her uses, though – if you know what I mean.' Chris winked at the guy.

'I saw, don't you worry.'

'You going to get your shoes on then Jake, and grab your stuff? Then we'll be heading off.' Chris saw his way out of the room and away from this monster.

'I've had a change of heart, Joe. Why don't you stay here with Jake and I'll just sit and watch? Who knows? Maybe I'll join in as well.'

Chris' blood ran cold, and the bile rose in his throat. He put his hands into his jeans pockets and fingered the panic button. 'I'd prefer it if it was just Jake and myself, if I'm honest with you.'

'I'll just watch then. Don't mind me.'

This was going to get very difficult. *How was he going to get out of this one?*

Chris moved over and stroked Mikel's hair. He was amazed that the boy didn't flinch or cower away. He just sat there watching TV.

'Okay then. It'll be more fun if you stay, but at least tell me your name. I can't keep calling you "X" all night, can I?'

'Clive, Clive Bigsby.'

Things were suddenly starting to make sense – Clive was probably just a fake name. Chris couldn't believe he was stood there talking to this bloke while gently stroking a poor child's hair.

'You look familiar though, Joe.'

'You've probably just watched my wife too many times on the CCTV footage.'

'I feel like I've seen you somewhere before. What is it you do for a living again?'

'I live off the money I made before the banks crashed. I bet big and it paid off.'

'When was that, ten years ago?'

Chris' knowledge of the banking crisis was being tested.

'Oh no, before that. I got my money out in 2007. I had reinvested heavily and I was lucky.' Chris forced a chuckle. 'It now funds my lifestyle and, when wifey is out with her dumb friends, I explore some of my darker vices ...'

'Young boys and class A drugs,' Kevin finished his sentence for him.

'They're so pure, especially at this age.'

'I know what you mean. Jake, will you turn those damn cartoons off and come and sit here with me?' Kevin ordered the boy, who obeyed immediately.

'I looked through that catalogue you sent me in great detail. Tell me, where do you keep all these kids?' Chris was determined he was going to get something positive out of this at least.

'Now that would be telling – but I keep them close, don't you worry.'

'I think you and I are going to have a great working relationship, Clive. Especially if you can provide me with boys like this, and drugs as pure as those I took the other night.' Chris couldn't believe the words that were coming out of his mouth as he tried to meet Mikel's line of vision. The boy was now looking into the middle distance, almost as if he'd been switched off. 'Why don't we order room service, get something with a little sparkle in?' he said, trying to sound jovial and turning back to Kevin.

'I don't think they do room service, Joe. Not that kind of place.'

'And no mini bar either,' Chris said as he stalled for time by looking through the cupboards. 'Why don't you go down to the bar, Clive? Give me and Jake some time to get to know each other, open a tab and I'll pay it off when I leave.'

'Or you could just give me your card?'

Chris reached into his back pocket, glad that he'd been reminded to take his fake ID out with him. 'Here.' He passed it over.

'Why don't you take your clothes off, Jake?' Kevin ordered as Mikel stood up and began to remove his clothing in a sort of robotic way. How far was Chris going to have to go before he could get Kevin out of the room and Mikel to safety?

'Why don't you two make yourself comfortable?' Kevin suggested. 'And I'll go and get us something to get the party started.' There was no reaction from Mikel as he stripped and got into the bed.

'Splash out on some champagne; I think we're going to be celebrating tonight,' Chris said as he began to take his shirt off .

'You know, I'm sure I know you from somewhere. Are you sure you're not a police officer from Nottingham?'

Chris laughed. 'Do you seriously think I'd be caught naked in a hotel room with a young boy if I was?' That was the first honest thing Chris had said all night, and his delivery would have been spot on too.

'Don't have too much fun without me,' Kevin said as he left the room.

How the hell was he going to get both of them out of this situation before Kevin arrived back with the drinks? He looked around the room for a way out, then remembered they were on the ground floor. Maybe that was part of Hannah's plan, so they could get out easily if there was a problem.

'Listen, Mikel, we've not got long before he gets back. I'm going to throw this chair through the window. I need you to climb out the window and run, okay?' Mikel didn't answer, and Chris was unsure if he realised who he was. 'Mikel, listen to me. I'm with Lisa Carter and we're going to get you out of here, but I need your help, okay?'

Mikel's eyes lit up as he began to climb out of the bed. 'Man with the car with blue flashing lights?'

'Yes, exactly! Here I brought you this,' Chris said as he reached into his jacket pocket and pulled out the matchbox police car. 'Mikel, as soon as the chair goes through the window, I need you to run like you've never run before. Don't worry about any cuts or anything, just run and someone will be there to take you to safety, I promise.'

Chris hoped that the whole conversation had been heard by Hannah and the team on the other end. He picked up the chair.

'You coming too?' Mikel suddenly asked.

'I'll be right behind you, I promise,' Chris lied. 'Ready …'

'What about my mum? Will you take me back to her?'

Chris knew his time was going to start running out as he stood there semi-naked with the chair in his hand. He didn't have the heart to lie to the child again but, at the risk of him breaking down or causing a scene, a white lie wouldn't do any harm for now, as long as it got Mikel to safety and out of this dangerous situation.

'She's waiting for you back in Nottingham.' Chris heard the key card activate in the door and the sickening click that followed. 'You've got to go now, Mikel.' Chris threw the chair through the window, watching as Mikel climbed out just as Kevin stormed through the door.

'What the fuck?' Kevin dropped the tray of drinks he was carrying and launched himself towards the window. Chris had to do everything in his power to make sure Mikel got away and clear. It hadn't crossed Chris' mind that Kevin might have a gun as he stood there shirtless, and he had no time to find the panic button either.

Without a second thought, he threw himself at Kevin, trying to grab for a broken glass bottle as they both landed on the floor in a heap. Kevin wasn't going to go down without a fight either, and the two of them exchanged punches as the shards of glass embedded themselves into Chris' bare back. *Did they not have a bigger hotel room they could have been put in for this eventuality?* Chris knew that all he needed to do was to make sure Kevin wasn't able to get to any gun that he probably was carrying. As another shard pierced his skin, he heard the sound he'd been waiting for.

'I suggest you stay very still, Kevin Teddington, or I will not hesitate in putting a bullet through your skull.'

Did Sam even know how to fire a gun? Did he still need to work out a strategy of how to get the guy off him? Then a gun fired and Chris winced, wondering if he was about to feel the searing pain of a bullet as it burrowed through his skin.

'I will not miss next time,' came Sam's voice and, at that moment, more people piled into the small hotel room, and Chris let himself think for a second that this was all over and he could go back to being a DI in the quiet city of Nottingham. Instead, he felt the full force of Kevin's fist connect with his nose and the distinct cracking noise he'd heard so many times on the streets but never with the pain. Seconds later, the weight from Kevin was lifted off him by men in balaclavas. Chris found himself lying half naked on the floor, shards of glass embedded into his back, and pain like he had never felt before radiating from his face as he looked up at the team who had assembled around him. He watched from his position as the gun was taken out of Sam's hands, who was clearly shaken by the whole experience.

'Can you sit up, Inspector?' a voice from above asked him.

'I think so.'

'We'll take it steady. I'll get two of the team to help you.'

'In this space?' Chris tried to laugh as he attempted to move himself. 'Mikel? Did Mikel get out okay?' He suddenly remembered.

'He's with the medical crew as we speak, Inspector.'

He sat up and cringed at the pain in his back, followed by the realisation his nose was broken.

'If we get you off this floor, I'll get someone to assess your back before we send you to A&E.'

'Would you fill out a feedback form for me and put a request in that they make the rooms a bit bigger?' he joked through the pain.

'Just found this bath mat. If we put it on the floor in front of him, we should be able to get him out of here without glass in his feet too.' Chris heard another voice, and a second paramedic stood in front of him.

As the paramedics moved behind Chris, they helped him onto his feet. That was when he heard Hannah, and the sound of her voice gave him a renewed energy to get out of there. As he walked over the bath mat and out of the door, someone put a foil sheet over his shoulders.

'We don't want to put a blanket over you because of the embedded glass. This was the lightest thing we could find.'

Chris almost laughed. Was he really about to be paraded into the car park in a foil sheet and his torn and bloody jeans? It wasn't going to be the most glamorous shot of him for the next day's paper.

'Don't worry, we're parked round the back,' one of the paramedics said, seemingly reading his mind. 'We'll get you comfortable and have you straight into A&E.'

'There was me hoping to make the front pages in the morning.' Chris smiled and regretted it as the searing pain from his face reminded him of the broken nose.

As they led him through the now empty hotel, he caught sight of Hannah, finally, as she looked over at him as smiled, mouthing the words 'hope you're okay', before she returned to running the show and what was about to be the clean-up operation. Chris didn't know if he would see her again that night, or even if he'd get to return to their offices to help with the clear up. He was a victim now, and he was going to be processed as one.

Jen Garner

Jen had been sat in the team's office waiting for news since her phone call with Max. They'd arrested Jill and had her sat in the cells, waiting to see how things played out in London before they pressed her for more information. Jen studied the silver photo frame she had retrieved from Kevin's desk. She now knew that Kevin was one of the people in the photo, but it was the second person in the photo who really worried her. *How the hell were Kevin and Jessica connected?* Could Kevin be the mystery person who had sold her and Chloe out? It made sense, if he lived and worked in the area ...

'You okay? You look deep in thought?' Greg asked.

'Yeah, there is something about this photo that's bugging me.'

'Want me to get it scanned onto the system?'

Jen was about to take a breath to answer when the office phone rang.

'Jen Garner,' she said, snatching it up before anyone else could.

'Jen, it's Max. I can't talk for long, but I knew you'd all be waiting for news. We've got him, Jen. We've got Mikel, and Chris Jackson is okay. He has some minor injuries, but nothing to worry about.'

'Thank God. Okay, boss. Talk later.' Jen turned as the rest of the team looked in her direction. 'They've got Mikel.' A cheer went up in the room. 'Chris is okay too. Some minor injuries, but nothing that can't be fixed.'

Julie came straight over to Jen and hugged her. 'Thank you,' Jen choked out, unsure where the emotion came from as she broke down. After everything that had happened in the last week, they now had Mikel; he was safe. She would make sure he would never have to go through the same thing again.

As Jen pulled away from Julie, she noticed that Julie was crying too. 'You did it, Jen. You saved that little boy,' Julie sobbed.

'I'm pretty sure your DI played a big part in it too.'

Epilogue

Jen Garner

When everything had been tied up in Nottingham, Jen had returned home. She hadn't said anything to the team regarding her concerns about the photograph as they were all in a celebration mode. She'd managed to scan a copy for herself to send to Max. If there was a connection between Kevin and the Crawfords, they'd find it – but right now she needed to concentrate on her family.

She sneaked in to see Melanie and Alex while they slept and kissed them both, telling them she was home safe. She had sobbed into James' arms that night, because there was so much about Dana they still didn't know. It would no doubt take weeks, if not months, before everything came out. Although, just before she'd left the Nottingham offices, Julie had handed her a package.

'This was found in Gordon Parks' office. It's addressed to Lisa Carter. I've not submitted it into evidence, just in case it was something important.'

Jen had taken it from Julie and placed it in her bag as she left. *What on earth could it be?*

What had really worried Jen was that there had been another connection to her past life in Nottingham. She wondered again how often Chloe had been in touching distance without her realising.

'What's this in your bag?' Alex asked the next morning as he pulled the package out. 'Who's Lisa Carter?'

'A friend of mine. I forgot to post it last night as I wanted to come home and see you guys,' Jen said as she kissed his head.

Alex seemed to accept this and skipped off.

Jen took the package into the living room and began to open it. She'd completely forgotten that Julie had given it to her last night, and now her interest had been sparked again.

Dear Lisa,
I never thought it would end this way ... I had been
drug running for several years before it happened ...

DI Chris Jackson

Chris was tired and looking forward to getting back to his flat. His nose had been fixed, though he still had to keep the medical tape and bandages on it. Plus he had been told to see his GP as soon as he got home. Well, that was one way to finally get round to discussing the headaches that had plagued him all this time. He hadn't told anyone at the station that he was visiting, but he'd decided to pop in before heading off to the doctor's.

'Just thought I'd swing by to let you know I got out alive,' Chris announced as he walked into his team's office. A huge cheer went up and Julie rushed over to hug him.

'I'm so glad you're okay,' she said. 'We've had the news on since we heard last night,' she added as she looked up at him.

'Careful of my back though, DS Ryan. I lost count of the number of shards of glass they removed.'

Julie laughed and moved away. 'Sorry, we're just all so glad that you're okay.'

'I know, Julie, it's fine. I've just come in to pick a few bits up, then I'm going back to the flat for some well-deserved sleep.'

'Is Mikel okay?'

'He's as okay as he can be. They've got a team with him in London. He doesn't know about his mum yet, but I'm sure they'll be breaking it to him soon. Then it's probably into witness protection for the rest of his life.' Chris sighed.

'And young Hannah?' Greg asked.

'Ha, she didn't even break a fingernail.' Chris forced a laugh. 'Right, team. I'll see everyone on Monday bright and early. Catching criminals in Nottingham is surely going to be a lot easier than the last couple of days.'

Chris grabbed the stuff from his office that had been left there since the day he visited Shelham. He hoped that his cat wouldn't be too pissed at him for leaving her home alone for the last couple of days – he'd made sure his neighbour checked on her in his place.

He had managed to snatch some time with Hannah before leaving the hospital and, with promises to speak to him as soon as she could, she'd disappeared again. He also needed to have a debrief but, right now, home and sleep were calling him.

He jumped back into his car, cringing as he forgot about his back. Then he picked up his phone.

'Medicalview Doctors' Surgery. Can I help you?'

'Hi, yes. I was involved in an accident recently, and the hospital have advised me to see my GP. I was wondering if there were any appointments today at all?'

'Let me look … oh yes, we can fit you in at 3 p.m. Can I take your name and date of birth?'

Chris gave them his details.

'Okay, Mr Jackson. Dr Ross will see you at three.'

'Great, thank you.'

Chris wasn't sure how he'd managed to score a doctor's appointment in a matter of hours; maybe it was because he'd mentioned the hospital? He couldn't help but start to wonder what they would say about the headaches, especially when he also factored in the blurred vision and balance issues. He wanted to believe it was just stress … but he wasn't sure he could any more.

Detective Hannah Littlefair

Hannah was about to go into another interview with Kevin Teddington when her phone made a noise. It was a voicemail from an unknown number.

'Hannah, I'm really sorry to contact you like this, but I didn't know who else to call. Chris has been taken into hospital. He said something about them wanting to give him a brain scan? I think it might be something to do with these headaches he's been having. I'm going up to Derby Royal now to be with him. Phone me back.'

Hannah's heart felt like it had stopped momentarily, and she rushed into Max's office.

'I'm sorry, Max. I need to go. Something has happened to Chris.'

'Take my car,' he said, throwing the keys at her. 'Call me when you know more.'

Hannah ran out of Max's office and down to his car, navigating it out of the car park while typing Chris' postcode into the satnav. She waited for the Bluetooth to pick up her phone, scrolled back to the message she had just received and pressed the call button.

'Julie, tell him I'm on my way …'

Thank You

Wow! Book two! A little over a year ago I didn't think *Perfect Lie* would happen, and here I am writing to say thank you for reading *A Silent Child*.

Like *Perfect Lie*, the journey with this book has been just as challenging if not more. I have probably cried more than all my characters put together, and there is so much more to come for all of them.

I'd love to hear what you thought of this book and my characters, so if you could leave a review on Goodreads, or the retail site where you bought the book, that would be great.

Until next time,

Claire
X

About the Author

Claire lives in Nottingham with her family, a cat called Whiskers and a dog called Podrick.

She suffers from Multiple Sclerosis and as a result of the disease had to reduce her hours working in insurance for an Insolvency Insurer. This spare time enabled her to study a creative writing course which inspired her to write her debut, *Perfect Lie*.

When Claire isn't working she enjoys reading crime novels and listening to music – the band Jimmy Eat World is her biggest muse! Claire is also an avid reader and book blogger. The inspiration for her novels comes from the hours spent watching *The Bill* with her grandparents and auntie; then later, *Spooks* and other detective programmes like *Inspector Morse*, *A Touch of Frost* and *Midsomer Murders*.

To find out more about Claire,
follow her on social media:
Twitter: @ClaireEESheldon
Facebook: www.facebook.com/clairesheldonauthor

More Ruby Fiction

From Claire Sheldon

Perfect Lie

Book 1 – Lisa Carter Files

What is 'perfect' trying to hide?

Jen Garner tries her best to be 'wife and mother of the year'. She helps organise school plays and accompanies her husband to company dinners, all with a big smile on her face.

But Jen has started to receive strange gifts in the post ... first flowers, then a sympathy card.

It could just be a joke; that's what she tells herself. But then the final 'gift' arrives, and Jen has to question why somebody is so intent on shattering her life into pieces ...

More from Ruby Fiction

Why not try something else from our selection:

One by One
Helen Bridgett

Professor Maxie Reddick Files

When practising what you preach is easier said than done ...

Professor Maxie Reddick has her reasons for being sceptical of traditional policing methods, but, in between her criminology lecturing job and her Criminal Thoughts podcast, she stays firmly on the side lines of the crime solving world.

Then a young woman is brutally attacked, and suddenly it's essential that Maxie turns her words into actions; this is no longer an academic exercise – this is somebody's life.

But as she delves deeper, the case takes a sickening turn, which leads Maxie to the horrifying realisation that the attack might not have been a one-off. It seems there's a depraved individual out there seeking revenge, and they'll stop at nothing to get it ... little by little ... one by one.

Visit www.rubyfiction.com for details.

The Final Reckoning
Margaret James

What if you had to return to the place that made you fall apart?

When Lindsay Ellis was a teenager she witnessed the aftermath of a violent murder involving her lover's father. The killer was never found.

Traumatised by what she saw, Lindsay had no choice but to leave her home village of Hartley Cross and its close-knit community behind.

Now, years later, she must face up to the terrible memories that still haunt her. But will confronting the past finally allow Lindsay to heal, or will her return to Hartley Cross unearth dangerous secrets and put the people she has come to care about most at risk?

Introducing Ruby Fiction

Ruby Fiction is an imprint of Choc Lit Publishing.
We're an award-winning independent publisher,
creating a delicious selection of fiction.

See our selection here:
www.rubyfiction.com

Ruby Fiction brings you stories that inspire emotions.

We'd love to hear how you enjoyed *A Silent Child*.
Please visit www.rubyfiction.com and give your feedback
or leave a review where you purchased this novel.

Ruby novels are selected by genuine readers like yourself.
We only publish stories our Tasting Panel want to see in
print. Our reviews and awards speak for themselves.

Could you be a Star Selector and join our Tasting Panel?
Would you like to play a role in choosing which novels
we decide to publish? Do you enjoy reading women's
fiction? Then you could be perfect for our Tasting Panel.

Visit here for more details ...
www.choc-lit.com/join-the-choc-lit-tasting-panel

Keep in touch:
Sign up for our monthly newsletter Spread for all the latest
news and offers: www.spread.choc-lit.com. Follow us on
Twitter: @RubyFiction and Facebook: RubyFiction.

Stories that inspire emotions!